Praise for Lauren Dane's *Taking Chase*

Taking Chase is a 2006 CAPA nominee in the Best Romantic Suspense category!

FIVE Blue Ribbons "These stories are fun, fast paced, and full of heart (...)I'll definitely be watching for the rest of the books in this series." ~ *Romance Junkies*

Recommended Read "There are unfortunately only two more Chase brothers, but with Ms. Dane telling their stories, they will be worth the wait." ~ *Fallen Angel Reviews*

"As with Giving Chase, I really cannot recommend this book enough. The storyline grips you right from the start. You care about these characters. You root for them and their relationship. Lauren Dane left me panting for more." ~ *Don't Talk Just Read*

Recommended Read "Lauren Dane's writing continues to amaze me, and it gives me great pleasure to Joyfully Recommend Taking Chase!" ~ *Joyfully Reviewed*

Five Flags "Lauren Dane definitely knows how to weave a reader's attention into the tale and keep it moving. I was captivated from the first few sentences and didn't want to stop reading." ~ *Euro-Reviews*

Four and a half Lips "Taking Chase is a book I never wanted to end. I am eagerly awaiting for the next book in this wonderful series by Lauren Dane." ~ *Two Lips Reviews*

"Suspense, steamy eroticism, and downright likeable characters are what readers are in store for when the open up Lauren Dane's TAKING CHASE." ~ *RRT Erotic*

"Taking Chase is an endearing story about what faith, a strong will and a patient soul can survive. I love this book for the hope it inspires and that it does not shy away from what needs to be said. I can't wait until the print release of this book. It will definitely go on my keeper shelf." ~ *A Romance Review*

Taking Chase

Lauren Dane

A Samhain Publishing, Ltd. publication.

Samhain Publishing, Ltd.
512 Forest Lake Drive
Warner Robins, GA 31093
www.samhainpublishing.com

Taking Chase
Copyright © 2006 by Lauren Dane
Print ISBN: 1-59998-383-4
Digital ISBN: 1-59998-301-X

Editing by Angie James
Cover by Scott Carpenter

First Samhain Publishing, Ltd. electronic publication: November 2006
First Samhain Publishing, Ltd. print publication: February 2007

Dedication

I can't say it often enough because it's such a miracle to me. But Ray, thank you for being my heart and the person who completes me. Always thanks to my incredible beta readers, who kick butt and take names and always have my back, even when they tell me something sucks and that I'd better fix it. And not being one to forget my manners and while on the subject of butt kicking—thanks Angie. Being an editor is a thankless job I know, so let me say it again, thanks for being the guardian of my words and the wielder of the grammar whip. Heh.

The name change project is real. Sadly, it's necessary for some women to change their identities to run and hide from their former partners. The program and countless advocacy programs for domestic violence across the nation saves lives. Abused women come from every class grouping, every race and background. They are your neighbors and friends and chances are, you know someone who is being physically or mentally abused by her partner. I used to be a domestic violence victim's advocate, Cassie is for every woman who had the courage to leave and for every one who lives in her own personal hell every day.

Chapter One

For the first time in years Cassie Gambol felt as if she wasn't being watched. She couldn't remember the last time that had been true. But as she drove down Main Street in tiny, way off the map, Petal, Georgia, her muscles relaxed just a bit.

It was Friday night yet most of the businesses along the street were closed but for the restaurants and what looked to be a bar or tavern. The place was pretty quaint. Definitely not Los Angeles. But that was okay. It was off the beaten path and that's where she needed to be.

The last thing she needed or wanted was for Terry to find her. Ever. She planned to keep her head down and get on with her life. Because she *was* alive and that wasn't something she'd take for granted ever again.

While she was stopped at a red light, she looked down to check the address she'd written down. She had no clue that the giant Cadillac was heading right for her until it rear-ended her, slamming her car into the intersection.

Muzzy but rising back toward full consciousness, Cassie did a mental inventory of her body. Everything seemed to be in working order. She could move her fingers and her toes. Great, teach her to relax her muscles.

The airbag deploying kept her from getting her head split open by the steering wheel, a good thing because she was pretty sure her skull had taken all it possibly could. Still, as she began to regain her senses, she knew she'd be bruised and sore as hell in the morning.

Cassie opened her eyes. The bag lost air and she was able to turn her body enough to see the group of people running from the bar toward the intersection. Oh, *special.* One of them was a cop. She hoped like hell those new documents Brian had given her a week before would hold up. The social security card and driver's license were legit but the rental documents and that kind of stuff were based on faked information.

Get yourself together, Cassie, you've dealt with cops before. Just keep it simple. She gave herself a mini pep talk as she took in the freakishly tiny woman with the huge hair standing next to the car wringing her hands.

"Oh my lands! Honey, are you all right?"

Cassie blinked several times to see if she was hallucinating or not but the woman was apparently real.

"Momma! Damn it, I told you a hundred times to stop putting on makeup while you drive," the cop, a very big man, hissed at the tiny woman with giant hair and four inch heels.

"Shane, we can deal with that later." One of the other bystanders, clearly related to the cop, peered into the car, opening the door carefully. "Miss? Are you all right?"

Could the situation be any more ridiculous? Twenty seconds after she'd driven into town and she got rear-ended by a pixie with aspirations to drive NASCAR. Of course the tiny woman in the giant car had to be related to the giant cop. And the giant cop was droolingly sexy. Yes, her libido which had died years ago chose to come back to life at that very moment. A strange giggle tried to escape her belly.

The guy standing at her car door smiled at her as he looked her over carefully. "I'm Matt Chase, a firefighter and paramedic here in town. I'm just going to look you over to check for injuries, all right?"

Blinking slowly, she licked her lips and nodded. Gentle hands felt her head and neck, flexed her fingers and arms. He turned her toward him and checked over her legs and ankles. The experience was far from unfamiliar and the old fear began to well up. She hoped he took her trembling hands as shock from the accident.

"I'm all right. Just a bit shaken up."

He looked up, as though startled by her voice. "Can you stand?"

"Let's see." She took the hand he offered and stood, unsteadily at first but it wasn't very long until she was much stronger and didn't need to lean on the car. "Yeah, apparently so."

"Do you know your name?"

Her old one and her new one. "Yes, I'm Cassie Gambol."

"I'm glad you're okay, Cassie. I'm afraid your car isn't so all right. I called a tow truck to take it to Art's. He's the mechanic here in Petal. He'll get to you first thing."

"No thanks to Mario Andretti there." Cassie turned her gaze toward the tiny woman.

"Oh honey, I'm so sorry. It's totally my fault." The woman at least had the decency to really look upset about it.

The giant groaned. "Ms. Gambol, can I get a statement and your insurance information for my report, please?"

"For cripe's sake, Shane. Let's at least get her into The Pumphouse so she can sit down and get a drink of water." Matt rolled his eyes.

"Why aren't you asking Crash there for her insurance info?" Cassie motioned at big hair.

"Believe me, miss, I know her information." The giant heaved a put upon sigh.

The tow truck arrived.

"Can we get anything out of your car for you?" Cassie turned to find a smiling redhead. "I'm Maggie Chase." She pointed at the hottie firefighter and the giant. "Their sister-in-law."

"I'm supposed to meet my new landlord in about ten minutes. I need my purse and that bag on the floorboard on the front seat. Oh and I have a few suitcases in the trunk and my overnight case."

Maggie turned and waved at the assembled men. "Get to it. Put it all in my car. I'll run her where she needs to go." She looked back to Cassie. "Well, isn't this a wonderful welcome to Petal. Where're you meeting your landlord? I'll get you there in time if he's here in town."

"I uh..." Cassie leafed through the papers in the bag someone handed her. "It's 1427 Riverwalk Drive. He said it was a fourplex just off Main Street."

"It is." Matt turned to Maggie momentarily. "It's my place, you know where to go." That bright, white smile moved back to Cassie. "You're going to be my neighbor. I live in apartment C. Chuck said he had a new tenant moving in to A. He's a good guy."

Maggie nodded and grabbed her purse from another bystander. "Okay, Shane you can come by in half an hour and take her statement then. We can't have her be late."

The cop scowled but moved to the side to let them pass. "Fine. I'll be there in a few minutes." He crossed his arms over his chest, looking imposing and suddenly, Cassie found him far less attractive and a lot more scary.

"Don't mind him. His bark is worse than his bite." Maggie ushered Cassie to a sedan across the street.

On the quick ride over Cassie was aware that Maggie Chase was sizing her up. It annoyed her but she supposed it wasn't unusual. After all she was a stranger in town, it would be natural to be curious. Still, it made her nervous.

"I apologize for my mother-in-law. I hope you don't think poorly of her. She's really a very good person. She's just a terrible driver and she gets distracted. I think it's all the hairspray she uses to keep her helmet hair lacquered. Anyway, I just wanted you to know she'll make it right. Heck, if I know her, she's already working on making you enough food to last you until Christmas."

Cassie just wanted the ride to be over so she could be alone again. She needed a shower, a cry and then a lot of sleep. "That isn't necessary. She doesn't need to do anything but be sure her insurance takes care of any repairs for my car."

"If it doesn't, she'll deal with the difference. So, where are you from? What brings you to Petal?" Maggie pulled her car into a driveway in front of a well kept fourplex with a big oak in the front and brightly colored flowers in beds that hugged the walk.

"This is nice," Cassie murmured, avoiding Maggie's questions. The place felt friendly, open.

"Matt lives in the top apartment on the left. You're next to him on the right. Oh, there's Chuck." Maggie waved.

Thank goodness the woman was as ADD as her mother-in-law. Cassie knew she'd have to deal with the questions sooner or later but after the last two months, hell, after the last year, she was exhausted. It was hard for her to be rude but it was self preservation at that point. If she didn't get rid of them and

11

get some privacy, she'd lose her shit in front of her new neighbors. "Uh, thank you, Maggie. It's very nice of you to have brought me here."

"Oh no problem. I'll wait here for you. Kyle and Shane will be here and they can help you move your bags in."

Cassie couldn't figure out if Maggie was being purposely obtuse or was just really nice. "That's not necessary. I can move my own bags. It's not a big deal. Really." Cassie got out before Maggie could reply.

Not that that stopped the redhead from getting out. "Chuck! This is Cassie, your new tenant. Polly rear-ended her right in front of The Pumphouse. She's had a rough night."

Cassie ground her teeth and tried to remember that Maggie meant well. But she'd had enough being managed. Stepping forward she held out her hand to the man walking toward her with a sympathetic smile. She'd had enough of those too.

"I'm Cassie Gambol, it's nice to meet you."

"I wish it was under better circumstances. That Polly." He chuckled and shook her hand. "Come on up. Your furniture was delivered earlier today. I didn't know where you wanted everything but I had them do the hump work and bring it upstairs." He led her up those very stairs as he spoke.

When he opened the door, Cassie knew immediately she'd be okay. The apartment was right. It felt safe. Second floor. One entrance. She'd put on all the window alarms after everyone left.

"You just let me know when and where you want this stuff moved, okay? You surely don't need to be hefting anything heavy after a car accident." He dropped a set of keys into her hand and pulled out an envelope. "Here's a copy of the lease you sent me last week. Rent is due the fifteenth. But as you paid the first two months, you're good until September."

She walked through the place in a daze. Her muscles were sore and she wanted everyone to leave her alone so she could shower and sleep for about twenty hours. He showed her the various highlights, where the circuit breaker was, the air conditioner and heating controls.

When they walked back into the living room Shane and Kyle entered with Matt and each carried one of her bags.

"Do you want these in the bedroom?"

Numb, she just nodded. The giant looked at her with suspicious concern but took the big suitcase into the other room as she got rid of Chuck. Only four more to go.

Telling herself to just hold on a bit longer, she thrust her new insurance card and driver's license at Shane when he came back into the room. "I was at the light. Stopped. Because it was *red*. Your mother hit me and knocked me into the intersection. My airbag went off. She wasn't going super fast but fast enough." Her recital of events was delivered in a flat voice.

"Would you like to go to the hospital?" Maggie looked concerned.

"I'm fine. I'm just exhausted, so if you're done, you can all go and I'll sleep." Her nails dug into her palms, trying to stave off the shakes.

"You could have a concussion. You should go in just to be checked," Shane said, his voice rumbling along her spine, eyes flicking over her body.

She wanted to scream and shove them all out the door. If any woman knew what a concussion felt like it was her. Terry had given them to her more than once.

"I said I'm fine. Honestly. Now, are we done? Because I'm dead on my feet. I need a shower and to sleep. I've been driving for three days."

Shane looked the lush, raven-haired beauty over carefully. His mental alarm was blaring. There was something off about Cassie Gambol. He didn't like it when people hid things from him. Petal was his town, it made him nervous to wonder what sort of secrets this woman was bringing in to it. And she was hiding something. He was sure of that much. Her hands shook and her voice trembled here and there.

There was also no denying she was the most beautiful thing he'd ever seen. Something about her drew him in. Made him feel protective as well as suspicious. He found himself gripping the insurance card to keep from touching her hair where it had fallen loose from the clip thing holding it away from her face.

Taking a step back and a deep breath, he handed her back the insurance card and license. He didn't miss the half moon imprints on her palms from where her nails had dug in. "I'm done. Your account matches my mother's. You'll need to follow up with Art tomorrow about the car." She took the business card with the mechanic's information on it from him and put it in her wallet, nodding her thanks.

"He told me he'd get on it first thing. If you need a rental he can hook you up with that too. I can assure you my mom's insurance will cover the repairs." He sighed heavily, he was sure he'd end up having to take her license away if she didn't stop driving like a maniac.

Officially done with the small talk, Cassie crossed the living room to the front door, holding it open. "Thank you for carrying my bags in. I appreciate that. And Maggie, thank you for the ride."

"Any time. I'm in the book. Please give me a call when you get settled in. I know it's got to be hard to be in a new place. I'd love to introduce you around. Folks around here are pretty friendly." Maggie patted her arm as she left.

"Just pound on the wall if you need anything." Matt grinned at her. "You'll probably need a grocery run. I brought some milk, bread and eggs over from my place. They're in your fridge. A few cans of soup are on the counter there."

Something warm and long forgotten bloomed in her gut. She smiled past the lump in her throat and blinked back tears. "Thank you. That's very thoughtful of you."

"No problem. Neighbors help each other. The grocery is only two blocks west. But if you need a ride there or anywhere, just let me know. I have tomorrow and the next day off and I'd be happy to run you wherever you need to go."

Shane pushed his brother out the door but kept his eyes on Cassie. Perceptive cop eyes. They both knew she was hiding something. "I think Miss Gambol wants us to go." He nodded curtly in her direction.

"Thank you all again." She refused to let herself even look at his ass in those uniform pants as he retreated. Refused. Okay, okay so one peek before closing the door. To help calm her nerves.

And she closed the door. Locking it. Alone. Alone and safe.

Methodically, she went into her bedroom and pulled the window alarms out of one of her suitcases, installing them one by one, checking the locks as she went. It was a warm night but the air conditioner seemed to do a good job keeping the place cool enough.

Pulling the blinds tight, she made a final pass through the place, making sure it was secure and then kicked off her shoes. She knew she should eat but the very thought made her nauseated. At that point, she was on auto pilot, finishing all her safety tasks would be her sole thought until she could assure herself she was locked in and safe. That if someone did break in, the safeguards would be enough to wake her up. She knew you couldn't defend yourself if you were sleeping.

Getting a change of clothing, her toiletries and one last item, she headed into the bathroom, locking the door behind her. After putting the doorstop alarm down and in place, she hung her towels and put the washcloths in a drawer.

As always, Cassie avoided looking in the mirror as she undressed. The fear was enough, she didn't need to see the scars. Anyway, the scars on the inside were just as bad and she couldn't look away from those. She cursed Terry for making her this way. Creating a scared rabbit from a woman who'd been so confident and self-assured. And she'd let him.

The water heated quickly but she made sure the safety on her gun was off and that it was within reach before she stepped into the stall. Her breath came out in a long exhale. Alone at last. Safe to let the tears come.

CRED

"So how about my new neighbor, huh?" Matt winked at his brothers as they all sat in his living room.

Shane heard laughter from the kitchen. Maggie was in there with her best friend Liv, making up some nachos and he also suspected, gossiping about the evening.

"She's something else, huh? It's not like I haven't seen pretty women before but this one is up there in the top five. Did you get a load of her legs?" Matt laughed. "Biggest blue eyes I've ever seen. Pretty lips. And that voice. Holy shit that voice. Made me hard just hearing it."

"She's hiding something." Shane wanted Matt to shut up about Cassie's body.

Kyle and Matt looked at their oldest brother. "Yeah? What makes you say so?" Matt asked.

"I'm a cop. I know what it looks like when people have something to hide. Her hands shook. She avoided eye contact. She wanted us out of her house pretty darned bad."

Maggie walked in and put food down on the coffee table with a stack of paper plates. "Of course she was shaking, Shane. She'd just had a car accident. She didn't know any of you and hell, I know what she must have felt like with all these giant handsome men in her living room. Give the woman a break. But she was nervous. Really nervous. Could just be her nature, though." Maggie looked up at her brother-in-law. "But I don't think it's a prosecutable offense to be nervous."

"She had some considerable scarring on her scalp and the back of her neck. I felt it when I checked her over. It could be that she'd been in another bad accident before. I've seen victims at the scene with major trauma from past accidents," Matt said around his nachos.

"Maybe. But I'm gonna watch this woman. I don't trust her. I don't like people coming into my town carrying trouble."

"Jeez, Shane, cut the woman some slack. Do you need to go from zero to the Terminator in three seconds? Not all women are out to hurt people," Kyle said.

"It's my job to watch people and I never said all women were out to hurt people," Shane growled at his brother.

"Okay, this needs to stop before it gets started. Kyle, lay off. Shane, give her the benefit of the doubt. And anyway, I saw you watching her. Did you think she was hiding something in her bra? Maybe her back pocket?" Matt snorted.

"Okay, so she's easy on the eyes. But I don't know what she's bringing into my town and I'm not going to be comfortable until I figure it out."

Chapter Two

When Cassie opened her eyes the next morning, it almost felt like she was a new person as well as living in a new place. Sun streamed into her bedroom and she heard the birds singing just outside. Peace. How long had that been?

As she got dressed she contemplated the importance of where she was at right then. She wasn't on the verge of taking the first step into her future. She'd taken it. And she was still moving ahead. For so long it had been about just surviving. It seemed monumentally scary to have her life be about living again.

Cassie decided to walk to Main Street, have breakfast and then deal with the car situation. Get to know the town a bit better.

While she was out she'd also look for a place with wireless so she could email Brian and check in. Or at the very least call him on a payphone. She hadn't spoken with him since she left the hotel the morning before and she knew he'd be worried.

After she got some makeup on, she pulled her hair into a ponytail and made sure her shirt collar hid the scars at the back of her neck. It wasn't until she'd locked the door that the heat hit her. Like a thick, wet blanket. If it was this bad now, she knew she needed to get out and finish her errands before noon.

The trees cast nice, cool shade as she began to walk. People out working in their yards actually waved hellos at her. And taking a deep breath, she waved back. She had to claim her life again.

Once on Main Street she crossed over to a little diner she'd seen the night before, The Sands. It was everything she'd imagined a small town diner to be when she walked inside. Crowded and full of people talking and laughing, waving to folks as they came and went. Steeling her nerves, Cassie slipped into a spot at the counter and grabbed a menu.

"Hiya, sug. You must be the pretty girl that Polly Chase ran into last night."

Surprised, Cassie looked up into the face of a woman behind the counter. Big brown eyes sparked with good humor. Cassie couldn't help but smile back.

"That's me. I suppose this is my introduction to how fast news travels in a small town?"

The woman laughed and patted Cassie's arm. "Now you're catching on. I'm Ronnie Sands. I own this place." She put a coffee cup in front of Cassie and filled it.

"I'm Cassie Gambol. Nice place you have here. I like it. Looks like I'm not the only one." She ordered the pancake special and complimented Ronnie on the fresh juice.

Ronnie grinned. "Be right back with your pancakes. Welcome to Petal, Cassie." Ronnie bustled off to help another customer.

Well, you're looking a mite better today." Cassie turned to see Maggie Chase hop up into the chair next to her. "Although I don't like those dark circles under your eyes. How are you feeling after last night?"

"I just need a few good meals and some rest. Thanks." Cassie felt torn between the idea of actually making new friends and the vulnerability that created in her.

Damn it, she used to be so good at this. She had friends and a vibrant social life. She used to be a lot of things before Terry.

The woman who'd come in with Maggie leaned forward and smiled. "You must be the Cassie everyone is talking about. Hi, I'm Liv Davis. Nice to meet you."

Ronnie came by, put a heaping plate of food in front of Cassie, took Maggie and Liv's orders and hurried away.

Cassie waved back at Liv before digging into her breakfast. She'd forgotten what this kind of cooking tasted like. Terry had insisted on a cook to prepare low fat meals based on his menu plans and when she wasn't eating at home, she ate what she could grab at work. Hospital cafeterias weren't known for their delicious meals.

"What brings you to Petal, Cassie?" Maggie asked.

Cassie knew the question would be asked again and all the way out from her brother's she'd worked on the answer.

"I got tired of the big city. I wanted a change." She shrugged. "One of my friends was here a few years ago, on his way through to Atlanta and he's always gushed about it. So I checked it out on the internet and ended up talking to Chuck and rented the apartment."

"I admire that. You just up and moved? Changed your life because you wanted to, that's pretty amazing." Maggie's smile was genuine.

"Don't. It's not a big deal really. The city was killing me."

Or rather, someone in the city wanted to.

Maggie frowned a little before brightening again. "Well it's most certainly admirable. What city did you come from?"

She and Brian decided it was good to keep close to the truth. Los Angeles was big enough that it shouldn't ring any alarm bells.

"LA."

"And what are you going to do here? Do you have a job lined up?"

Well, she couldn't be a surgeon anymore. Three of the fingers in her right hand had had the bones shattered so severely she'd never have the range of fine motor skills she'd need. Hell, she could barely hold a fork in her right hand for nearly half a year after she'd gotten out of the hospital. On top of that, she couldn't practice under her new name without a whole lot of hassle and paperwork. Hassle and paperwork that would expose her. Futile rage swamped her for a moment, Terry had taken away her greatest love as well as her safety and nearly her life.

"No. I need to start looking." She shoved it all away, not allowing him to own her fear or her anger. Her days of letting him control her were over.

"Well, what can you do? Any special talents? Maybe we can give you suggestions." Maggie buttered her toast.

"Clerk, secretary, bookstore? Coffeeshop?" Cassie shrugged, trying not to resent Maggie's apparent ease with herself and her surroundings.

"You know, I think Penny is looking for someone over at Paperbacks and More. You should pop in. She's really nice, our age, I think it would probably be a really fun place to work. And wow," Maggie leaned in close to Cassie, "where did you get those earrings? They're gorgeous."

Smiling, Cassie touched them. "Thank you. I made them."

21

"You made those? Well they're beautiful. You're pretty talented, Cassie. Have you ever thought about selling them?"

"Funny you should mention that, I was thinking about it on the way here. Is there a craft market or flea market around here? I have a supply of things I've made that I'd love to sell on the odd weekend here and there." At least she could still make jewelry with her hands.

"As a matter of fact, yes. There's a Sunday Market. This is the first year for it but it seems to be doing pretty well. They close down Fourth Avenue, which is just a few blocks down. As it happens, our friend Dee is on the organizing committee. Here." Maggie dug through her bag and pulled out a pen and paper. "This is her number. Give her a call and let me know because I'd love to buy some of your stuff." Maggie grinned.

"Thank you, Maggie. I appreciate this." Cassie paid for her breakfast, a little bit of hope in her belly along with the great food. "Ronnie, breakfast was excellent and the juice made me feel a lot better. I'll be seeing you."

"Wait, Cassie. Do you need a ride somewhere?" Maggie asked.

She'd had just about all the small talk she could take. Cassie just needed to be alone to think. "No, thanks. I noticed from the card that the mechanic is only a few blocks away. After I check in there I need to run errands. Nothing I can't walk to and I need the exercise anyway. Thanks for the tip about your friend and the Market. Oh and do you know if there's a place in town that has wireless internet access? My phone won't be in until Monday and I haven't even thought about internet service."

"The Honey Bear. It's a bakery at the other end of Main. We'd be happy to give you a lift." Maggie's friendly nature was earnest and unvarnished. Cassie had to admit to herself she liked that. There didn't seem to be anything fake about her. The gorgeous best friend seemed nice too. But she wasn't ready for hanging out with the girls just yet.

"Oh thanks, but I'd like to get to know the town a bit. I appreciate it." Cassie backed away toward the door. "Have a great Saturday afternoon."

And she was free again. Free to do whatever she wanted. The walk down Main Street was quite nice. There were a number of little businesses along the way. A few cafés and specialty shops dotted the sidewalk. The town seemed to be thriving.

The mechanic shop was busy but when she walked in one of the men stopped what he was doing and came over to help her. "You must be Cassie. I'd shake your hand but I don't want to get you dirty. I'm Art."

Okay, so it was odd but she was getting used to everyone knowing who she was. Definitely *not* something she experienced a lot back home. "Yep, I'm Cassie. Nice to meet you. Just came in to check on my car. How is it?"

"Well, that big old Caddy is a menace. She's whacked your rear axle out of alignment and it's cracked. I've called in an order for the parts but I won't see them until Monday. The rest isn't too bad. The body work shouldn't take too very long and we can do the paint job here. But I wouldn't count on having a vehicle for another week or so. Do you need a rental? We have two on site. Polly's insurance will cover it."

Cassie laughed. "Everyone in town seems to be familiar with her insurance and what it covers."

"Well yes." Art blushed. "She's gotten into a few fender benders. But she really is a nice woman."

"So I'm told. And yes, I'll need a car if I won't have one for at least another week."

He completed the paperwork and she drove off half an hour later to the grocery store. But when she parked, she saw the small bookstore just a few doors down and decided to head over and check out the job lead.

"Miss Gambol."

Shit. The giant hottie of a sheriff came walking toward her. Stalking, like something big and bad but graceful too.

"Sheriff."

His eyes didn't miss anything on their slow circuit of her body. She knew that he knew she was holding back. "Please, call me Shane. How are you doing today?"

She resisted the urge to shift from foot to foot. "I'm all right. Just a bit sore. But I've got a rental and Art is taking care of my car." She shrugged. Cassie tried not to think about how his skin was so work-hard and firm and nicely sunkissed. She smelled him from where she stood. A bit of cologne, man and clean sweat.

Cassie doubted she looked as good. The heat made her skin feel clammy and her hair most likely hung like a limp rag. She chewed her lip, knowing the lipstick she'd applied first thing was gone. And then she smacked herself for even thinking it. No way. No more controlling men with power issues. And clearly this one had that in spades. He took up far more of the sidewalk than he physically occupied. His presence was overwhelming. And certainly he'd be hot in bed, but she was not going to find out. Oh no. Not her. She wouldn't even think about how he'd look naked and laid out on her sheets waiting for her. *Damn. Were vibrators legal in Georgia?* Yeah, she'd need to look that up online.

He was talking and she blushed when she realized she'd lost half of what he'd said. "I'm sorry. I missed part of that."

He smiled, with white predator's teeth. Oh my. *Okay, thinking about sex again! Stop it!*

"I was saying that you should be on the look out for a visit from my mother. She's still upset over what happened last night and she wants to make it right. Which means she'll hound you until you let her. I suggest you don't try to resist. It's pointless anyway. She might be small but she handles four very big sons with one hand tied behind her back."

Suddenly he was so charming he totally disarmed her and she laughed. "I see. Like the Borg? Only with big hair and a bigger handbag?"

He cocked his head and grinned. "You got it. You settling in all right? Can I help you with anything? You shouldn't move any of that furniture so soon after the accident. I'd be happy to help." Her heart sped up as his gaze pulled her in. He was thinking something naughty wasn't he? Or maybe she was projecting.

Wetting her lips nervously she shrugged. "I'm sure I'll be all right. Thanks."

His long pause alarmed her until he blinked slowly and cleared his throat. "Uh, okay. Well, I have to go. It was nice seeing you again. You be sure to call me at the station or go and get Matt if you need anything, all right?"

"Thanks again." Stepping back from his body made her feel a bit better. She could breathe without smelling his skin. It had to be the heat that made her feel so lightheaded.

With a wave she steered around him and headed into the bookstore, leaving him standing there, watching her.

Shane unfisted his hands as he took in her sway before she disappeared into Paperbacks and More. Nervous as a cat that one. Why? And where in hell did the persistent need to protect her come from? She was in his town carrying something she didn't want him to know about with her. That made her a threat. But he didn't see a threat when he looked at her.

He saw the shadow of fear in her eyes. He saw the lines of stress around her mouth. And what a mouth. That mouth of hers was made for kissing and other things he shouldn't be thinking about doing with a woman like Cassie Gambol.

He'd done a quick check on her that morning when he'd gotten to work. Not much to be found and that made him nervous. No one got to be their age without something. No speeding tickets, no fingerprints on file, he didn't find anything about her in any newspapers from Southern California either. It was like she just came into being a few weeks before. A woman built for a hell of a lot of naughty fantasies, made from smoke with fear in her eyes.

In his town. And if he had any say in it, he'd find out who the heck she was and what she carried so close to the vest.

CಣಞಞO

Cool air hit her skin as Cassie walked into Paperbacks and More. Being away from Shane and out of the heat, she found she could finally breathe again. Wandering through the store, she noted the cozy seating areas in the different sections and a good variety of genres. It was bigger than she'd thought it would be. The kind of bookstore she'd have found herself in every payday back in college.

Finally, she sighted the counter and smiled at the woman standing behind it. "I'm looking for Penny."

"You found her." The woman, dressed smart in a lightweight summer skirt and blouse looked Cassie up and down. "Hmm, you don't look like an IRS agent and my personal relationship with the Lord is my business."

Cassie laughed and put her hands up in surrender. "I'm Cassie Gambol and I'm not peddling anything. Well, that's not entirely true. I'm looking for a job. I'm new here in Petal and Maggie Chase said you might be looking for someone."

"You ever worked in a bookstore before?"

"Back when I was in high school and then later when I was in college."

"Who's your favorite author?"

"What a question. How can I just name one? That's impossible."

Penny grinned. "Well, I must say that's a very good answer to start with. Okay, who are your five favorite authors?"

"Margaret Atwood, Isaac Asimov, Frank Herbert, Nora Roberts—and I'll snag JD Robb while I'm at it since they're the same person—and Barbara Kingsolver."

Penny's eyebrow rose. "Nice group there. Okay then, so of those authors—give me your favorite book by each."

"Hmm, for Atwood it's a tie between *Handmaid's Tale* and *Cat's Eye*. Asimov would be *Foundation*. Frank Herbert? *Children of Dune*. Nora—and you know that's a hard one—but *Born in Fire*. JD Robb's, *Naked in Death*. I just love the beginning of Eve and Roarke. And Barbara Kingsolver's *Bean Trees*."

Penny Garwood knew people. She could do a resume check on the woman standing in front of her. Would do. She may trust her gut but she wasn't a moron. Still, she knew it would be fine. Her gut told her that Cassie Gambol was a good woman and would be a darned good employee. And Penny always went with her intuition. It'd never proven her wrong. And there was no doubt that the men would be coming into the store in droves just to get a look at her.

"Okay. When can you start, Cassie Gambol?"

"Are you kidding me? Really? Just like that?"

Penny couldn't remember the last time anyone had looked that overjoyed to be offered a job in a bookstore. The woman didn't look hard up for money, but looks could be deceiving.

"I have a rule, I listen to my gut. My gut says to hire you so I will. We'll start you on a trial basis. I'll give you a week. If it works out, I'll make you permanent. If it doesn't, no harm done. Let's start you part time for now. We're open from noon to five on Sundays. Why don't you come on in tomorrow and we'll set up your schedule?"

Cassie offered her hand and Penny took it. "Thank you so much. I'll be here tomorrow at noon. You won't be sorry for taking a chance on me."

"Make it eleven-thirty. Come around the back. We'll get your paperwork done first and I'll give you a bit of a run through before we open."

"You got it. Thank you again." Heart light and a smile on her face, Cassie headed out and back across the street to the grocery store.

It wasn't that she needed the job. Brian had changed her trust to pay blind to an account that fed into Switzerland and then back to her new name. Her father would have been heartbroken to know what a mess her marriage to Terry had turned out to be. But the money he'd left her when he died enabled her to run. Enabled her to get into the program to change all her identification like her social security number and name. Gave her a chance at a new life.

But she wanted to work. Wanted to do something with her time. Yes, she grew up with money but she'd worked from a very early age and it felt uncomfortable to not have some kind of major activity in her life other than being afraid. Working at a bookstore and making her jewelry wasn't the intricate and lifesaving vascular surgery she'd performed for the last four years, but it was something to help her take a step to move on with her life. And that's what she meant to do.

Matt Chase unfolded himself from his place, laying in a hammock in the shade of the big oak tree in the yard, when she pulled up. He was a work of masculine art. They sure did grow them handsome down in Georgia.

"Hey there, Cassie. Need some help?"

He ambled over and it was impossible not to notice the long, tanned legs in the cut off jeans and the flat, tight belly peeking from under the hem of his T-shirt.

Pulling out a few bags and balancing them she smiled, she knew just a bit thin at the edges. "Oh no, that's okay. It'll just take me two trips. Thank you, though."

But as she began to walk up the steps, she heard him grab the remaining bags and follow her up. "Now it won't take you another trip." He breezed past her into the apartment and put the bags on her kitchen counter before leaning a hip against it and watching her.

"Thank you. It really wasn't necessary."

"I know. It wouldn't have been neighborly if I'd been required to do it. I was just goofing off and taking a nap."

He seemed nice enough, he truly did. But having him in her apartment with the door closed began to make her feel queasy. She didn't know him. He could be anyone and scary often had a pretty face.

She took a step back and he noticed. Concern spread over his handsome face. "Cassie? You all right?"

"I...the heat, I need to cool down and rest." She went to the door and opened it up, gripping the jamb tight. She wanted to gulp the air, try to breathe in the calm but it wasn't working. "Thanks again for helping with my groceries, Matt. I appreciate it." The shaking was coming, she could feel it and she clenched her teeth.

"Are you all right, Cassie? Did I do something wrong?" Matt stopped very close to her but didn't touch her. Still, the fine tremors in her hands hit.

"Please. Just go. I'm not feeling well."

"I...just bang on the wall please if you need me." He backed out of the door and onto the landing. She slammed and locked it, sinking to the floor as her legs would no longer hold her up.

Her teeth began to chatter as the shakes came. Her breath exploded in sobs and she curled into a ball and closed her eyes, letting it wash over her. She knew it was useless to fight it once it got that far so she rode it out.

After a time, she sat up, her muscles still rubbery and slightly sore from the shaking and sobbing. Ordering herself to buck up, she stood up, bracing her weight on the door until she could stand on her own, and went to splash some water on her face.

Moving tentatively, she put her groceries away as her body and spirit regained control over itself. It was then that she remembered she hadn't gotten in contact with Brian and she knew he'd be climbing the walls with worry by then.

She didn't want to leave the house. She wanted to stay inside and hide. But she couldn't. She wouldn't. Instead, she grabbed her keys and her wallet, and headed out to the payphone she'd noticed earlier that day outside the grocery store.

But Shane Chase was waiting at the bottom of her stairs and she recoiled for a moment. *Damn!* He noticed that.

"Oh, Sheriff Chase. You surprised me." She tried to be nonchalant and force herself to go down the stairs but she froze three quarters of the way down because he remained standing at the bottom of the landing, effectively blocking her way. Making her feel trapped.

"Shane. Please. And you want to tell me why the very sight of me scared you?" His voice had an edge she couldn't quite place. "Matt said you had a panic attack earlier when he was at your place. Why don't you tell me what's going on? I can help you."

Anger replaced the fear and she pushed her way past him and down the walk. "I'm on my way out, Shane."

He moved his body to halt her progress and the fear was back at the edges of her anger. "What are you hiding?"

"Sheriff, you're blocking my way. And anyway, what's it to you? I haven't done anything wrong unless panic attacks are illegal in Georgia." Her voice shook a bit, mortifying her even more but thank goodness he stepped out of the way.

"I'm sorry I scared you. I don't know why you're afraid but I can't help you if you won't let me." Hands held loosely at his side, he kept his voice calm and low and she felt like an animal all the sudden. A cat spooked in a treetop. When had her life become so out of her control?

Oh how she wanted to tell him. To give it all to someone else and let them fix it for her. But that wasn't possible. No one could protect her but herself. And the last thing she needed was another big, dominant man who thought he could run her life far more efficiently than she could.

"I'm fine. Now if you'll excuse me." She walked around him, got into the car and pulled away, leaving him standing there, watching her go.

Matt waited on his landing as Shane came up the stairs. "Something has spooked that woman big time." Matt waved his brother inside and handed him a soda.

"I'd wager it was a man. Some asshole who beat her up a time or two. Maybe a daddy." Shane took a sip and sat down on the couch. "Either that or she's running from the law. I checked her out and she's clean but it's not like fake identification is a foreign concept to criminals."

"I don't think so, Shane. She doesn't come off as the kind of woman who's hiding something from others because of what she's done."

Shane nodded at his brother. His stomach clenched as he remembered the look on her face when she'd looked down the steps at him. No, that wasn't the face of a woman hiding from a drug charge. That was the face of a woman who'd been hurt by someone and was afraid it would happen again. No woman had ever looked at him like that and it bothered him deeply that she would be afraid of him.

That nagging protective feeling was back. "I think you're right. I think it's an ex. She didn't seem to have a problem being alone with Maggie or when she was with us all in her apartment. But men alone? You should have seen her reaction when she walked out and saw me on my way up the stairs to her place. She flinched. There's something bad there and I aim to find out what it is."

"I told you, she started shaking when I was at her apartment. I could hear her sobbing for breath after I left. I'm worried about her."

"Are you now?" Shane's eyes narrowed at his brother. "Leave that to me. It's my job and she's not going to tell us anything at this point. I just need to show her we're the good guys and hopefully she'll come to trust me...us, in time."

Matt raised a brow. "Oh, so that's how it is? You staking a claim?"

"I just want to help. I'm a cop, it's what I do." Shane paused and Matt made a rude noise.

"Puhleeze. Shane, I've known you my whole life. That look on your face says there's a lot more than your cop-type duty on the line here."

Shane started to argue but groaned instead, shaking his head. "Damn it, there's something about her. You should have seen how pissed off she got out there. First she's totally freaked and then I say something that makes her mad and she's spitting and hissing. She's..." Shane shrugged his shoulders. "But if you had your eye on her...oh hell, even if, unless you want to have some serious competition, you'd best back up and let me at her. That juxtaposition of timid ferocity gets to me. I can't say I've ever been this intrigued before."

Matt threw back his head and laughed. "Well, she's a looker. And those big blue eyes are haunted. But I'm still stinging over my break up with Liv. I don't think I'm ready right now. But I do want to help Cassie. So I'll keep an eye on her."

"I'm sorry things didn't work out between the two of you. I thought Liv was the one."

"Yeah. Me too. But after nearly a year of dating, she wanted to move to the next level and I just wasn't ready after all. I can't blame her for moving on. I look at Kyle and Maggie and I know that if I'd truly loved Liv, I'd have asked her to move in or marry me long before a year passed." Matt cocked his head. "Cassie may be able to get spitting mad at you but I don't think she's the plaything type. Don't play with her. I don't think she can handle it. And she deserves more."

Shane's lips tightened as he stood up and began to pace. "Hey, fuck you, okay? I don't play with women, Matt. I'm just not serious about them. I've made mistakes, I grant you that. But I have no intentions of harming Cassie Gambol. She's different. She moves me and I want to know more. A lot more." He ran a hand through his hair. "I should be running for the door right now, looking to hook up with a woman who'll make me forget those eyes. But she makes me want to stick around. I think I'm in trouble."

CRSO

Standing in the payphone she'd spied earlier that day in the grocery store parking lot, Cassie punched in the numbers and waited for Brian to pick up. The shaking had finally abated but the after effects of the attacks always left her feeling off balance.

"Hello?"

"Hey, B. I'm here safely."

"I was ready to get on a plane and come looking for you. Why didn't you call me last night? Is everything okay?"

"My phone won't be hooked up until Monday. And I got into a small fender bender and my car is in the shop but yeah, everything is okay. I got a job."

"Already? Great news. Doing what?"

She told him about the bookstore and the five favorite authors question. "She's giving me a week's trial and if she likes me, she'll make me permanent. Who'd have thought I'd be so excited about something like this?"

"You've been through an awful lot. Of course something like this job is exciting. You're claiming your life. Now, a fender bender? Did the new identification work?"

"I guess so. The sheriff hasn't arrested me yet. And it was his mother who hit me. Rear ended me at a red light. I'm all right but my car needs some TLC. My furniture arrived and there are people coming out of the woodwork to offer me help. It's all very stereotypical southern small town here. Lots of people calling me miss and ma'am and going out of their way to be nice. It's odd. Disconcerting and yet, it feels nice."

"Did you tell them?"

"Hell no. That's my past. I mean, they offer to drive me places and move my furniture, that sort of thing. The sheriff has taken it into his head to try and save me. He's like nine feet tall and four feet wide. I'm wagering he was the quarterback in high school. In any case, I'll have to disabuse him of the notion that I need saving."

Brian laughed. "Honey, you can let people in, you know. You haven't done anything wrong. There's nothing for you to be ashamed of and he won't find you. Maybe telling the sheriff is a good thing, he can keep an eye on you."

"You just said Terry won't find me so why do I need an eye kept on me?" And she was ashamed. She knew she shouldn't be but she was. She graduated at the top of her class and yet she'd let a man in her life who'd estranged her from her family and had nearly killed her. He'd taken away one of her greatest passions when he used a hammer to shatter the bones in her fingers. How she let things get that far, and more than once, was still something she didn't understand. And if she didn't how could she expect others to?

"You going to see that doctor they recommended? The one in Shackleton?"

"Yes, she has evening hours and I have an appointment on Wednesday night. I suppose I'll need to clear it with my job."

"You promised you'd go. She's a specialist with domestic violence survivors, Car—Cassie. Don't break that promise."

Closing her eyes, Cassie leaned her head against the cool glass of the enclosure. "I won't. I promised and I'll see it through. Even though I don't need it."

"No one can live through what you did without needing some help."

"It was a year ago."

"Yes and you spent months in the hospital. You were in a coma for three weeks. They weren't even sure you'd be able to use your right arm again. And then the trial and the fuckups. You need someone who can help you process it all. You've just been existing for the last year. Hell for the last several years."

"Fat lot of good the trial did when they found him guilty and he's out there free." Free and filled with violence and the need for revenge. She shivered against the ninety plus degree heat. Fear made her cold.

"I know, Cassie. I know. It's wrong. But you're alive and safe and damn it, you need to claim your life again and live. Get a boyfriend, go on dates, neck at the movies. If you like this town, buy yourself a house and settle there. When they catch him, I won't have to hide when I come and see you. Or you can come back here."

The mere idea of a life where she could have those things mocked her. Could she? Could she be normal and have friends and a boyfriend? A life where she didn't weigh every word and action out of fear? It seemed like such a ridiculous fantasy, rage bubbled up within her. But she didn't want to unleash it on her brother, who'd been her rock through everything. "I have to go. I need to get home and get some dinner. I'll email you and call you with my new info once my phone gets hooked up on Monday. Thank you, Bri. I love you."

"Good. Then you won't be mad when the cell phone I just bought for you shows up at your place early next week. You need one and it drives me nuts that you don't have one."

Cassie sighed. "Fine. Thank you. You're pretty peachy keen as big brothers go."

"I should have done more. I should have seen it. I'm sorry."

"Stop. Damn it, stop! Hell, I *lived* it and I didn't see it. Not all the time. Not until it was too late. But it's over. And I'm alive and you're alive and we're okay."

"I love you. Take care of yourself. You'd better call me on Monday when you get that phone working."

"I promise."

Before she got in her car, she went into the store and bought a gallon of chocolate chip ice cream.

Chapter Three

At eleven-thirty on the dot, Cassie knocked on the back door of the bookstore and a smiling Penny Garwood opened it and waved her inside. Penny's short, stylish brown hair had a pretty barrette on one side, holding it back from her face. Cassie liked the woman's style.

"Well that's a good start, Cassie. Right on time." Penny handed her a stack of paperwork. "Have a cup of coffee and fill all this out. I'll be out front getting everything ready to open. Come on out when you're finished."

She settled in with her papers and took a sip of coffee. She tried not to look at her hands as she wrote. Tried not to think about how much her life had changed in the span of not even an hour. Cassie had had to learn to write with her left hand while the fingers on her right healed. Her victim advocate had encouraged her to keep writing that way. Another layer to her new life. It'd been strange to think constantly about how to become Cassie Gambol and keep Carly Sunderland dead.

Still, she'd gotten to the point where she answered to Cassie like it was the name she'd been born with. She wrote her new social security number with her left hand on that paperwork and listed the past jobs as those people she knew she could trust to keep her secrets and back up her cover.

Cover. She nearly snorted. Once a respected surgeon, now she had to deal with cover. And she didn't even get a cool car like James Bond had.

Finishing up, Cassie went out to the front of the store and handed the papers to Penny who looked through them quickly, tucked them into a folder and smiled.

"Okay, that's all done. Let's get you to work."

For the next several hours, Penny showed Cassie the ropes. How to work the cash register, how to find stock, what went where. It wasn't complicated but it was more detailed than she'd expected it to be and after a while, Cassie fell into the rhythm of it all.

At five Penny turned over the closed sign and locked up. "Good job. Especially for your first day. I'm impressed."

Cassie hadn't felt accomplished in a very long time. It was a simple thing but it felt damned good.

"Thanks."

"Are you busy tonight? We need to set up your schedule and it just so happens I have chicken marinating in my fridge. As an added bonus, I've got sangria that I started last night so it should be nice and ready to drink."

With a little bit of effort she could make an actual friend. The first new one in a few years. "You sure I wouldn't put you out?"

"I wouldn't have invited you if that was the case."

For some reason, Penny's mixture of formal Southern charm and blunt manner put Cassie at ease. She didn't feel pitied or suspected. "All right then, sounds good."

Cassie followed Penny a little way from the center of town and into a neighborhood that overlooked a lake. Penny pulled into the driveway of a large Tudor style house with gorgeous

Lauren Dane

landscaping. The front yard had a huge willow tree that shaded the entire front of the house including the large porch.

She got out and caught up with Penny at her door. "This is some place you've got here." The inside of the house was gorgeous. Filled with period antiques but it still felt comfortable and homey.

"Thank you. I quite like it myself. It was my wedding present."

"Oh, I didn't even think to ask if you were married." Cassie blushed.

"I was. He died two years ago."

"I'm sorry. About your husband, that is."

"Well thank you, honey. He and I had a lot of good years together. I miss him of course, but this house has a lot of good memories." Penny hung her bag on a hook on a gorgeous oak armoire near the front door and Cassie followed suit.

Penny gave her the quick tour and they ended up in the kitchen. "I'm going to put the chicken on the grill. Can you throw a salad together? All the greens are in the fridge."

Expertly—salads were the only thing she could really do well in the kitchen—Cassie chopped up vegetables and ripped lettuce, tossing them all together in a big bowl as Penny tended the grill.

"You ready in there? Come on out and bring the sangria." Penny called to her from the deck.

The pretty glass pitcher of fruited wine in hand, Cassie paused a moment in the doorway as the full impact of the view hit her. The back deck overlooked a lawn that sloped down to the water. It was shady and cool there with a breeze coming from the lake. Peaceful. The kind of place you'd want to come out and sit at the end of the day with a man who loved you.

How wrong was it that a man who gave this to his wife for a present was dead while the man who tried to kill his was alive?

"This view is something else." Cassie came out and put the sangria down.

"One of life's greatest pleasures, sitting out here with a glass of wine and watching the sun go down. You hungry?"

Cassie nodded and for a few minutes they got down to the business of filling plates and sipping sangria until the edge was off. They made small talk as they ate dinner. Penny warmed up, losing a bit of her formality and Cassie began to remember what it was like to have friends and do normal things like have barbecued chicken on a summer evening.

"So why Petal, Cassie Gambol?" Deciding enough small talk had been expended, Penny cut to the chase. Perceptive eyes watched the woman seated across from her.

"A friend passed through a few years back and loved it here. I was sick of LA and wanted a change."

"Well, isn't that easy sounding? Somehow, I think it's more complicated than that. You married?" Cassie was a good person, Penny hadn't seen or sensed anything to make her believe otherwise. But she skirted around details, kept things broad and general. She was hiding something.

Cassie's mouth tightened. *Bingo.* There was a story there. "I was. We divorced."

Penny waited but Cassie didn't elaborate. "What did you do in LA?"

"All kinds of things. I worked for my brother. I ran his law office."

"You certainly do seem to be organized. I know a lawyer who needs some part time help, actually. One of my dearest friends, Polly Chase, her husband Edward is looking. She was just talking about this a few days ago."

"Polly Chase?"

Penny looked askance at Cassie when her voice cracked. "Yes. Do you know her? She's a pistol."

"She barreled into the back of my car at a red light night before last."

Penny's eyes widened and then she began to laugh. "Oh my. I wish I could say I was surprised but I'm not. Frankly, I'm waiting for Shane to take her license away. I love her like my own mother but she is the worst driver in the history of ever. I trust you're all right? I haven't seen her since Wednesday and haven't been out of the store much. I can't believe I missed the gossip on that." Penny sighed with a rueful smile. "She really is a good person. She's just the type to always be thinking about twelve other things and putting lipstick on at the same time."

Cassie just shrugged. "I'll have to take your word for it. My small bit of experience with the woman hasn't been all that encouraging."

"She'll win you over. It's useless to try to resist her. She's special in her own indomitable way. Fiercely loyal and loving. When Ben died, that was my husband, she came over here every day and brought me food. Did my laundry. The entire family has been there for me. Kyle, her son, he took care of the lawns and Shane—that's the sheriff, you may have met him after the accident—he was at my side the entire trial. Edward made sure they prosecuted that rat bastard within an inch of his life."

"What happened to your husband? If you don't mind my asking."

"He was murdered. A hit-and-run. That scum had a record of drunk driving as long as my arm. He hit Ben when Ben was on his evening jog. Left him bleeding by the side of the road. Didn't even call the cops anonymously. By the time they found Ben, it was too late. He had massive internal injuries." Penny's shoulders fell. "Anyway, one of that murderer's co-workers saw the damage to his car and called to report him. They found Ben's blood on the bumper. He confessed. And then he tried to say it was allergy medication that went wrong. He's doing ten years. That bastard killed my husband and all he got was ten years."

Penny's smooth veneer slid away and behind it, Cassie saw something she recognized. Reaching out, she squeezed Penny's hand. She knew what it felt like to be failed by the legal system, even when most of the people involved had done all they possibly could for her.

"I'm sorry. I don't even have words so I won't try."

Penny sighed and shook it off. "I'm mostly past it. I have my days, but you have to move forward. I met Ben in my last year of high school. He and I had twelve years together, that's more than a lot of people ever have. Living in the past kills you and I know he'd hate it if I couldn't let go." Penny smoothed down the front of her skirt as she pulled herself together.

"If you decide you'd like the work, I'd be happy to introduce you to Edward. He's a very nice man. And if you haven't seen those Chase boys yet, well, you're in for a treat." Penny winked.

Not being able to help it, Cassie laughed. "Yeah, I've seen 'em. I live next door to Matt, and Shane took my accident report. I met Kyle and his wife Maggie too."

"All of them are single except for Kyle." Penny's face tried to stay innocent and nonchalant and Cassie snorted.

"Oh, well, I don't think I'm ready to date just yet. Maybe later."

The humor slid from Penny's face. "That bad, was it? Your ex?"

"Yes."

Penny let the one word answer go because it spoke volumes. Whoever Cassie's ex-husband was, he wasn't a nice man. She liked Cassie and hoped one day she could confide in her. Penny knew that every story had to be shared in its own way so she'd back off for the time being. She would ask Edward about the job too, though, because she wanted to help Cassie all she could.

ꕥ

The following Sunday, Shane pulled his truck into his parents' driveway and hopped out. It was just in time for the weekly family dinner. He cut it close but he'd had a call and had driven past Cassie's on his way back. Just to make sure everything looked all right.

Opening up the front door, he smiled as he was greeted by the hoots of his father and brothers watching baseball in the TV room. Moving toward the insanity of noise, his attention was snagged by the feminine laughter of his mother and sister-in-law across the hall in the sitting room.

Baseball was for suckers when you could grab some attention from two of your favorite women. And he wanted to talk to his mother about a few things, anyway. Tossing his stuff on the bench in the hall, he joined them as they sat drinking lemonade and talking.

"Hey, Momma, Maggie." He bent and kissed their cheeks and tossed his long body on the couch.

"Hey, puddin'. How are you today?" Polly grinned at her oldest son.

He pretended to glower at the pet name and Maggie just laughed as she handed him a glass of lemonade.

"Be better if you didn't call me puddin'. You get out to talk to Cassie Gambol yet?"

"I do believe that girl is avoiding me. Not that I blame her. Some way to greet her, plowing into her and all. But she can't evade me forever."

Maggie snorted a laugh. "She'd be a fool to even try, Mom. But from what I've seen of her, the woman is very shy. There's a story lurking just below the surface but I doubt she'll part with it easily. Liv and I had breakfast with her last week and I've seen her at the bookstore. She's friendly enough but she reminds me a lot of an animal that's been abused. Her eyes," Maggie paused, looking for the right words, "there's a shadow there." Maggie looked to Shane. "I thought you suspected her of being the leader of a drug cartel and smuggling through Petal."

"She's hiding something, but I'm willing to admit I think it's more of her running out of fear than running to hide a dark history as a master criminal." He rolled his eyes at his sister-in-law.

Shane told his mother all about how Cassie had reacted to Matt and then him the week before. "I think she needs someone to turn to, Momma. I want her to know she can trust us. Er, the people here in Petal, I mean."

Polly's very perceptive gaze took her son in. "Well, aren't you sweet? You are, aren't you? Sweet on this girl?"

Shane gave up trying not to smile and sighed. His mother was too damned smart for her own good. "Yeah. Okay so yeah, I like her. There's something about her that draws me. I don't know what about her makes me just want to scoop her up and wrap her in my arms to protect her. It's not that she's giving me a line or anything. Hell, I can barely get three words out of her. I've tried to talk to her here and there but she's so jumpy.

"And sometimes I see her and she's so afraid. I don't want her to be afraid of me. I hate that. I may have been a jerk a time or two," he looked quickly at Maggie, "but I've never physically hurt a woman. I want her to trust me. I want," he scrubbed his hands over his face, "I want her to look at me without fear. I want her to see me as a man and not a threat." And he hated that she made him feel that way but he'd fought it since the moment he saw her and had given up. He was more than sweet on Cassie, he had a major jones on for her.

"Well, I'll talk to Penny about her. Maggie, you said she worked at the bookstore?"

"Yeah, a few days a week. And Shane, she's...you'll be careful with her, won't you?"

"I'm not a villain, damn it!" Frustrated anger coursed through him but the look on Maggie's face calmed him down. "Look, I know I was a jerk to you. But I'm trying to be better and I really do want to know Cassie. I won't hurt her if I can possibly help it."

Maggie nodded. "I don't think you're a villain, Shane. I think you're a good man who needs the right woman to love. So okay we'll reach out to her."

"My heart breaks to think about that woman all alone here and scared." Polly's face shadowed for a moment before she recovered herself.

Shane watched his mother's face and realized he had such wonderful examples of womanhood in his life. His mother cared so much about people and so did his sister-in-law. He could finally begin to see that his own woman could have a place there, in his family and his life. And he wanted to know if Cassie was that woman.

CRER

Cassie worked out on her front porch filling the pretty planters with bright flowers. She wanted to make the apartment her home. Each week she decided to do one more thing to claim the space. The flowers were the first step, the next week she planned to try and make some curtains for the windows in her bedroom.

"Hey there, Cassie."

She looked down the stairs and into the upturned face of Polly Chase. She'd been trying to avoid the woman for the last week and a half but Penny told her to give it up because Polly would eventually find her.

She couldn't help but smile back at the woman as she teetered up the stairs toward her on spiky heels. "Hello, Mrs. Chase. How are you today?" Time was up, she'd been caught like quarry. Cassie got up and poured water into the planters while she waited for Polly to reach her.

"Better now that I've finally found you home." Polly got to the landing and thrust two bags at her. Cassie took them with a puzzled look on her face.

"Would you like to come in? I've made some iced tea." Cassie may have been annoyed at Polly plowing into her but it was impossible not to respond to the tiny woman's smile.

"That would be lovely." Polly walked past Cassie into the apartment.

"Have a seat, I'll bring it out. What's this?" Cassie held up the bags.

"Oh just some casseroles and a cobbler. Peach. I hope you like peach cobbler."

"Like it? I never had it before until I moved here and it's solely responsible for two extra pounds. It wasn't necessary for you to do this, you know." Cassie began to put the pans in her freezer and the cobbler on the counter. She filled two glasses with ice and tea and brought them to Polly.

"It wasn't necessary but it's neighborly. You're new to town and I got you into a car accident your very first day here. Lordy, I can't believe I did that. I hope you don't think worse of me." Polly blushed furiously.

Cassie had of course but found herself unable to hold her anger now that she was face to face with Polly. "Everyone in this town adores you, Mrs. Chase. I appreciate you coming by, I really do. And no, I don't think worse of you. Accidents happen." Especially if you're Polly Chase apparently.

Polly laughed and drank her tea. "Not bad for a Northerner." She winked.

"Northerner? I'm from Los Angeles."

"Exactly. If you're not a Southerner, what are you then?" Polly waved it away and Cassie just laughed and tried not to stare at how high Polly Chase's hair was. It was like an engineering marvel.

In the end, Polly stayed for an hour and wrangled a promise that Cassie would come to dinner sometime within the next month.

Bowled over, Cassie watched her whip away from the curb and nearly hit an oncoming car. The capper was the gay wave she sent to her near-victim as she drove away.

Chapter Four

As the days passed, Cassie began to truly live her new life. No one knew about her past and it was like a weight lifted from her. Most days she even forgot about Carly until some odd thing would remind her that a year ago she'd been someone else.

Three days a week Cassie worked at the bookstore, spending her spare time making jewelry. She'd spoken with Dee and would begin to sell her stuff at the Sunday Market that coming weekend. The detailed work took time and attention and she found it really good physical therapy for her fine motor skills. She wouldn't do surgery again, but she was able to hold the tools without shaking and manage all the finish work.

Her friendship with Penny had continued to deepen and damn if it didn't feel good to have a girlfriend again. Terry had never allowed her to go out with friends, wanting all her free time to be spent with him. He was always jealous of friends and family. Over time she'd pushed them all away rather than get into continual fights with him over it. In any case, her friends had all been pretty smart cookies, they'd seen his behavior, commenting on it and it was just easier to not have to deal with the embarrassment.

She'd even begun to see a therapist twice a week and found that talking about her time with Terry had started to help. Began to understand how it all happened and also that she wasn't a bad person. Still the guilt and shame were hard to part with.

Petal began to be home to her. Her residents like an extended family. Cassie got to know her neighbors in the fourplex, most especially Matt Chase. She certainly had no plans to complain that because of Matt she saw Shane Chase nearly as often. It seemed like he was at Matt's all the time. Truth was, she was beginning to like him too. He knew she was skittish and respected her space. He never rushed up on her or surprised her. For a big man, he was surprisingly gentle with her each time their paths crossed. There was something disarming about the way he treated her. Not so much like he felt sorry for her or pitied her but he was careful, respectful of her.

As a whole, every Chase family member she met she'd taken a liking to. Polly, as predicted, was impossible not to like. There was something irresistible about her. Maybe it was that Polly just sort of accepted Cassie, warts and nerves and all and didn't seem to notice. It just felt so *normal.* And normal felt good.

CR80

Three weeks after Cassie had started at the store, she and Penny were closing up when Maggie came in.

"Hiya, Penny. Hey, Cassie, I saw you had some pretty flowers on your front porch. Looks nice. Kyle was impressed when we stopped over at Matt's on the weekend."

Cassie just smiled. It wasn't like she could get a word in edgewise with Maggie Chase if she tried. But as it turned out, Maggie, like the rest of the Chase clan was simply a nice person and fun to be around.

"It looked so forlorn, I wanted to make it more colorful. Just trying to make it a home, you know? What are you up to?"

"Well, I have an ulterior motive for being here. You and I haven't really hung out much and I'm on my way to The Pumphouse for some beer and staring at some Chase brothers. Tonight is their pool game and really, we just gossip and watch tight butts in faded jeans. Sounds good doesn't it? What do you say? You and Penny should come and hang out."

How long had it been since she'd gone out with girlfriends for beer and burgers? And pool? "Pool?" Cassie grinned. "Really?" She loved pool. Before marrying Terry, she'd played several times a week at the tavern near the medical school. After they'd gotten married, he'd bought a table for the house. Of course he couldn't deal with losing so eventually she refused to play with him.

But as Brian was so fond of telling her, she had to start living her life again and who cared what Terry did or didn't do? He was long gone.

"From that slightly scary look in your face I take it you play? Those boys play every Friday night. I'm sure they'd love for you to join them."

"Shane would," Penny said as she locked up the back door and came toward them.

Cassie blushed and Penny chuckled. "Come on, Cassie. Anyone with eyes can see how he looks at you. He's smitten."

"I uh. Well, he's just being nice. And I think he suspects I'm up to no good. But yes, I love pool. Or I did. I haven't in a few years. I used to be pretty good."

"Well then I think some beer, gossip and watching you play pool with some handsome boys is just the ticket." Maggie grinned and they all headed out.

Liv and Dee were already waiting at a table near the doors when they arrived. Once seated, Cassie tried to pretend that she wasn't watching every move Shane Chase made. The man was so big and bad but there wasn't anything threatening about him despite that. She loved the color of his hair, sort of coffee brown with a hint of blond. He had a savage kind of handsome that she found herself thinking of during the day. Many times during the day.

Forcing herself to focus on the women at the table, she tried to put him out of her mind. She did not need any more men.

As if he felt her gaze on his skin, Shane turned and noticed her there with Maggie and the others. So tall and striking. She stood out every time he saw her. The woman was seriously beautiful.

"Oh for cripes sake! Just go over there already." Kyle took his shot and rolled his eyes as he straightened. "You look like a starving man. It's pathetic."

"Yeah, the last time I saw that look *you* were wearing it." Marc chuckled. "Go on, Shane."

"I will, only because you three won't shut up until I do. Bunch of old women." He leaned his cue off to the side and headed toward their table.

"Hi, Cassie. Nice to see you here."

Cassie looked up at him and smiled hesitantly. She'd lost most of her fear with him but there was still a shadow of it in her eyes. He wanted to wipe it away.

"Hi, Shane. How are you all tonight? Who's winning?"

The sound of her voice, smoky sex and velvet seduction, stroked over his skin and made his gut tighten.

"Cassie here loves to play pool," Maggie said with a grin.

Shane adored his meddling sister-in-law at that moment. "That so? Well, show me what you've got, then." He held out his hand and Cassie scooted out of the booth, grabbing his forearm instead to help herself stand.

The shock of the cool, soft skin of her hand touching his arm shot through his body. As always, she seemed so many things at once. Strong and independent, yet vulnerable and scared. And he was seriously messed up if a woman's hand on his arm made him cow eyed. He was so pathetic he wanted to kick his own ass.

He motioned toward the table in the back and she walked ahead of him. Which was fine with him. He had no problem at all watching the delectable sway of her denim-clad ass. And it was a mighty fine ass, Round and high and juicy. Did she wear a thong? Boyshort type panties would look nice too, just a nice little slice of her cheeks showing out the bottom. Okay that had to stop or he'd be embarrassed in about a minute or so.

"Cassie's gonna play a game with us. She says she used to be pretty good. So let's take it easy on her." Shane cleared his throat and thought about the college football scores to get rid of the substantial hard on she'd given him.

Rolling her eyes, she grabbed a cue and chalked the tip. All four men watched, rapt, as she blew off the excess. Annoyed, Shane elbowed Matt and glared daggers at Marc but both men just shrugged and Kyle laughed.

"Rack 'em up, boys."

Oh, the way she said that made his heart stutter. Didn't matter what she said, he was sure she'd sound drop dead sexy ordering a grilled cheese sandwich.

"Ante's ten bucks," Matt said with a wink.

Cassie snorted, pulled a ten out of her jeans and slapped it down on the side of the table.

"Ladies first," Shane said, motioning for her to go ahead.

"You sure about that?" She stood, hand on her hip.

"Of course. Guests and ladies first."

Cassie shrugged and took her first shot and proceeded to wipe the floor with them. Shot after shot, she'd call and sink it. She cleared the table without breaking a sweat.

Turning back to them, a sexy grin broke over her lips. Satisfied, she grabbed the money and tucked it into her pocket. "Thanks boys. That was a very profitable few minutes."

"You're a pool shark!" Shane had been dumbfounded but now he found himself even more attracted by this mystery woman. Okay, so watching her bent over the table as she played helped a bit too.

"Nah, not anymore. See I could have played dumb and suckered you in until the pot was much bigger and then kicked your asses. But I played true from the first shot. I wasn't even sure I could still play this well. I'm glad I still have it." She smiled and Shane's cock sprang from hard to impossibly hard.

"You guys underestimated me." She patted her pocket. "The element of surprise, boys. Kept me in milk money." Her laugh was honeyed sexual heat.

"Another game?" Shane wanted her there longer.

"I need to be getting home. I have to be up early to get all of my stock ready for the Sunday market day after tomorrow. It was a pleasure taking your money, though. Enjoy the evening." She waved back over her shoulder as she walked away.

"Totally devious." He shook his head in wonder. "She's the perfect woman." Shane watched her go to the table and say her goodbyes to the women there. "I'm going to be sure she gets home okay." Blindly, he shoved his cue at one of his brothers, heading toward the door that she'd just walked out of.

"Cassie." He'd noticed how prone to spooking she was so he made sure to always make a lot of noise when he approached her.

She turned, a bit startled but relaxed when she saw it was him. "Hello, Shane. What's wrong?" He looked good coming toward her. Handsome and masculine.

"I just thought I'd offer you a ride home. Police escort and everything."

"Oh, that's all right. I have my car just up in front of the bookstore."

"I'll walk you to it then."

He didn't give her much chance to run away when he fell into step next to her. The heat of his body rolled over her as they walked. The more she was around him, the less he scared her, but still, it was hard to not cringe when he walked so close to her. He just took the world for granted. Lived without fear of being assaulted or raped. Men his size could walk around any time without worry. She wished she knew what that felt like. For even just a few minutes.

He was patient as she unlocked her car but stopped her from getting in with a gentle hand at her shoulder. "Cassie, uh, would you like to get dinner sometime? Maybe go dancing?"

"I...well, I don't know if I'm ready to date just yet." Her words came out in a rush and the tenderness she brought out in him bloomed through his heart. Damn, what was it about this woman that got to him so deeply?

"Just yet? Are you with someone? I should have asked." He knew she was divorced of course. Nothing stayed a secret very long in Petal. Hell, her landlord share that tidbit innocently enough the first night she'd landed in Petal and Shane had done a background check as well.

"Not anymore. I'm divorced."

He wasn't sure what emotion was in her voice as she'd said it. Sadness? Did she miss the ex? Pain? Was she afraid? It was petty of him but he far preferred that she hated her ex than her still wanting him. "Oh, it's still new. I'm sorry."

He tried to stay patient as possible, watching as she took deep breath and licked her lips before deciding to answer him. "It's not really new. I'm not pining away for him or anything. It's...complicated." Her voice trembled at bit at the end and he locked his knees to keep from moving to her.

The fear was there, unmistakable. "I know you're afraid of something. You can trust me, you know. I want to help. You can share your story with me. I like you, Cassie." His voice was soft and he had to grip the top of her car door to keep from reaching out to touch her.

Her big blue eyes looked up at him for long moments, wavering. But at the last minute she looked away for a split second and when she looked back, the moment had passed. "I'm...it's not something I like to talk about. Anyway, I should be getting home."

"Just come as my friend then. I won't rush you. I want to get to know you. Unless you're not attracted to me at all. In which case, I'll back off anything other than just being friends."

She sighed. "I'll think about it." She got into the car and then rolled down the window. "And any woman not attracted to you is blind or a damn fool."

Before he could respond, she'd pulled out and was driving away, leaving him wearing a goofy grin.

CRES

He took those words as a sign along with her pool game. Later that night in his bed he stopped pretending he wasn't totally gone for her and just accepted it. He'd never failed at pursuing a woman and he certainly didn't plan to start. He wanted Cassie Gambol and not just for a few nights in his bed. At first it had been a mild crush, then an interest and now he'd developed a serious fascination with Cassie. She made him think about her in ways he'd never thought about a woman before.

The very specter of the feelings that had sent him running out on Maggie two years before seemed totally right and he realized he was ready for Cassie. The issue was that he had to make her ready for him.

He'd take it slow even if it killed him.

CR80

He made himself promise to not rush up on her as he walked toward Fourth Street the next morning.

She sat there, ebony hair glossy in the sunshine, pretty blue eyes shaded by sporty black sunglasses and he was drawn to her immediately.

He'd thought she was gorgeous as he caught sight of her but the smile she gave him once she'd recognized him made her a goddess.

"Mornin', Cassie." He stuck his hands in the front pockets of his shorts to keep from touching her.

"Good morning, Sheriff. What brings you out here on such a sweltering Sunday?"

She did. He'd tossed and turned and finally had to take matters into his own hands in the shower. The woman drove him to distraction, turned him on, electrified him with her presence and it drove him wild. That she apparently had no idea she affected him that way was even more irresistible.

"Oh just looking." He motioned to her wares on the table. "You made all this?" Her creativity was impressive. He admired her skill and the craftsmanship of the things she'd made.

"I did. What do you think?" Her voice had gone soft and shy.

Reaching out, he fingered a pretty beaded necklace that she'd hung on some sort of stylized branch thing. "I think you're amazingly talented. This is all beautiful. In fact, I think this would look good on Maggie, don't you? And this for my momma?"

Her smile returned, brighter than before. "This amber color would go really well with Maggie's hair, yes. I've seen her wear something similar to this before. But this," she touched the necklace he'd indicated for his mother, "is too delicate for your mother. She's much bigger than this necklace. Her jewelry should be bolder."

"She's barely five feet tall." Shane chuckled.

"Ah yes, but your mother is ten feet tall in personality. That's what I mean. Her hair is very..." Cassie chewed on her lip and he grinned, waiting to see what she'd say. "It's so festive and her accessories are all very large."

She looked over the things on the table and shook her head. "I don't have anything that's right for her." Reaching down, she pulled out a plastic container and flipped it open, rustling through it for a few moments. "Aha!" She held up a pretty piece of glass swirled with blues of all hues and a thread of silver. "This. Let me make her something with it. I'll let you know when I've finished it. If you don't like it, no harm."

"You'd do that for me?"

"Sure. I was thinking of having it hang vertically, I think it would draw out her neck."

He smiled at her, not knowing what the hell she was talking about but it sounded good. And it gave him the chance to see her again. "Thank you. That's very nice of you. Her birthday is next month. Can I buy that necklace there for Maggie now though?"

"Oh." She blushed and he liked that the blush was for something innocent and sweet between them and not her usual shyness. "Sure. Thank you. Would you like me to wrap it up for her?"

He nodded, without words. He watched her graceful hands draw the necklace from where it was hanging and lay it in a box and then proceed to wrap it up so fancy he was sure he'd fuck it up by the time he got it to Kyle and Maggie's.

She handed it to him and he paid her. He didn't want to leave but people had come to her table and were browsing.

"Well, thank you again, Cassie. I'll see you around."

She waved at him as he walked away.

Cassie watched him walk away, feeling giddy. Oh man, she had a crush on the sheriff. She wanted to put her head down on the desk and sigh wistfully. Wanted to write his name on her notebook and ask Maggie if Shane liked her.

This was bad. She couldn't have a crush on the damned sheriff. She didn't need the big goon, damn it. She—if and when she decided to ever date again—needed some nice, easygoing man about half a foot shorter. With like, a third the testosterone. Shane was a walking testosterone factory. He emanated masculinity. It disturbed and attracted her all at once. What she needed was a plumber, an accountant or a carpenter. She didn't need law enforcement or men with god complexes.

That made her wince. She was being unfair and she knew it. Shane Chase had been very sweet to her and while he was obviously arrogant in some ways, he didn't appear to have a god complex. Still, what the hell would she do with a man like him?

A smile crept back onto her face as she pondered the answers to that question.

CRSO

Several days later, Shane walked into Paperbacks and More and held up a take out bag when Cassie looked in his direction.

"Hi there, darlin'. Care to share a couple of sandwiches and some soft drinks with me?" This was just another step in the "get to know me" plan. He wanted to just sort of barge in and order her to come have lunch with him. It probably would have been how he'd have handled another woman. But this one needed special handling and he wasn't sure where his patience was coming from but he was thankful for it nonetheless.

"I don't know. I..."

Before Cassie could finish her sentence, Penny poked her head out of the back. "It's lunchtime anyway. You came in early and worked late day before yesterday. Flex out the time. That's a Honey Bear bag he's holding. Best sandwiches in town. I'll see you in an hour."

Cassie's mouth moved a few more times but Penny simply took over and pretty much pushed her into Shane. He'd have to thank her for that later on.

"I guess I can, yes. Thank you, Shane."

"There's a big ol' shady spot near the fountain at City Hall that's got our name on it." He held out his arm and after a brief hesitation, Cassie took it.

"Shady sounds very good."

They walked the few blocks to City Hall. He liked the way she felt next to him, her arm in his. Liked the way she fit against him even as she'd forget herself and lean a bit before pulling herself away.

Shane wasn't a fool, he wanted her to himself so he'd chosen a time after the lunch rush and had scoped out the bench earlier that day.

"This is nice. Thank you very much. How much do I owe you?"

He snorted, handed her a soda and unwrapped her straw, poking it in the top of the lid. "Please. It's not going to ding my retirement account to buy you a sandwich, a lemon bar and some soda."

"A lemon bar?"

He grinned, liking the sound of eagerness in her voice. "You like them huh? Me too. Turkey okay? It was the special today." He handed her a sandwich wrapped in wax paper. While she unwrapped it, he flattened the bag between them and put a bag of potato chips there for them to share.

She toed off her shoes and dipped her feet into the cool water of the fountain, sighing. He wanted to groan aloud at the sight of her pretty red toenails.

"Uh oh. Are you gonna give me a ticket now?"

He nearly choked on his sandwich and looked up at her. "What?"

She gestured toward her feet. "You were staring at my feet in the water. I figured I was breaking the law somehow."

He laughed, if she only knew just what he'd been thinking. "Nah. I like your toenail polish. It's sexy. And if I didn't have work boots on, my feet would be in there too."

"This heat is spectacular. Thank goodness for the shade. I don't know how you all deal with it." She leaned her head back, her spine arched.

He coughed as the erotic carnival of delights returned to his head. "Uh, yeah, it's bad but you'll get used to it. How's the sandwich?" *Must not think of sex, must not think of sex...*

"It's as good as advertised. I didn't realize how hungry I was. Really, thank you for thinking of me." Her voice suddenly turned shy and he saw a delicate blush work up her neck.

"Well, it's not hard. Thinking of you, that is. So uh, what did you do back in Los Angeles?" Jeez, the woman had the power to make him babble. Him, Shane Chase, a man thought of as smooth and cool, turned into a mass of babbling, lovesick fool. His brothers would have a field day.

She blinked at him a few times and he wasn't sure if it was about his question or the comment about thinking about her.

"A little of this, a little of that. Nothing major really."

He may be a small town cop but he was still a cop. He knew when someone wasn't telling the whole truth and Cassie Gambol was not telling anywhere near the whole truth.

"Okay, if you say so. Do you have any family?"

"I have a brother." She smiled.

"Ah, progress! Older or younger? Parents?"

"He's older by three years. My mother died when I was twelve and my father nearly two years ago now."

"I'm sorry. It must have been hard to grow up without a mother. And then to lose your father at a young age too."

"It was, yes. But my brother was always there for me and my dad was a good man. He worked a lot but he was home every night for dinner. We survived as families do."

"Did you grow up in LA then?"

"Born and raised. My father too and his father before him."

He liked the way her voice changed when she talked about her family. There was a fondness there that appealed to him.

"Which high school did you go to?"

She snorted and balled up her wax paper as she finished the sandwich. "Where's my lemon bar?"

He laughed and handed it to her. Her eyes lit up with greed as she pulled the plastic wrap free, amusing him. The way her eyes slid half closed and she moaned as she took a bite did other things to him entirely. He had to put his napkin over his lap to hide the ridge of his cock pressing against his zipper.

"That's so good."

"You have a sweet tooth to go with that sweet voice, huh?" His voice was hoarse.

"I love sweet things. My big failing." She smiled sheepishly, avoiding the rest of his comment.

"You're doing well being friends with Maggie then. She's quite a hand in the baking department."

"You seem very close to her. To all your family."

"I have a great family. My parents are the best, they've supported me in everything I've ever done and Maggie is my family now too. She and Kyle are great together." He leaned forward and drew the pad of this thumb over her bottom lip. Her eyes widened and he saw the pulse at the base of her throat flutter. "You had a bit of powdered sugar there."

She brought her hand to her lips briefly and the moment between them stretched until she licked over the spot he'd just touched. The unwitting eroticism of it sent him reeling.

Clearing her throat she took a deep breath. "Uh thanks. That's lovely. About your family I mean. Oh, I'm nearly done with your mother's necklace. If you like, I can leave it at Matt's for you in a few days. Or I can bring it to work on Friday and you can get it then. When is her birthday? I didn't want to miss it."

Impulsively, he took her hand and held it in his own for a few moments. She turned, her gaze locked with his. Relief rushed through him to see there was no fear in her eyes.

Bringing her hand to his mouth, he brushed his lips across her knuckles ever-so-softly and laid her hand back in her lap. Her taste tingled on his lips.

"Her birthday is Labor Day. So you have three weeks. And I'll drop in the shop Friday. We can have lunch again."

She bristled. "I don't know. I told you before, I don't know if I'm ready to do this yet."

He turned to her, bending his knee between them. "Do I make you feel pressured?"

"No."

"You said you didn't have any feelings for your ex, right?"

She shuddered and he dug his fingers into his calf, wanting to demand she tell him about it. Instead he waited.

"No. God, no. Well, not any good ones. It's just, I don't know if I'm ready for a relationship or dating."

"We'll take it one step at a time. This is step one here, friendship. It's going pretty well, don't you think?"

She cocked her head and studied him carefully. "You're running a game on me, aren't you?"

"A game?" He fought a smile, liking her pluck.

Sighing, she sat back.

"It's just lunch. Look, you know I'm interested in you, there's no pressure there at all. You know where I stand and I know you're interested in me too. You're the kind of woman who'd tell me to hit the road if I got too uppity."

"I used to be." Her voice was quiet, sad.

He paused a moment, not knowing how to approach and not wanting to put her off or make her upset. Aw, hell, he could only be who he was. "Cassie, you know you can tell me. You'll feel better for sharing it. Not as the sheriff, tell me as your friend."

She shook her head. "It doesn't matter. But you've won this round, Shane. Lunch Friday would be nice."

"Don't think I don't know you're changing the subject. But as it got me what I wanted I'll let it go. For now." He winked and she snorted.

The rest of their lunch was quiet and comfortable as they finished dessert. Standing after he'd tossed the trash into a nearby can, he reached down and offered her a hand up.

This time, instead of avoiding his grasp, she took it and let him help her. But he didn't let go and she didn't insist so they walked the few short blocks back to the bookstore hand-in-hand.

"Thank you very much for lunch, Shane. Why don't I deal with lunch Friday? I'll bring us something."

He grinned. "Nope. I got it. Friday is peach pie day at The Sands. We'll go there if you don't mind, sit in the air conditioned cool and have the special of the day while I pretend not to look at you a lot."

Her hand went to her throat. "I don't know what to say when you lay stuff like that on me. You're really good."

"Do I offend you?"

"No. It's flattering."

Quickly, he brushed a kiss across her forehead and stepped back. "Then my work here is done. For now. Go on back inside. I'll see you Friday." With that, he turned and headed down the sidewalk and she had to grab the door to keep from melting into a puddle.

"How was the sandwich?" Penny's mouth twitched as she hid a smile. "Pretty good if you're having trouble staying on the ground, I'd say." A single eyebrow rose as Cassie floated back into the bookstore.

"I don't know what to think about it. About him. He's so...big. He takes up so much space. He's overwhelming and charming and he knocks all good sense right out of my head every time he looks at me."

"Well, Cassie, I think you need to ask yourself why it's so necessary to think about it at all? I've grown up with Shane, he's a good man. Up to this point he's not always been so careful with women. He's been the kind of man who flits from flower to flower if you know what I mean. But with you? He's different. Not cautious so much as gentle. It's clear he's interested in you and he's being patient and letting you set the pace. And if you're going to dip a toe back in to the dating life, why not with a man like Shane? Let's be honest here, he's so hard and hot you just want to take a big bite."

Cassie froze for a moment in surprise at Penny's—for her—racy comment, and then laughed. "No kidding. But I don't know. He's so...big and in charge. I don't know if I need any of that."

Penny shrugged. "No doubt the man is one of those take charge kind of guys. Being in a relationship with Shane would take a lot of work. I think he'd want to protect his woman all the time."

"Well, I already had a man who thought he knew what was best and that didn't end very well at all."

Penny reached out and squeezed Cassie's shoulder. "I want you to know you can tell me how much you want whenever you're ready. I get the sense it was very, very bad. But despite being a big, bossy man, Shane is not like that. He's not the type to hurt a woman. I like seeing you with a carefree smile. Let him make you happy why don't you? If it turns in a direction you're uncomfortable with, you can always take a step back. You're young, Cassie. Let yourself live." With a final squeeze of Cassie's shoulder, Penny went into the office again and Cassie went to finish putting the new releases out on the shelves.

Chapter Five

Penny smiled and waved as Maggie and Polly walked into the Honey Bear and joined her.

"The tea and brownies are on the way."

Polly tossed her gargantuan bag on the floor and sat with a happy sigh. "Good. How are you, sugar?"

"I'm doing well, Mrs. Chase. Hey, Maggie, looking great as always. Thanks so much for meeting me here."

"An offer of blonde brownies and planning for Cassie? What's not to like about that?" Maggie grinned and took out a pad of paper and a pen.

"I was thinking of something like a welcome barbecue. We can invite folks to come and spend the day mixing. She could get to know people and feel like a part of something." Penny sipped her tea.

"That's a great idea. We can do it over Labor Day weekend. We were going to do something for my birthday but we can make it a combination thing. That way she'd have to come or risk insulting me." Polly raised a smug eyebrow and the other two women laughed.

"It's a good thing your powers are harnessed for good, Mom. She's so shy sometimes that I agree she might turn down something that was just for her but if we link it to your birthday she'd come. Plus, Shane can have her for the whole day then." Maggie bit into the just delivered brownie and groaned in delight.

"He's shown up twice to bring her lunch this week. Just this afternoon he brought her flowers and escorted her like she was some precious object. She's bowled over. He's putting on the full court press with her. It's impressive to watch," Penny told them.

"I haven't seen him this interested in a woman since before Sandra. He talks about Cassie all the time. I like her a lot. She's a sweet girl and smart. I think she's good for him because it makes him think about someone else. Not that he's selfish but he's never really put a woman first before. Whatever it is she's hiding, it's not anything she's at fault for, I can tell that just from dealing with her. I worry for him but if anyone can help her, it's my Shane."

"Polly, I think it's about her ex-husband. She hasn't shared much but I think there was some bad stuff there. She's nervous as a cat about men but she's not a criminal. Hard working. Kind."

Polly sighed sadly. "I hate to think that any man would do something bad to his wife. But I'm glad she's here and we'll just have to show her that."

They planned the party, deciding to have it at Penny's house, right on the water with food and drinks and lots of fun. They'd invite enough people for Cassie to mix and get to know but not so many she'd feel overwhelmed.

CR&O

Cassie's thoughts were filled with Shane as she watched him approach her table at the Sunday Market. His jeans clung to his long, powerful looking legs and his T-shirt fit snug over his upper body. His muscles positively rippled as he moved, blue-green eyes only for her. She loved the way his hair looked a bit messy but still soft and silky as it touched the top of his collar.

"Hi." She waved as he stopped. She wished she had something more articulate to say but the man sapped her IQ as all her blood moved away from her brain to her nipples. Shifting and squeezing her thighs together to ease the ache his presence brought, she smiled up at him.

"You look beautiful today. Well, you always do. How's business?" He reached out and touched the scarf she had around her neck. The scarf she used to hide the scars.

Still, it was a major victory for her that she'd stopped hiding so much of herself. Yes, she hid the physical reminders of her years with Terry, but she was opening up in ways she hadn't in years. She'd had beer and burgers with Penny and Maggie and the others on Friday night after a really lovely lunch with Shane where he made her blush with his love of the necklace she'd made his mother. She'd beaten the Chase brothers at pool again and Shane walked to her to her car. The kiss had been on her lips, brief but still made her all shaky.

She'd gone into her growing feelings for Shane with her therapist and her brother. Cassie was beginning to feel normal again. She had a life with friends and grocery shopping and a paycheck. Normal was a gift and she'd agreed with her therapist and her brother that she needed to grab it with both hands and live it.

Starting with letting Shane Chase catch her if he wanted to. Or, at least let him take her on a date.

"I'm all right. Apparently your mother and Penny have got some big party planned to welcome me to Petal. They're saying it's for your mother's birthday so I can't refuse."

He threw back his head and laughed. "You're right. They've got your number. Not that it matters, she's got you on the ropes. You're coming, right?"

She grinned. "Yes. I've been promised peach cobbler *and* lemon bars. You're a terrible man to expose my weakness so it can be used against me."

He'd never seen her so flirtatious. He liked it. Liked seeing her lighthearted and unafraid of him.

"Darlin', you've been in Petal nearly six weeks now. By now, your brand of toothpaste isn't a secret. That's the price of living in a small town."

She blushed and he decided to forge ahead. "Would you like to go to dinner with me? Dinner and maybe some dancing at The Tonk? Dinner would just be us two. Well, 'cause I want you all to myself. But dancing would be a group of folks. Kyle and Maggie, Matt and Marc will have dates, too, of course. Liv will be there with her new boyfriend Brody."

"Okay."

He'd been readying his next line of attack when he realized she'd just agreed to a date. "Okay?"

"Yeah. When?"

"Tuesday? I have Wednesday and Thursday off this week."

"All right. I have Wednesday off too."

"Pick you up at seven then? Is Italian food okay with you?"

She nodded and he stood there grinning at her for several long moments.

"I'm gonna go now before I do something stupid and you change your mind. I'll see you tomorrow for lunch."

Before she could argue, he turned and headed off with a wave. Still didn't stop her from watching his ass as he left though.

CR&O

As satisfied as she'd been with the profits from her Sunday Market, the best part was that she got to use her hands to create. Truth was, she ached to practice medicine again.

There had been very little in her life she'd been more passionate about than being a doctor. She loved it. Loved helping people, loved improving lives. She missed it and found herself thinking about starting again with a new practice specialty.

Oh, she knew she'd have to go back and get more training. That didn't seem as daunting as it might have before. Before she'd decided on her surgical residency, she'd been fascinated by family medicine and one of her old mentors was a family practitioner in Orange County. The thought of taking care of entire families had a lot of appeal.

At the same time, it scared the hell out of her to imagine risking herself over something and losing it again. She couldn't work at the bookstore forever but it was good for the immediate future and her creative side was nourished by the jewelry making.

At the close of the day, Cassie went to a movie with Penny and called Brian once she got home.

"So, the sheriff asked me out today again."

"Yeah?" She could sense his grin.

"I said yes. We're going to dinner and dancing afterward."

"Well it's about time. Go Sheriff Chase. Good for you, Cassie. I'm proud. So proud."

"You know what? I'm proud too. It feels good not to live in fear. He's a nice guy, Brian. I really like him. And his family, they're like a dream come true. Every last one of them is adorably sweet."

"They'd better be. You deserve it."

They spoke for a long time after that, sharing their lives in a way she'd been unable to do since before the last years with Terry. She finally had part of herself back. Even better, she was sharing it with people who mattered to her. It was a kind of connection she'd missed so much. It felt so good she wondered when the other shoe would drop and something bad would happen to mess it all up.

Chapter Six

Tuesday morning dawned and Cassie puttered around the house all day. To keep her mind off her first date in a year and a half, she'd painted one of the tables she bought at a yard sale. It sat drying on her deck as she realized it was longer than a year and a half. It was six because Terry didn't really count. Hell, the first time she felt lighthearted about a simple thing like dinner and dancing since the first year she and Terry were together. Gah! So much for not thinking about it.

To get away from the apartment, she splurged and went to the beauty salon to get her hair and nails done. On the way back, she bought a sexy pair of shoes. Which would of course go with the jungle of sexy shoes in her closet right now. She had a weakness for shoes. Okay, an addiction. But hey, as addictions went, it wasn't that bad.

After a brief nap she still had an hour to go before Shane showed up and she began to get nervous.

"This is stupid. I should not be going out." She began to pace, mumbling to herself.

A knock sounded on her door and she looked at the clock. No, still an hour away, it couldn't be Shane. She'd kill him if he showed up an hour early. What kind of man showed up an hour early?

Stomping over to the door she looked through the peephole, fingertips caressing the baseball bat leaning against the wall.

She opened it and Maggie, Penny and Liv all rushed in. "Afternoon, Cassie." Penny gave her a brief hug. "I do like your hair. I think I see Tate's handiwork. She's a genius with those scissors."

Before Cassie could answer, Maggie and Liv followed with hugs and all three simply strolled past her into her bedroom.

"What are you all doing here? I mean, sorry, that's terribly rude of me. Hello, how are you all? Now what the hell are you all doing here?"

Liv laughed and gestured to the endless rows of shoe trees and racks lining her closet floor. "You're a shoe whore! My word, I don't think I've ever seen so many shoes in one place. What size do you wear?"

Cassie narrowed her eyes. "I don't know if I've known you long enough to share shoes with you. That's a very intimate thing. I'll need to run a credit check and do a few home visits to see what sort of environment they'd be in."

Liv looked startled and then laughed. "You've got a sense of humor. I knew it was in there somewhere." Her eyes moved back to a pair of red patent leather slingbacks with open toes. "Oh my lands. Cassie, I don't care what you were going to wear, you will plan an outfit around these shoes."

"Wait, I think I know the dress for them." Cassie reached into the closet and pulled out a white dress with a big red O ring on the bodice where the fabric gathered. It was backless and tied around the neck. The skirt of it had a handkerchief hem. The perfect sexy summer dress.

Of course, she hadn't worn it since the...what the fuck could she call it? It sure wasn't an accident. Was your husband trying to kill you an incident? Whatever, maybe she'd write Miss

Manners to see. But for now, she'd have to choose something else because backless wasn't an option.

"Oh, no. Let's see what else there is." She moved to hang it back up but Liv grabbed it.

"This is perfect. Cassie, you've seen yourself in a mirror, right? You know you'll look like a sex goddess in this dress. Shane will be under your spell the minute you open that door."

"I don't feel comfortable showing so much skin on a first date."

Liv started to speak but Penny put a hand out and touched her arm. Instead, Liv nodded and hung it back up. "Okay. Well that's fair enough. What else do you have?"

In the end, they decided on a different white dress with a wide, red patent leather belt and tiny, heart shaped buttons. The cuffs on the short sleeves were red where they folded up and the sweetheart collar was also lined in red. It hugged every curve and the shoes made her legs look ten miles long.

No one seemed to mind when she shooed them all out of the room to change, although she did laugh when Liv told her to leave off panties or they'd show a line.

After she got dressed, the four of them crowded into the bathroom while Cassie put on makeup and did her hair.

"Man, you're a knockout. I'd probably hate you if I didn't have such high self-esteem." Liv winked and Cassie laughed. "You do know you're going to stop traffic tonight, right? I don't know if The Tonk can take it. Shane is gonna freak."

"Oh puhleeze!" Cassie blushed and rolled her eyes.

The other women stared at her in disbelief. "Are you telling me you can't see how beautiful you are?" Penny asked.

"Gorgeous? I'm attractive enough, I'll give you that. But I'm just average looking. Not all siren sexy like Liv or athletic sexy like you, Penny or that sweet, fey kind of sexy like Maggie. I'm too tall, too leggy and I have an ordinary face. I do have nice boobs though. I got those from my mom."

Maggie shook her head as she stared. "Don't take this the wrong way or anything but I'm pretty sure I've never seen a more beautiful woman in person before. Cassie, you're long and curvy and your features are seriously perfectly proportioned. And your hair, who has Elvis blue-black hair all thick and shiny? And back to the not taking it the wrong way thing? Your voice is so sexy it kind makes me all tingly and I'm as straight as they come. You were stunning without makeup and in jeans but now, all dressed up and polished—you're a knockout."

"Girl, you must have hit your head if you can't see it. You're like, 'Top Ten Most Gorgeous People' beautiful. So shaddup. And take a compliment. And look in the mirror without whatever the hell happened to you. Because it's robbing you of your life," Liv said seriously.

Cassie spun and looked at Liv, heart pounding. "I wish I could," she whispered. "You have no idea how much."

Liv went to Cassie, bringing her into a tight hug. "Honey, I'm sorry. I didn't mean to be flip. It's obvious whatever it was, it was bad and I shouldn't make light. I just don't want you to hide your light under a bushel. Even if you are big time competition." Liv winked.

"Thank you. I appreciate all of you coming over here and being my friends. It means so much to me."

"Well, that's what friends are for. And now I have to get home and get ready. Kyle is making me dinner before we meet you guys at The Tonk. You look fabulous, Cassie." Maggie kissed her cheek quickly.

"And I have to meet Brody at his place, we're having...uh, okay, we're having sex before we meet you all at The Tonk."

Cassie grinned and shook her head.

"And I have dinner in the crock-pot. I will see you at The Tonk later on. You look beautiful, Cassie." Penny joined Maggie and Liv at the door and they all headed out, leaving Cassie in the quiet, alone with her thoughts and her racing nerves.

Luckily, they'd all eaten up so much time, it was just a few minutes until the doorbell sounded and after a peek through the peephole, she saw Shane standing there.

Taking a deep breath, she opened the door. It would be step one of the challenge to be comfortable with him alone in her apartment. She hadn't had a panic attack in a few weeks and the mental exercises her therapist had given her really seemed to help.

His smile fell off his face as he stared at her.

"What?" She smoothed down the front of her dress. "Do I look awful?"

He shook his head slowly. "No. You look fucking amazing." He blinked quickly. "Oh shit, I'm sorry. Oh," he grimaced, "sorry, I tend to get a bit profane when I'm nervous or agitated. That outfit has me in both states. You look beautiful. Sexy. Outrageously hot."

His flattery washed over her, making her feel warm and tingly. She smiled, blushing. "What are you standing out there for?"

"I was waiting for you to invite me in. I know you've been uncomfortable alone with Matt, I didn't want to scare you."

Her euphoric mood was cut by the reality of her insane life. "Come on in, I'm sorry. My manners are bad. I'm all right. I didn't know Matt then, I do now. I'm really not crazy, I swear."

He caught her hand and raised it to his lips. "I don't think you're crazy, Cassie."

They stayed long enough for her to gather her wrap and a bag and they were on their way to the restaurant.

Vincent's was a small, family-owned Italian restaurant. The interior was beautifully intimate. Candles in pretty glass holders cast a golden glow about the room, bouncing off the sheen of the polished wood furniture. The place smelled of garlic, marinara and roses from the two large bouquets at the hostess stand at the front door.

The hostess smiled at Shane, her expression all but turning into a snarl when her eyes reached Cassie.

"I had reservations, Stella. For seven." Shane was crisp and efficient and kept his arm around Cassie's waist. It wasn't possessive, though, so Cassie relaxed a bit and walked ahead of him with his hand, warm and solid at the small of her back as they went to their table in a far back corner.

The hostess was ready to break her own neck as she vascillated between flirting and simpering at Shane, who did his best to ignore it, and shooting daggers at Cassie. At last, seeing she didn't have a chance, she flounced off.

Cassie smirked at Shane. "My. I think I've upset your admirer. Is she an ex?"

"Stella?" Shane's voice was shocked. "Cassie, the girl is barely twenty. I'm thirty-four years old. I assure you, I don't date women who are fourteen years my junior. I'm not a letch."

Cassie laughed then and he stilled, closing his eyes a moment. "You do know that your laugh should be a registered aphrodisiac, right? Your voice in general but your laugh...well, if I could bottle it, we'd make a million dollars."

"You're full of compliments tonight and I haven't even told you how handsome you look. I really like that color on you."

She did. The dark blue dress T-shirt he had on brought out the chocolate hues in his hair and the blue in his eyes. The

Tommy jeans were a rust color and hugged a very nice ass and hard thighs. He was a seriously dreamy man. And he smelled good, too.

"What cologne are you wearing? I like it."

"Oh, it's Ralph Lauren Black. A birthday present from my momma, believe it or not." He blushed.

"Are you blushing? Don't tell me you aren't used to women falling over themselves to compliment you, Shane Chase."

"I'm not going to answer that. I've been a man long enough to know better than that. But I will say that what matters is that *you're* the one complimenting me."

They ate a leisurely dinner and got to know each other better. Cassie found herself more able to relax with him each time they got together. Those lunches had made a difference because he wasn't really a stranger.

"You ready to go grab a dance or five with me? I have to show you off. I bet you'll fit against me just right." He stood and they walked out to his car.

"Do you write all this stuff down? Seriously, you're smooth."

He laughed and avoided the answer as he navigated into a spot to park. "Wow, crowded tonight. It's not usually this bad on a Tuesday."

"We can do it another night if you like."

"Oh hell no. You owe me a dance. Come on now. Let's show 'em how it's done."

He sprang out and walked around but she'd gotten her door open. He frowned and she took his arm.

"I can open a door, Shane. Stop pouting. I already see you have nice lips."

"I don't pout. And I like to do things for you."

She stiffened and halted. "Let's get this straight before we go inside. I can do things for myself. I'm a grown woman. I am capable of opening doors, making phone calls, ordering my food, buying my clothes and generally living my day-to-day life without being managed and done for."

He narrowed his eyes, ready to argue but saw her eyes and took a step back instead. Fear and anger. He'd pushed a button and his cop brain began to piece together whatever the hell her ex must have done.

But he wasn't going to be put in the same category as some control freak asshole who fucked her over either. "I never said you weren't capable of doing things and I didn't order your food or manage you. I just wanted to open your door. But if it bothers you, I won't."

She sighed and looked him up and down. "Listen, maybe you should just take me home."

He closed the distance between them slowly, careful not to spook her or frighten her with his body. Gently, he took her hands in his own. "Cassie, clearly I've struck a nerve. I didn't mean to upset you. And I didn't mean to sound pissy. You have a right to be treated how you want to be treated. It wasn't my intention to offend you. I am a bossy guy, it's just how I am, but I'm not trying to control you. Come on, let's go inside. Okay?" He brought her hand to his mouth and kissed the inside of her wrist.

Slowly, he felt the tension leave her body and she nodded.

Inside, the place was chaos. Cassie was thankful for his size when he plowed his way through the crowd and led her to the table where their friends had gathered.

Matt's eyes widened and he whistled when he saw her. "You look fantastic, Cassie."

Shane pulled a chair out and then indicated that she sit. She appreciated that he didn't do it all for her. Appreciated his control and the fact that he seemed to be trying hard to let her be.

She chatted with Maggie and the others and tried to ignore Matt teasing his brother.

Shane leaned over and spoke in a low voice. "Eyes back in your head, Matt. Don't let the fact that you're my baby brother stop you from understanding I'll hurt you if you continue staring at Cassie."

Matt threw back his head and laughed so loud and hard that everyone turned to look at him.

"Shall we dance, darlin'?" Shane murmured in Cassie's ear.

"Uh, sure. What was that all about?" She looked back at Matt, who was wiping his eyes, as they walked to the floor.

"He's just being Matt. A dumbass."

"Mmm hmmm. If you say so."

"I do, darlin', I do." He winked and pulled her against his body, resting his arm around her waist, holding her hand with the other. They fit together perfectly. He was a big, tall man but she was tall, too, and in her heels, it was softness to hardness in all the right ways.

So right, Cassie was pretty sure she'd need to think about it. With her eyes closed. In the dark, in her bedroom, after he dropped her home that night.

Relaxing, she put her head on his chest and melted into his body, breathing him in.

Their rhythm matched. Both with such long legs they moved over the floor gracefully, sinuously. She was aware the music changed here and there but really, it was all about Shane holding her against his chest.

Until they got bumped into. First and then again. The floor got crowded and they had to stop moving and just sway. Which was all right to start. But the people began to press in.

Every few minutes she'd get jostled again and she felt the edges of the panic encroach. Her hands started to sweat and the trembling built up in her muscles as she tried to hold it back.

But she couldn't calm it with breathing or meditation.

Shane stopped and leaned in. "Cassie? Darlin', are you all right?"

She shook her head, lips tight. Breaking from him, she headed off the dance floor to their table but people kept getting in the way. And being Petal, she was handled over and over as the men kept saying "excuse me" and helping her past. They weren't manhandling her, it was all to help her and be neighborly but it wasn't good.

By the time she reached the table the panic was gray at the edges of her vision. She knew she had to get home fast.

"I have to go. Please." She grabbed her wrap and bag and ran out the door.

Shane looked at his brothers and tossed down money for the drinks and moved to follow her but Maggie, Liv and Penny stood up.

"Shane, let us. I don't know if a man is what she can deal with right now. I promise you, we're going to her house right now. She's just a few blocks away. I'll call you and let you know she got home all right. Let us help her." Maggie begged him with her eyes and Kyle looked worriedly between them.

"She's right, Shane. Let them go so she won't be alone very long." Kyle squeezed his brother's arm.

He sighed. "Fine. But call me. Promise. Tell her I'll see her soon. I'm not walking away from her."

Maggie tip-toed up and kissed his cheek quickly. "I promise." She gave Kyle a brief kiss and the three women rushed out to follow Cassie.

Cℛℰℴ

Cassie had finished throwing up when the knocking on the door started. Shakily, she rinsed her mouth out and wobbled back into the living room.

She tried to ignore the knocking, it wasn't pounding but it was insistent. "Cassie, it's us. Please, let us in. We're worried about you."

Penny. She'd expected Shane and she *so* wasn't ready to deal with him.

"I'm all right. I swear. I'll see you all later." Cassie leaned her head against the door she spoke through.

"No way. We aren't leaving until we've seen for ourselves," Maggie called out.

Sighing, Cassie opened the door, ready to shut it after they saw her in the flesh but they pushed their way into the room.

"Now, do you have any tequila? Because I think this calls for some margaritas." Penny went into the kitchen and began to look around.

"I'm fine. You see? Now you can go. I'm not up for company right now. I don't feel well." Cassie followed them into the kitchen where they had her blender out and were assembling ice, tequila, limes and salt.

"You even have mix."

"I don't want to have drinks. I want to go to bed."

"Too bad. You're going to talk to us and if some margaritas make that easier, great. If not, we're still drinking them and you can tell us all about whatever the hell has you so spooked." Penny began to assemble everything in the blender.

"Oh, Penny said hell, I'm telling," Liv teased.

Smiling and shaking her head, Maggie pulled out her cell phone. "I'm going to call Shane to let him know you're all right. He's worried about you. He didn't come here himself because we were concerned about how you'd react to a man right now."

"I..."

Maggie held a hand up to silence Cassie while she made the call and Cassie sighed heavily and went to sit on the couch. Liv laughed and plopped down next to her.

"We're your friends, sugar. You need this. You may not even know how much but you do. Friends will sit your ass down and give you the 'Come To Jesus' talk when you need it most. And girl, you need it."

Penny brought a tray with the pitcher of margaritas and glasses and even a bowl of snacks.

"You're a pretty good hostess with my stuff." Cassie snorted.

Penny laughed. "Why thank you, I do try. Now stop being so damned difficult. Drink up and tell us what the hell brought you here today. And see, you made me curse. Three times in twenty minutes and Liv is going to call my mother and tell on me. So you'd better make this worth it."

Cassie blinked a few times and couldn't help but smile. Penny didn't swear much and it was sort of funny and hell, why not? Why not just let part of it go?

Maggie and Penny moved the small coffee table out of the way and they all moved to the floor on pillows.

"I don't suppose I could just say I had a bad ex-husband and it makes me wary of all men, can I?"

Penny arched a brow at her and Cassie sighed.

"Okay, the truth is that I did...do have a bad ex-husband. Really bad. He didn't start out that way. I met him when I was nearly done with school. He was so sweet. Funny. Concerned about my well being. He went out of his way to be sure I slept enough and ate well." She didn't want to talk about being a doctor, she wasn't ready to reveal that much just yet.

"At first, I thought it was wonderful. He brought me roses and took me to lovely places. He bought me clothes. Lots of clothes. I didn't think anything about it. But really, that's where it all started. They were not the kind of thing I'd normally wear. But slowly, he made me into another person. The person he wanted to marry."

Cassie shrugged and drank several gulps of the margarita. Of course she'd thrown up everything in her stomach so it hit pretty fast and she felt the alcohol began to work on her inhibitions.

"And we did of course. My father liked him well enough and I wanted him so that satisfied him. But my brother always disliked him. God, I should have listened to that.

"Over time, he took over every aspect of my life. Little by little. I didn't even notice it until it was too late. He controlled everything. Where I worked, what we ate—he even hired a cook to make things the way he wanted—we lived in a house he chose. My hair color was his choice, along with my hairstyle. I lost most of my friends because he thought they were unsuitable and many of them thought he was an arrogant ass and didn't want to be around him."

She closed her eyes and a tremor worked through her. While she'd been able to relate this to the therapist and even in court, it was not easy to talk about. Shame burned hot on her cheeks.

"Take it slow. We're all here as your friends, Cassie." Penny squeezed her hand.

"The hitting started. Well wait, back up a bit. The emotional and mental abuse started after the control. If I questioned anything he did, he'd grind me down. Make me think I was stupid or mean to him, that I didn't love him or appreciate what he did for me. I'm a smart woman, graduated at the top of my class but he made me feel stupid. Worthless. Invisible. Ugly." She gulped the last of her margarita and winced as the icy drink made her head ache. Still, she held up her glass and Penny refilled it.

"He didn't hit me all the time. He didn't need to really. I was so afraid to do anything wrong, I had no life outside of my job and our marriage. Being his wife was a full time job. He made me weigh in every Friday. If I gained a pound or lost more than two, he'd punish me."

The other women cringed but stayed quiet, letting her tell her story in her own way.

"He was a doctor. He knew just where to hit where it would hurt me but not do outward damage. Kidney punches so hard I urinated blood. He punched me in the head, no bruises that way but I developed a vision problem so he stopped that. All of the physical stuff was where it wouldn't show. On my stomach and lower back, my thighs were a favorite place." Her voice seemed so calm as she related it all. Almost like she was reading it, or even talking about someone else. It was the only way she could get through it.

"Anyway, it all started getting really bad two years ago. The physical abuse was getting severe enough that my co-workers began to suspect something was wrong. He was questioned by his boss, which only made things worse for me. Our sex life," Cassie shuddered, "was awful. He raped me more often than I consented. It was like this one part of me I could control. He couldn't make me want him or even pretend to." Her voice became choked and tears welled up. Maggie moved closer and stroked a hand over her hair.

"I wanted to leave. I don't know why I didn't. I was afraid. He told me he'd find me and kill me. I believed him. I had every reason to. I took birth control shots and thank heaven I never got pregnant because he really wanted kids.

"And then my father died and he deteriorated because I had money. A lot of it. In his crazy mind, enough to leave him. He became paranoid. He'd weep, begging me to forgive him one day and beat me nearly bloody the next. I was missing work and I knew it was a matter of time before I lost my job or he killed me."

She got up and went into the kitchen and took two shots of the tequila, wiping her hand on the back of her mouth before coming back. "Okay, I think I'm better now." Her words were slurred a bit but she wanted to finish it. Or at least most of it.

"My boss was...is a wonderful woman. Really supportive. I love her to this day. Anyway, she cornered me in her office and demanded that I tell her the truth. I'd been lying so long, hiding it that I started to deny it automatically but for some reason, I shook it off and told her the truth. Showed her the bruises on my back and stomach and she called the cops and my brother. The cops took my statement and pictures and my brother made me move out of the house and in with him.

"I filed for divorce and we started going through the process. It sucked but my ex couldn't do much. My brother is a hot shot family law attorney and he had my back. There were pictures and lots of evidence from people who'd seen my physical problems getting worse at work. I got my divorce but I gave him the house and the car and the vacation house and all the clothes he ever bought me. I wanted to be free, I didn't care about the stuff. I just took what I brought into that house and my books.

"But it wasn't enough. And he wouldn't stop. I thought I had my life back but he wasn't going to let me. He just pretended to and he attacked me. A little over year ago. Bad." She couldn't detail that night. Could not.

She shook her head hard and began to cry. "I can't say more."

The women, her friends, surrounded her and enveloped her into a hug as they murmured. Comforting her.

She cried a long time until she couldn't anymore and sat back, head on the couch.

"Girl, I don't know how you came out of that clusterfuck with such a good head on your shoulders. You're a strong woman, Cassie. I admire you."

Cassie moved her head enough to look at Liv in utter disbelief. "Strong? I let this asshole fuck me over and beat me up, *rape me*, for four years! I'm not strong. I'm a doormat. I was weak and stupid."

Penny moved, holding her upper arms. "You are not stupid, Cassie. Domestic violence happens to women across class lines, across educational backgrounds, across race and religion. It happens to all kinds of women. It's the frog in the pot syndrome. You didn't know the water was boiling until it was too late. That makes you *human*, not stupid."

"And that's what these asshole abusers do. They make you believe you deserve it. It's a mindfuck. He worked you over physically as well as mentally. But you got out. That's the key here, Cassie. I can't believe what you've gone through. No wonder you get spooked by men. It's amazing to me how totally together you are." Liv's voice was tinged with anger.

"I'm not some charity case you know. I heard all this at my group counseling. You must all think I'm such a flake. I thank God my father never lived to see how it ended."

Penny shook her head. "I think you're amazing. I've thought that since the first day you came into the store and I continue to think so. You're a *survivor*, Cassie. He took your life for four years but you took it back. You're here, working, living, dating even. This doesn't change the way I feel about you. You're my friend."

"You have nothing to be ashamed about. What happened was not your fault. It wasn't. He hurt you, that's on him. I hope that bastard got what was coming to him." Maggie's face held an emotion Cassie couldn't quite identify.

Cassie sighed. "He didn't. But I don't want to talk about it anymore. Thank you for listening to me. You don't know what it means to be able to share this with someone other than a therapist."

"That's what friends are for. Cassie, nearly two years ago now, I was kidnapped, assaulted and nearly raped by a stalker. It's not the same as what you endured but I understand the guilt and the shame. If you ever want to talk, please call me or come over. Anytime. I mean that." Unshed tears shined in Maggie's eyes.

And suddenly, a weight moved from Cassie's chest and she took a deep breath. Deeper and more relaxed than she'd taken in quite some time. Her brother and her therapist were right, it did feel better to share her burden with people.

They stayed a while longer and talked until Cassie was well enough to laugh again. Alone in her bed that night, she didn't feel the specter of Terry over her shoulder. It was just her.

Chapter Seven

After a long day at work, Cassie slumped into her superheated apartment, turned on the air conditioning and hit the shower before even considering what to make for dinner.

Shane had left her a phone message, checking on her earlier in the day. He'd wanted to come by for lunch but it was a big new release day and she'd been rushed off her feet and had worked several hours overtime.

She'd called and left him a voicemail that she couldn't do lunch but hoped to see him later on if he still wanted to. She hoped like hell she hadn't freaked him out. Gauging by his wanting to have lunch with her, she didn't think so but hell, he may have wanted to lay it all out that he thought she was a freak and to stay away from him. Maggie was his sister-in-law after all, she probably told him all about the craziness of the night before.

Standing in front of her open fridge, hair in a ponytail, feet bare, legs exposed by a pair of cut off shorts, she jumped when someone knocked on the door.

A quick check showed Shane Chase waiting on her doorstep. Taking a deep breath, she opened the door, wincing at what a mess she must look.

He looked her up and down and shook his head. "Darlin', how do you manage to look as gorgeous in cut offs as you do in a dress that hugs every curve? You're magic."

Taken by surprise, she smiled and blushed. "Oh, well, thank you."

He held up a bag. "Take out from China Gate. You hungry?"

Stepping back she waved him inside. "Come on in, it's hot out there and I'd never say no to those spring rolls."

She put out plates and silverware as he opened all the containers and put spoons in them.

"I hope you like it spicy." He grinned and grabbed her wrist, pulling her to him carefully.

"I do." Her voice was low, sultry.

"I'm gonna kiss you now, Cassie Gambol."

"Why? I mean, why do you want me? I don't understand it. I can't lie and tell you I don't know you've been regarded as a player here in Petal. I like men, yes, but I'm afraid of being a casual indulgence to a man like you."

"There's not a damned thing about the way I feel about you that's casual. Now, I've been dying to do this for so long." He closed the last bit of distance between them and he brushed his mouth over hers. His lips were lush and delicious, spicy and masculine, just like the rest of him. They both groaned as he moved away.

"Cassie, you fascinate me. I'm shocked by how much I want you. I think I started wanting you when you kicked my ass at pool. No, I'm a damned liar. Since you stumbled out of your wrecked car and called my momma Crash." He put his face into her neck and inhaled deeply. "God, you smell good."

"Shampoo, sweat and a little bit of Delice," she breathed out, running her tongue over the lips he'd just touched with his own. A sense of unreality washed over her. The connection between them was warm and sticky. Lethargic with want, she let him hold her against his body. The heat of him blanketed her skin. Her nipples hardened against the wall of his chest and a libido that she'd thought beaten out of her roared back to life. There was a moment where she wondered if she was dreaming. Hell, if it wasn't she sure didn't want to wake up.

"Mmm." He licked his lips as she'd just done and a shiver ran through her. "You taste good, too. Better than you should. I ought to be running out the door but damned if you don't make me want things I'd thought I'd never want with a woman again."

His hand rested at the small of her back, hot and inescapably present. The other rested on her shoulder. He held her in his orbit physically and mentally. His presence was so intense it boggled her mind. Things tightened low in her gut as her skin tingled everywhere he touched her. And yet, aside from general nervousness, she wasn't afraid.

She caught her lip in her teeth and he groaned softly. "I know you want me too." Leaning in, he pressed a hot, wet kiss to the hollow just below her ear. "I can feel your nipples against my chest," he murmured, breath stirring the wisps of hair around her ear. His tongue darted inside and then he caught the lobe between his teeth. She shivered, going weak in the knees. "But I want more than your physical need of me. Let's have dinner. Some snuggling on your couch. A liberal smattering of smooches. Let me get to know you as a woman."

"I...yes." She nodded, incapable of further speech. Especially when his grin widened and he looked like a predator.

They sat down and began to dish up the food, digging in. He watched her and she laughed. "What? Do I have a bean spout between my teeth?"

"No," he chuckled. "I just like the way you look here with me." He shrugged. "And I like that you eat. Not like some dainty thing who wants everyone to believe she survives on air and mist, but you eat like a real person."

"Is that your finessed way of telling me I eat like a pig?"

He threw his head back and laughed. "Oh the unwinnable guy question. Darlin' you do not eat like a pig. You eat like a human who likes to eat. I *like* that."

She narrowed her eyes at him for a moment and shrugged before going back to her plate. She'd only just put the weight on she lost from the hospital and afterwards in the last three months or so.

They kept a wide berth around what happened the night before but Cassie was pretty sure Maggie had told him about Terry. He didn't seem freaked, which made her more comfortable.

After they'd eaten, he helped her clean up and get the dishes in the dishwasher before they retired to the couch.

"Let's get comfortable here, shall we, darlin'? Because I have some serious smooching planned and we should do it right." He winked and pulled her into his lap, her body straddling his.

The hard ridge of his cock fit up against her and she undulated, grinding herself over him without even thinking of it. Little flares of pleasure played up her spine and the muscles inside her pussy fluttered and contracted.

One of his eyebrows rose slowly and his hands slid to rest at her waist. "So that's how it's gonna be, huh? Mmm. You feel so damned good, Cassie. I need to kiss you again." Arching his neck up, he brought his lips to hers with crushing intensity.

Her head swam as she drowned in him. In a myriad of ways he affected her, overwhelmed her, turned her on and turned her out. Helpless to do anything more than hang on, she slid her hands up his chest and neck and into his hair. The soft, cool silk of it flowed over her skin, his skull solid and sure beneath her palms.

Grunting in satisfaction, he slanted his mouth to get more of her. His tongue slipped in between her teeth and he tasted her, met her warmth with his own. Her elemental flavor rocked him, he couldn't get enough. When she sucked at his tongue, he pulled her to him tighter and delighted in the moan that came from her lips. Swallowed it down with the rest of her that he took from the kiss.

God he wanted more. The luscious flesh of her bottom lip seduced him as he sucked it into his mouth. Arching into him with a breathy sigh, she traced the outline of his upper lip with the tip of her tongue. Down over the seam of his mouth where her lip was captured, the wetness of her tongue, the tentative and yet utterly carnal way she responded, drew him in.

It'd never been like this with a woman before. Intense, sure. Really good, that too. But so good, so right that it made his chest ache with want and need of *this* woman in his arms? Never.

Damn, he was falling for Cassie. Scratch that—had *fallen* for Cassie and he wasn't running. No, he wanted more. Wanted to gorge himself on every drop of her he could get as long as he could get it. He wanted to see what kind of tomorrow he could build with this woman. Cassie Gambol wasn't a casual indulgence at all, she was big league addiction and instead of fear, there was only joy that he'd found it at last.

It took every bit of his self control to keep his hands resting at her waist instead of sliding down to cup her ass. She was so soft against him, so warm and pliant—everything sexy and earthy, he wanted to take her in the grass under the moon, the dew on his naked skin as he watched her in the silvery light. She was a goddess come alive in his arms.

Her head tipped back as he kissed down her neck. To keep her balance, one of his hands, splayed open on her back, moved up to her neck. He gripped her, sure but not hard. Still, she stiffened and pushed away.

"Whoa! What's going on?" he asked as she scrambled off his lap and put some distance between them.

"I'm sorry. I...you touched a nerve. He did that to me when he...damn, what you must think. I don't know why you even came over here after Maggie told you."

"Told me?"

"About all the abuse, the..." her voice lowered, "...rape. I don't know if I can be normal."

"Rape?"

Cassie paled. "Maggie didn't tell you?"

"She told me you had problems with your ex-husband. She said she couldn't tell me any specifics because she didn't want you to not be able to trust her."

"Shit. Never mind. It was bad. It's over. But there are things that happen and I don't even see them coming and I don't know if I can be a normal person again. I seem to have a minefield of emotional shit because of him."

"Sit down." He pointed to the couch and went to retrieve a glass of iced tea. Coming back into the room, he pressed it into her hands and sat next to her. "Now I want you to tell me. Damn it, Cassie, trust me. Please. I can't help you if I don't know. We can work through the minefield together but I can't if I'm blind."

Closing her eyes a moment, she began to relate all that she'd told her friends the night before. She kept looking blankly out the windows as she did and Shane didn't interrupt her.

By the time she'd finished, the sun was down and her tea was empty.

"I don't even know what to say. Cassie, you're so strong. Why didn't you tell me before? Why hide this? Of course it freaked you out when I grabbed your neck like that. He must have when he hurt you, didn't he?"

She jumped up. "Yes! Yes, okay? I don't want to do this. I didn't tell you because I hate it. I hate that it happened to me and that I let it happen. I hate the person I was and I hate that anyone would know I allowed someone to do those sorts of things to me."

Gracefully, he stood and went to her. "You didn't allow it. It happened to you and you got out. And damn if you did all the right things but were failed. I'm sorry." A gentle hand moved to her cheek and his fingertips traced the line of her jaw.

"You're not disgusted? Freaked out?"

"Of course I'm disgusted. But not by you, Cassie. How can any man do that to the woman he's supposed to love and cherish? How can a man turn that love into something sick and twisted? Look at you. How can any man have had you at his side and perverted it instead of rejoiced in it? Fuck, I want to kill him for harming you!" Dropping his hand, he began to pace.

"Okay so here's what we'll do, you'll be sure to get me the order of no contact from LA. My father can help you and get you in to see a judge to get it extended to here. Does the bastard know where you are now? We should assume he's looking for you and take precautions. We'll get you some better locks, a security system too. One of the guys I work with does installation of security systems on the..."

"Whoa!" She yelled, making the time out motion with her hands. "I'm fine. I'm dealing. I'm moving on. I am so fucking done with the legal system right now it's not funny. Let's talk about something else please."

"Hell no we won't talk about something else. Cassie, you can't just ignore this. You have to take care of the legalities so I can protect you better if he comes to town. In fact, why don't you give me the name and number of the cop you dealt with and I'll give him a call and he can fill me in and I can handle things for you that way."

Her eyes widened. "This is not going to happen. Do you understand me, Shane Chase? You will not manage me. I can take care of myself."

"Yeah, sure! That's why this guy hurt you so bad that when people bump into you in a nightclub you totally shut down."

"You think you can wish all that away? Step in and make it gone? Poof, Cassie was never beaten up and raped by her ex? Stalked, nearly fired because of the harassment at the workplace? You. Can't. Save. Me! It's done. It's over."

"I have some skill and expertise here. I'm willing to overlook the fact that you didn't even tell me until tonight about the years of abuse, but it's unacceptable that you won't let me help when I have the damned ability. I want to protect you. I know what you need."

"I have had *enough*, and I mean always and forever, of men thinking they can protect me and that they know what I need more than I do. I do not need another pushy, overbearing, control freak man in my life. I do not need to be taken care of. Never again. Never again, do you understand me? I will not ever let anyone take me over and make me feel like I deserve to be beaten and treated like nothing. I like you, Shane, but not enough to give you my soul."

"Are you comparing me to your ex-husband? Oh fuck no. You will not. I've made a lot of mistakes with people in my life. Trusted the wrong ones, didn't trust the right ones, hurt those who trusted me. But I am not that filth you were married to. I care about you, Cassie. More than I've cared about a woman in..." he shoved a hand through his hair, "...damn it, I've never cared about a woman this much. Have I harmed you, Cassie? Have I used my size to intimidate you? Does my wanting to be a cop and help you and keep you safe begin to compare to a man who'd punch your head?" His eyes were vivid with emotion and it cut straight to her gut.

"I don't want your soul. I want your heart. I can wait for it and I want it of your own free will. But I'd never harm you to get it. If you'll let me, I'll cherish you, not control you. I can't promise not to be an arrogant ass. Hell, I *am* an arrogant ass. But I can't bear to think you'd class me with him. It's not fair of you."

Standing there, arms crossed defensively over her chest, she realized she'd just had a heated argument with him but he'd never jumped at her or menaced her. He'd raised his voice, yes, but not once did she feel afraid. Irritated, hell yes. The man irritated the heck out of her and it was clear he had white knight tendencies. But he was right, she wasn't being fair and he wasn't anything like Terry.

Sighing, she moved forward one step and then another until she reached him. She placed her palm over his heart and looked into his face. "You're right. It's not right. And I don't think you're like Terry. God, you're a million miles away from his zip code." She pulled back.

"But I don't know if I can promise not to react again to something like this. Or anything. The panic attacks happen less and less frequently but when they do, they're pretty bad. And I can't be managed. You're a very in charge type, Shane. I have to make choices for myself. Even if it seems stupid to you, it's everything to me. You should move on. Find a normal woman without baggage."

"Are you dumping me?" A smile played at the corners of his mouth.

"Are you mocking me?"

"If you're dumping me, I'm mocking you, yes. Cassie, darlin', I knew you were hiding something that first night you came to town. I knew you had something that was eating at you. But I pursued you anyway. You know why?"

"My sparkling wit?"

He grinned. "Yeah. And your smile. And your intelligence and beauty and damned if you don't have the nicest tits I've ever seen on a woman and I would very much like to see them naked and in a bed very soon." He held up a hand to continue. "I know it won't happen tonight, we're both a bit ragged. I'm just saying."

His arms encircled her waist and he held her to him. "Are you interested in me? In a relationship? For me, this is getting serious. You said you knew my history, well, it's true. Not that I've been a womanizer, but I've played around a lot. I had one serious relationship but I never should have moved in with her much less asked her to marry me. Looking back, I thank my lucky stars that she cheated on me and got caught.

"I want you to know you mean something to me. I'm going to try to be totally up front here because I want this to work. I want us to be together. Let's work through your panic attacks. I'll try to curtail my need to take care of the people I...uh...care about. I can't promise to stop, it's who I am, but you can yell at me and I'll never, ever, raise my hand to you in anger. I might be an asshole from time to time but I'm not a thug or a bully. Let me in. Let's see where this can go."

Her forehead rested against the hard muscle of his chest as she thought. Thought about what a relationship with Shane would be like after the morass of messed up she'd been married to. He made her smile. He cared about her and wasn't afraid to say so. That touched her deeply. And without a doubt, he was the sexiest, handsomest and downright wonderful man she'd ever met.

"Are you sure? I'm a mess, Shane."

"I'm totally sure, Cassie." The bass of his voice vibrated through his chest.

Taking a deep breath, she leaned out and looked into his face. "Okay. But don't manage me, Shane, or I will chew you up and spit you out. I mean it."

He grinned. "Promise?"

Startled laughter bubbled from her gut and she rolled her eyes.

"Cassie, do you trust me to touch you? I know we won't sleep together tonight but I'd very much like to touch you."

To demonstrate, his hands slid down the curve of her back and down to cup her ass.

"Oh, *that* kind of touching." Cassie couldn't help but smile.

The tips of his fingers brushed against the satin of the exposed skin just below the frayed hem of her shorts. Shane felt the gooseflesh erupt there as he stroked that sweet spot where the curve of her ass met her inner thigh.

He watched her eyes, waiting for her to refuse before moving his hands anywhere else. He needed her terribly but he also knew he'd have to take it slow with her at first. She had some wounds and he intended to heal them. Okay, to *help* her heal them.

Step by step he moved her back to the door behind them. He stopped when her back met it. The eyes locked with his showed trust and no small amount of desire and curiosity.

His mouth moved down and took hers. Her lips called to him, her taste tantalized and seduced. Unable to resist, his teeth caught her bottom lip, giving it a sharp nip before sweeping his tongue along the sensual curve there, laving the sting.

She sighed and his mouth caught the sound, swallowing it, taking it into himself greedily. Her palms slid up the muscles of his forearms and biceps, up his neck and into his hair as he feasted on her lips.

Their tongues slid together, sinuous and sex laden. He knew that once they got into bed together it would be incredibly powerful. Their chemistry was off the charts. That knowledge helped him stay in control. As much as he wanted to be inside her, he wanted to be inside her heart first. Wanted her to be totally sure she could trust him not to hurt her.

He brought a hand up to free her hair and it tumbled down, the scent of her shampoo filled his senses. "Everything about you smells good," he murmured as his lips moved to the column of her throat and ever-so-slowly, one palm slid up her stomach, beneath the hem of her T-shirt and found her breast.

Emboldened when she arched into his touch, he moved his other hand, slipping down into the front of her shorts. The skin of her belly was soft and warm. Fingertips traced over the front of her panties, against the silky fabric. He felt her heat, her wetness through the material.

A soft moan slid from her lips, vibrating against his mouth on her throat. The hand on her breast moved out of the way and he caught her nipple between his teeth through the cotton of her shirt. She cried out, rolling her hips forward.

Clever fingers moved the panties out of the way and slid through the heat of her pussy. Shane groaned at the same time Cassie did, finding her so wet, knowing she wanted him as much as he wanted her.

She tried to reach down to his cock but he held himself out of reach. "No, not right now. Let me love you, Cassie." She made a sound of disapproval until his fingertips found her clit and her head knocked on the door behind them. He only barely resisted chuckling, instead, he moved to the other nipple, his hand replacing his mouth on the one he'd just left behind.

Cassie hadn't had an orgasm given to her by another person in several years. Since the second year she and Terry were married. She'd wanted Shane for weeks now and her body was primed to his touch. There was no fear, only the roar of desire in her ears and the burn of want in her muscles.

The way he touched her was reverent. It made her want to weep. This big man treating her with such gentleness in the middle of his wicked carnal assault on her senses wrecked her.

She felt her orgasm coming, begin to burn in her muscles. He had two fingers inside her and his thumb applied just the right pressure to her clit. There was something to be said about a man who'd been with a lot of women. He certainly had experience.

Shane moved his mouth to her ear. "Let me have it, darlin'. Give me your orgasm. I want to feel you come around my fingers, I want to hear the sounds you make when you climax."

A cry, low and deep, broke from her lips as orgasm opened up around her and swallowed her deep. Pleasure soaked her, sapped her strength and she held on to him as it buffeted her over and over again.

Her parched cells filled up, replenished, and she began to feel whole after being broken for so long. Serotonin flooded her brain and lethargy, warm and heady stole over her as a smile crept over her lips.

It was his chuckle that made her open her eyes finally. His face was flushed, eyes desire-dark as he put her shorts back to rights and planted a kiss on her lips.

"I do believe I have never seen a more beautiful sight. Your neck arched, lips parted, a flush on that gorgeous face. You're amazing, Cassie."

She felt the tears in her throat but she didn't free them. They were bittersweet tears but she felt like giving in to them would have let Terry win and continue to fuck with her head. Instead, she embraced happiness and the thought that she might be able to have a real life, a real future and that just maybe, Shane Chase would be a part of it.

"You're good with the compliments, Chase. Now, it's your turn." She raised a brow and he laughed and shook his head.

"Not tonight. I want this first time to about you. We have so much time, Cassie. We'll take our baby steps and when we end up in bed, it'll be right and incredible."

She must have had a distressed look on her face because he laughed and kissed her again. "That look is almost as good as sex, Cassie. I like that you want me too. But we're not ready to go there yet."

She wasn't? She didn't know. She didn't think it was a problem. She wanted him to fuck her and right then. But she also didn't know if she'd freak out either and so close to their fight and the panic attack yesterday, he was probably right. She vowed to make it extra good when she did get her hands on him. She hoped she could.

Shane led her to the couch and pulled her down with him, pulling her into his side and snuggling with her. "A whole lot is going on in there." He tapped her head. "You wanna share?"

Terry had seriously eroded her confidence about sex. Not just about her own sexuality but her ability to please men. He'd always told her she was frigid and lousy in bed. What if he was right? What if she couldn't please Shane?

"Hey, no, get that look off your face right now. Talk to me, please. We can't move forward if you don't share with me."

"I'm fine. I'm working on getting past all this stuff with my therapist. Man, I never thought I'd say, *my therapist* in this context, you know? It's just something that Terry, my ex, made me feel like."

Shane took her hand and kissed her fingertips. "Like what, darlin'?"

"Unattractive. Frigid. Like I couldn't please a man." Her voice went quiet. She *knew* Terry was wrong, but what your mind knew and what your heart knew were sometimes very different.

"Cassie, your ex-husband is an asshole. You're the sexiest woman I've ever laid eyes on. I'm not lying. And the way you just flew apart in my arms? You telling me that's frigid? He's the one with problems. Any man who'd force a woman has big issues with sex and power. That is not about you. And I'd scare the bejesus out of you if I put your hand over my cock to show you just how pleased you make me. Trust me, you do."

With a soft sigh, she snuggled into his body and he held her tight while they watched a movie.

He waited until she'd fallen asleep in his arms and then carried her to her bedroom. Checking to be sure everything was locked up tight, he set the air conditioning and left her a note, telling her he'd call her the next day.

Outside, he double checked that the door had locked behind him and scanned the area for anything amiss. The lighting was good on her porch. He'd noticed she'd put in a higher watt bulb and made a note to himself to put some security lights out back for her. He was sure Chuck wouldn't mind him doing it. The added security was a plus for any future tenants anyway. He'd also put in a new deadbolt for her, after he figured out a way to make it seem like her idea.

Chapter Eight

"Is there anything I can do to help planning this shindig?"

Penny looked up at Cassie, who'd just come into the room, bearing the day's receipts.

"No. And you can give those to me and go meet Shane. I know he's out there flitting around, waiting for you."

"He can wait." Cassie sat down. "Penny, do you date at all?"

Penny pushed her glasses up her nose and paused. "It was hard, losing Ben. He was like the other half of my heart. For the longest time I couldn't even imagine being with anyone else. In the last year or so I've been on a few dates here and there. I haven't met anyone who could hold a candle to Ben's memory. Still, it hurts less and I feel like I'm waking after a long sleep. Why? You're not planning on fixing me up are you?"

Cassie laughed. "Hell, Penny, I don't know anyone other than you and the Chases. Matt's pretty hot. And Marc, well, a younger man could be just what the doctor ordered."

Penny burst out laughing. "I grew up with those boys. They're like my cousins so I while I can appreciate all that handsome, I can't see them like that. And I am quite sure Marc would wear me into nothingness. His prowess is pretty legendary."

Lauren Dane

"I was just wondering. After being married and having it not be the best experience, it's odd to be dating again and have it be so different. Better. I'm a bit giddy even but I'm not quite sure what to do. What to expect. I thought you might have some sage advice."

Penny patted her arm. "Honey, I'm no sage. All I can tell you is to go on and enjoy yourself. Anyone with eyes can see Shane thinks you hang the moon. You two are good people. The two of you can be good together if you just let go a bit."

Cassie stood. "We're headed out to The Pumphouse, you want to come with?"

"I have a date with a pedicure. I'll see you for brunch on Sunday."

"All right, come on over and show us your fancy new toes if you're up for it."

Shane nearly swallowed his tongue when Cassie emerged from the back of the store. She'd pulled her hair away from her face and was wearing shiny red lip gloss. Her sneakers had been replaced with sandals that showed off those sexy red toenails. The jeans and pretty T-shirt had been exchanged for a knee length skirt that rippled like water when she walked and a tank top-like blouse with buttons down the front. The casual professional look had transformed into something ultra-feminine and sexy with the addition of the sandals and some jewelry.

"I just needed to freshen up a bit."

He smiled and kissed her forehead. "A bit huh? You look gorgeous."

"And you smell good and look handsome. It's going to be a shame beating a man at pool who looks so good."

"You're awfully cocky."

"For good reason. Now come on."

Chuckling, he led her out the door where she locked up and they took the two block stroll down to The Pumphouse.

"Go on and play with your brothers for a while. I'm going to have a few beers and gossip with Maggie, Liv and Dee. Then I'll be over to kick your ass."

One handed, he wrapped an arm around her waist and pulled her flush with his body. "If it wouldn't smear that sexy lip gloss, I'd lay a kiss or two on you," he murmured, eyes locked on hers.

"Go on ahead, Sheriff. It's kiss-proof. And even if it wasn't, it's cherry flavored and I have more in my purse."

Her eyes fluttered closed as his lips met hers in a soft, brief and yet bone melting kiss. He didn't even use his tongue and she was nearly panting when he pulled back.

He licked his lips. "Mmmm, cherries. Very nice, darlin', very nice indeed. I'll see you in a while."

Cassie waved at him and stumbled into the booth where her friends waited.

"Uh, hello? The two of you have so much chemistry I'm all hot and bothered now. Sheesh, I'm going to jump on Brody the minute he gets off work tonight."

Blushing, Cassie grinned at Liv. "He'll thank me then, won't he?"

"I don't need to ask if you two had worked everything out from Tuesday night then." Maggie poured Cassie a beer and pushed it in her direction.

"He came over on Wednesday and we talked for hours. And kissed, a lot. He's a great kisser."

"He is. Not as good as Kyle, but definitely award winning."

Cassie stilled. "How do you know?"

Maggie blinked several times and stammered a bit. "I thought you knew."

"Knew what?"

"Shane and I dated before I got together with Kyle. It was just a few times and he dumped me and acted like a total ass. He's long since made up for it and has really grown. It was nothing, Cassie. God, he never looked at me with half the emotion he shows when he looks at you. I thought you knew."

"I can't believe no one told me!"

"Are you mad at me? It was nearly three years ago. I swear to you, Cassie, it was nothing. He really cares about you. Talks about you all the time."

"Well, I don't know. I'm not used to being around people who've kissed my boyfriend. It's weird."

Liv sighed and leaned toward Cassie. "Cassie, I'm going to say this as your friend and I want you to listen and take this to heart, okay? Shane has been with a lot of women in this town. I'm not going to lie to you about it. In this bar alone I count at least eight he's dated and it's early yet. He wasn't a slut as much as a guy who loved a lot of women. He's thirty-four, that's a lot of dating years.

"I want you to also hear me when I tell you that he's never dated a single one of them, including Maggie, for more than two weeks at a time. Shane hasn't dated since the night you came to town. You're it for him, Cassie. When a man like that falls, he falls hard and all the way. There's no middle ground for a guy like Shane." Liv smiled.

"And you *will* have to deal with jealous women, Cassie. I'm sorry to tell you but I know from experience. Not that I'm jealous of you and Shane," Maggie added hurriedly, "but I've had to deal with a lot of it with Kyle. If you let them get to you, you're letting them win. Don't. I can tell you without a doubt that Shane is not interested in any woman on this planet other than you. And I'm sorry if finding out Shane and I dated a few years ago bothers you or caught you by surprise."

Cassie sighed and looked toward the pool table. When she did, she saw the interested glances of women trying to catch the eyes of the brothers there, including Shane. But when he looked up, it was she his eyes sought out, not anyone else.

He must have seen her distress because he handed his cue to Matt and came toward them.

Not wanting to have a conversation at the table with the other women listening, she got up and met him halfway, near the arches that separated the seating area from the games section with the pool tables, darts and pinball machines.

Stopping just a hair's breadth away from her body he lifted a hand to touch her face. "You okay, darlin'?"

"Why didn't you tell me you dated Maggie?"

He looked over her shoulder toward the table but Cassie's voice brought his gaze back to her face.

"That's the kind of sneaky thing that bugs me. Why look over there for clues if you didn't have anything to hide?"

"You looking for a reason to push me away, Cassie? Hmm? Because I am quite sure Maggie told you what it was between she and I—nothing. Two dates. I dumped her because she was nice and I was worried I may actually have feelings for her at some point. I was an asshole. But it was her and Kyle from day one. Once they got together it was forever.

"I didn't think to tell you. It happened years ago. You said you knew about my history. I've dated a lot of women, hell a lot of women in this bar right now."

"Yes, so I've heard."

One of the corners of his mouth lifted and the furrows in his brow smoothed. "You're jealous, darlin'? Because flattering as it may be, it's unnecessary. I'm with you. You and no one else. Not ever again. But I can't change my past. I'm sorry if that hurts you. I really am."

"Jealous? Puhleeze."

He laughed out loud that that. "Darlin', you don't think it's hard for me to see the men watch you as you walk through any room you're in? I also have a history of being cheated on. It's hard to trust you. All I can do is take it on faith that you wouldn't do that to me. And all I ask is that you do the same."

"It's weird, knowing one of my friends has had sex with you."

"Maggie told you we had sex?" His voice rose a bit.

"No, not in so many words. You dated, you're a very...sexual man, I just put two and two together."

"We did not have sex. Do you want to know how far it went? If you do, I need another drink because it's kinda creepy now that I think of her like my little sister."

"Was there naked?"

He thought about it. "I can't remember. There wasn't orgasm. Nothing like what we shared in your apartment on Wednesday."

She shivered at the memory and he nearly purred in her ear. "Oh, darlin', seeing you react that way as you think about my hands on you, my mouth, your taste in my throat, it does me in."

"Wh-where do you get all this stuff?" Her voice was shaky. The way he affected her shook her to her core.

"That's not a line. I want to tell you all the things you do to me, all the things I *want* to do to you. You have no idea how you make me feel do you? Standing here in the middle of this crowded place, I want to back you against the wall and take you. I want to lay you on one of the pool tables and look down on your body as I thrust into it. I want you so much my hands are in my pocket because I'm afraid they'd shake."

A flush ran through her. "Oh. My."

"Oh my indeed, darlin'. I'm going to kiss you now, here in this bar and I don't care who sees it."

"Oh, okay," she said faintly as her arms encircled his neck like they'd wanted to all along.

He kissed her, not with the raw sexuality he'd shown in her apartment but it was still a kiss that she felt all the way to the tips of her toes. Holy cow the man could kiss. He tasted of beer and the spearmint of his gum and Shane and everything in her body tightened in response.

When he released her, she dimly heard applause and some hooting from his brothers.

"Wow." She licked her lips.

"Wow isn't a big enough word for the way you make me feel, Cassie. There is no one else. There hasn't been since the first moment I clapped eyes on you."

"You make me weak in the knees, Shane Chase. And you make me think I may not be as broken as I'd feared."

He smiled. "That's the best compliment I've ever gotten."

"Yeah? Come on back to my apartment and I'll give you a few more."

His joyous smile turned wicked. "Is that so?"

She nodded.

"Give me ten minutes to finish up with my brothers. Why don't we go to my house? You haven't seen it yet and you can, if you want to, sleep over. In my bed or in my guest room. I'll let you decide that one, I'm rather biased on the subject."

"Got any food there?"

He grinned. "I just went grocery shopping earlier tonight. I have fresh peaches and strawberries. I can think of a few things to do with them before eating them."

"Oh?" Her voice was faint as she pondered the possibilities.

"I'll let you think on it. Be by in ten to grab you. You okay? Are *we* okay?"

She nodded. "I don't like being taken by surprise. I don't expect you to be a virgin. I knew you were a player and all. But that it was Maggie just surprised me. You haven't been with Penny, Liv or Dee have you?"

"No, darlin' I haven't."

"I'm going back to the table. See you in ten."

"Go on then, I'll just stand here and watch."

She rolled her eyes.

"Is everything all right?" Maggie's voice sounded sad.

"I'm not mad at you, Maggie. I was just surprised. It's fine. I talked to Shane. He and I are fine. You and I are fine. It's all fine."

Maggie leaned back, sighing in relief. "Thank goodness."

"That was some kiss. I don't think I've seen him kiss a woman in public twice in one night and certainly not like that. Whew. I need to go home to Arthur. I'm sure Michael is in bed by now and I'm all hot and bothered." Dee shoved her way out of the booth and stood.

"I'll see you soon, Dee." Dee and Cassie hugged and Dee hurried out the door toward home and her husband.

"And I'll be going soon too. Shane and I are nipping out early."

"To do what?" A single eyebrow rose and Liv struggled not to smile.

"To play Scrabble." Cassie's voice was deadpan.

"Naked Scrabble?" Liv asked, laughing.

"I've never thought of that. Dude, that's a great idea. Strip Scrabble. I'm so getting the board out tonight to see if I can't lose badly to Kyle." Maggie winked.

ᘏᘒᘓ

"Just wow. Man oh man, Shane. I don't think I've ever been jealous of you over a woman before but Cassie is sinfully beautiful. And incredibly sexy." Marc leaned his butt against the table next to theirs.

"What was that all about?" Matt interjected before his little brother could goad Shane any further.

"Maggie mentioned she and I dated a few times. Cassie was caught off guard. It's all fine now."

"I saw that. That was some 'all fine now' liplock there, Shane." Kyle took a shot and sank it. "You find out anything about this ex of hers? I'm looking forward to finding him and helping you kick the shit out of him."

"Nothing. I've done some snooping with her name and social security number but I can't find any records. Some domestic violence records shield the victim so that may be the case. All I have is that the husband's first name is Terry. I couldn't find anything on Terry Gambol but she may not have taken his name when they got married."

"Does she know you're doing this? Obviously not if you're having to piece it all together this way." Matt sighed uneasily. "I don't think she's going to be pleased if she finds out you're investigating without her knowledge."

"I know, I know. But I want to protect her. God help me, I am falling so fast for this woman I'm in a tail spin. The idea of anyone hurting her kills me. It's just a little bit of snooping. Just to help."

His brothers looked at him skeptically.

"I'm out of here. She and I are on our way to my house and if any of you losers calls me and interrupts me with a flat tire or any kind of police emergency, I'll kick your ass."

He heard their laughter as he turned and saw the woman he was well on his way to being in love with, waiting for him, wearing a smile.

CR80

Nervousness began to creep into her stomach as the drove. The sex, or foreplay she supposed, between them two nights past had been wonderful but Terry's words were still in her head.

Shane held her hand as he drove them to his place in his big truck. She watched the light of the streetlamps and then the moon, on his face.

"Oh hey, this is Penny's neighborhood. I didn't know you lived so close." Cassie didn't know why but the thought of Penny's nearness made her feel better.

"Yeah, she's just three houses down. Ben and I were good friends, went to school together along with Penny."

He pulled into his driveway. His house was built in the Craftsman style, not something she'd seen often around Petal. Two large oak trees dominated the front yard, providing shade to the front of the house. The entire front lawn was beautifully landscaped with wildflowers and roses.

"Wow, this is so not what I expected." She joined him and they walked up to the porch.

"What? You expected some two room bachelor pad with potato chip bags strewn around?"

"No, not really. But this is truly beautiful. So well put together. I don't think I've seen a Craftsman style home around these parts at all. And the landscaping is just gorgeous."

"The landscaping is all Kyle. Wait until you see the back. One of my friends, the faithless asshole who cheated with Sandra, my ex, was...is a builder. He helped me with the plans and then my brothers, father, uncle and cousins all came out here and did a lot of the work, from the framing to the paintwork. I love this place." He opened the door and motioned her inside.

She watched as he turned off and re-set the alarm system. "Just for the front of the house. I'll show you the back. I want you to know you're always safe here. Come on through."

He led her through a big, open living room with exposed wood beams, hardwood floors and large windows. Dark greens and brick reds accented the space. It was a very masculine space dominated by leather couches and deep club chairs. A large fireplace fronted with river rock took up most of one wall.

He opened up glass doors to a view that took her breath away. The large wooden deck overlooked a grassy lawn that sloped down to the lake's edge. Pretty citronella candles hung on stands around the railing and furniture surrounded a sizeable, built-in outdoor grill.

117

The moon's light reflected from the glassy surface of the lake, illuminating the whole yard. Hedges lined the boundary of his property and she saw little seating areas dotted here and there. Roses climbed the trunk of an oak and she smelled the star jasmine in the air.

"You're full of surprises, aren't you, Sheriff?"

"I'm glad you like it here. It's an oasis for me. A place I can come home and leave all my work bullshit at the door. My family comes out and we barbecue and watch the sunset. It's a good life." He looked down into her face. "And now it's better."

He turned into her body and she rose to meet his kiss as he bent his head to hers.

Cassie's body melted into his embrace. Her heart beat in time with his, pounding reassuringly against her palm on his chest.

After he broke the kiss, he murmured against her lips, "Would you like to take a walk in the moonlight with me?"

She nodded, leaning down to kick off her sandals. The grass felt cool under her bare feet and his hand in hers felt anchoring and strong.

"You've really built a place for yourself here, Shane. It's beautiful. The inside and the outside."

"I'm glad you like it. I really am." And he was. Ridiculously so. That she approved made him happy. He realized he wanted her approval on the thing he cared about so much. His house was an extension of him and he'd worked hard on every last bit of it, had a hand in everything. He liked having her there with him. A lot.

"Wow, you even have a dock."

He chuckled. "I do. It's more to jump off for swimming than for a boat. The lake isn't that big or deep really."

"Do you sail?"

"I've done it from time to time. A friend of our family has a boat and I go out a few times a year with him. I take it you do? I can hear the affection in your voice."

They stopped and she bent to pick up a stone from the rocky lakeshore and skipped it. "I used to. When we were first married, we lived in an apartment in Newport Beach. Not very far from the marina. We had a boat for a while but Terry didn't like to sail and he sold it. I haven't been in some years now."

"Did you live near water too, then? I love hearing the sound of the shoreline, the water lapping against the rocks."

"Our house was in the hills overlooking the ocean. I gave it to him after the divorce. I just wanted to be free of him. I didn't care about the stuff."

"Do you miss it? Your house?"

She shook her head. "No. It was never mine anyway. He bought it. He decorated it. It was his. I was just another one of the things he owned."

Shane's jaw clenched and unclenched. "I hate hearing you talk that way."

"It's the truth, Shane. For years I was a thing. An accessory and at times, not even a very good one according to him. I know he was wrong. But that's what I was." She shrugged. "I'm working to be more than that now."

"You're not an accessory to me. I just can't wrap my head around it. How any man wouldn't cherish you with every fiber of his being."

"I don't want to talk about it anymore. I hate that it's this constant thing in my life." She turned her body away from him and looked out at the water. "Damn it, I'm more than the poor battered wife. Fuck, I feel like I should wear a nametag or something. It's why I didn't want to tell anyone about it. That's all you see. That's all anyone sees."

He moved to stand behind her, encircling her with his arms. "That's not true, Cassie. It's not all I see. It's part of your past, yes. It goes into making you who you are now—a strong woman. A survivor. You're smart, and competent and the most beautiful woman I've ever seen. Inside and out, I like you, Cassie. You. Not your past, not your zip code, but *you*. But I can't deny, and neither can you, that what happened to you shaped who you are now. Just like the things that happened to me shaped me. We don't have to talk about it any more tonight. There are far better things to do with our time."

He brushed his lips over her neck where it met her shoulder and she lost the rigidity in her spine, relaxing into him. He felt good behind her. The water from the lake lapped against her toes over and over with the beat of her heart.

Silence stretched as he held her, kissed her neck and shoulders with soft heat. She asked herself if she could have sex with this man and her body agreed right off and soon enough, her mind agreed. It was something she'd been thinking over a lot. But she wasn't afraid of him. She trusted him to take care with her and if she was going to live beyond those years with Terry, she had to move on with her life. Build a future and that included sex. Or she hoped it would.

"Stay right here. I'll be back in a minute." Her back felt cool when he moved away and jogged up to the house, disappearing inside.

She wandered up a path lined with sweet smelling flowers and bushes. His steps sounded against the decking and down onto the grass. He hesitated and she called out softly, "I'm here on the path."

"Ah." He showed up around the corner and held up a blanket. "I thought we could lay under the stars. What do you think?"

"Lay?" One corner of her mouth quirked up.

"Well, uh, if you wanted to just lay, that would be fine. I'd be happy to hold you in my arms as we looked up at the stars. On the other hand, I'd be even happier to see your skin bathed in moonlight as I made love to you. I want you, Cassie. But I want you to be okay with that. I don't want you to feel rushed or pressured."

"Hmm. Well, why don't you spread it out in this little area here, it's totally walled off by the plants and no one could see us. You know, if we got up to something no one should see."

Moving around her body, he spread the blanket out and held his hand out to her.

Taking a deep breath, her brain and her body in accord, she grabbed his hand and let him draw her down onto the blanket.

On her back, she looked up into his face and smiled. A lock of his hair slid forward rakishly. She could tell he was being very careful but she was sick of it.

She put her hands on his shoulders. "Shane, don't be so careful with me. I won't break. I can't guarantee something weird won't trigger something but I don't want this thing between us to be so fragile. I wasn't always this fucked up."

A look so tender slid across his face it made her draw breath quickly. His mouth covered hers in an intense kiss. The kind of kiss that makes a woman forget to breathe.

Cassie's hands pulled at his shirt, as she gave in to her sudden need to feel his bare skin. Breaking the kiss quickly, he sat up and pulled the shirt off over his head and she put a hand on his chest to stay him.

Lauren Dane

Impossibly broad shoulders led to a wide chest, covered with just the right amount of the same brown-blond hair on his head. The hand that had stayed him slid over the hard muscle of his pecs down to his flat, hard nipple and he sucked in a breath but remained still as she looked her fill and explored him with her hands.

Muscled arms held his upper body away from her as she traced down from his nipple to each ridge of his abdomen. One. Two. Three. Four. Five. Six. Dear sweet heaven, the man had a real six pack.

A trembling fingertip traced around his navel and south along the trail of hair that she was sure led to his cock but his jeans were in the way. She tapped the button. "This is a problem."

"I want to look at you, too." His voice was strangled. In it she heard how much control it took to hold himself still for her inspection.

She licked suddenly dry lips. "I..."

He watched her as he slid off the skirt and looked at her long legs and panties. Boy was she glad she wore the pair of pretty ones she'd bought a few weeks back on a whim.

"Your pants." She tipped her chin in his direction.

What should have been awkward for any regular person, he made graceful as he shimmied out of his jeans while still sitting. One eyebrow rose as he touched the waistband of his boxers, asking how far she wanted to go. At her nod he pulled them off and she widened her eyes and blinked a few times.

"Wow."

He stopped for a moment and then laughed. "Oh, Cassie, you're so good for me."

"Shane, you're beautiful. So big and muscled and, damn, I'm drowning in testosterone. I don't think I've ever seen a naked man who was more masculine and handsome. Hell, any man more masculine and handsome."

"Thank you. Now, I'm at a bit of a disadvantage here, Cassie. I'm buck naked and you are not."

Oh how she wished she didn't have fourteen scars on her upper back and neck from where Terry had stabbed her with the broken handle from the hammer he'd used to break her fingers. Wished she had a body she could show him without reservation. But her breasts weren't as high as they'd been when she was in her twenties and Terry always complained about the roundness of her thighs and the swell of her belly. She already felt overexposed with her skirt off, she really didn't know how she'd hide the scars if she didn't have her shirt on.

"That's some internal dialog you've got going on in there, darlin'." He tapped her forehead. "You want to stop?"

"No." She shook her head vehemently and to underline that, she took his cock in her fist and pumped. He was so hard she felt him throb in her palm.

He hissed. "Holy shit!"

"Do you have condoms?"

"Condoms? Plural? My, you're ambitious. I like that." He leaned over and pulled three foil packets out of the pocket of his pants and held them up for her to see. "Three. I know, it's very hopeful of me."

She laughed and slid her thumb over the head of his cock, smearing his come there.

"Okay, hold it back there, Ace. You keep doing that and we won't be needing a condom. I'll come in your fist like a freshman in the backseat of a Chevy and be so embarrassed I won't be able to face you in the morning. I keep telling you, we have time, Cassie. Let's take it. And yet, you still have your shirt on."

She laid back and pulled each button on the front of the camisole free and the two halves of the eyelet cotton slid apart, exposing her bra and her belly. She figured she'd leave it on and between that, the dark and her hair, her scars would stay hidden. And to further distract him, she hooked her thumbs in the waist of her panties and shimmied out of them.

"Now, where were we?" Eyes locked with his, she watched as his gaze broke free and slid down her body. The intensity of his attention had her drawing her knees together and trying to cover her breasts with her hands.

Shane moved to stop her, placing his hands over hers. "Shhh, don't hide yourself from me. Cassie, you're amazing. More beautiful than I could have imagined." Letting go of her hands, his fingertips grazed over the curve of each breast, popping the catch on the bra. "I want to see your breasts bathed in moonlight."

The tenderness of his words, of his touch, moved her deeply. Tears stung the back of her eyes. How long had it been since a man had touched her that way?

"Cassie? Honey?"

She shook her head, lips pressed together to hold back the tears. Her hands came up to put his on her again.

Leaning down he laid a kiss on her chest, just over her heart. "I hate seeing you in pain. We can stop, go inside, watch a movie on the couch. I can wait for you. You're worth it."

The tears slipped free then. "Shane, I don't want you to stop. I promise. I'm sorry I'm such a mess."

"You're not a mess, Cassie. You're working to get past something terrible. Why are you crying?"

"It's nothing bad. Please, I can't talk about it right now. Just touch me again. Make love to me. I need you."

His lips found her cheeks and he kissed away the salt of her tears and then back down to her chest. His movements were slow and gentle, giving her the time and space to stop him if she needed to.

Shane gloried in the beauty of her body, in the fragile shell that lay around her heart. But she kept on and didn't quit. His woman was everything. He stilled as he insinuated himself between her thighs.

The enormity of that statement hit him. She was his woman. She'd held his attention from the first moment but each time he thought of her it built in him, attention became attraction became something more intense.

There was no fear though. The shadow of worry passed. The moment when he'd run out the door on Maggie became clear to him. It wasn't that they could have had this thing he shared with Cassie. It was that Maggie wasn't Cassie. His heart knew what he needed and it was the woman stretched beneath him.

He wanted to heal every hurt she'd ever endured. Wanted to let her know that even broken women deserved passion and love.

And suddenly his need for her was so intense that his hands shook with it.

Sliding his palms up her ribs, he took the curve of her breasts into his hands, holding them so he could taste the hard nipples begging for his mouth.

Triumph roared through his system when she gasped and arched into him, her fingers digging into his upper arms.

The moment Shane's mouth closed around her nipple, Cassie's hesitancy was gone. Instead, desire coursed through her with each pull of lips and tongue against the sensitive flesh of her nipple. The edge of his teeth just barely skimmed over her and a deep, shuddering moan came from low in her gut.

Her squirms placed his cock against her pussy, pressing against her slick heat and they both stilled on a gasp.

"Oh hell. Okay, let me move away a bit or I'm liable to just plunge into you without a condom. You feel so good." When he shimmied down her body he left a trail of kisses down her ribs and belly.

When he knelt between her thighs the sheer size of him held her legs apart. "You're so wet, I can see you glistening in the light." Two fingertips dipped into her and, eyes still locked with hers, he brought those fingers to his mouth.

The sheer carnality of the action rendered her utterly speechless. Instead, she opened her mouth but no sound came out as her eyes widened.

"So good. I need more. Are you ready for that, Cassie?"

She nodded quickly. Oh hell yes she was ready for that!

He chuckled as he settled himself on his belly. His thumbs spread her open to his gaze just before leaning forward to take a long lick from her gate up and around her clit.

Her hands slid through the softness of his hair, thick and cool against her fingers. His tongue flicked up quickly over her clit until she began to see white lights against her closed eyelids, until she began to feel the burn in her thigh muscles and the flush working its way up her body.

He angled his hand, sliding two fingers up and into her pussy, twisting his wrist to find that sweet bump, the pressure against it feeling so good it nearly hurt.

There was no time to think about how Terry hadn't gone down on her in years and how he'd never made her feel good and delicious and sexy like Shane did at that moment. There was only the intense sensation of his mouth on her, his fingers inside her and the open sky above them.

When climax hit, an arc of pleasure shot up her spine with blinding intensity. Her back arched as she rolled her hips into him, helpless to do more than bite back the cry of joy, instead, whispering his name.

Shane remained there, nestled between her thighs, until her pussy stopped spasming around his fingers.

"You're very good at that," she gasped out, eyes still closed.

"Darlin', you're the tastiest thing this side of the Mason Dixon."

She laughed and he loved the sound. It wasn't one he heard that often from her so he treasured it all the more. So damned beautiful and sexy and she had no idea.

"It's my turn now. I want to taste you." She tried to sit up but he moved quickly, leaning over her, reaching for a condom.

"Darlin', if you do that, it'll all be over before it starts. I want to be inside you when I come. I've been dreaming of it. Later, I promise you can suck my cock all you want." One handed, he rolled the condom on while keeping his weight off her. "Are you still okay with this?"

She reached up and caressed his cheek. "Yes. So okay with it I'm shaking like it's my first time."

"Well, it's your first time with me. That's what counts."

She laughed then. "Of course."

Without breaking his gaze with hers, he reached down and guided himself to her gate and slowly began to push inside. She was slick from her recent climax and relaxed but still blindingly tight. Beads of sweat broke out over his forehead.

"Fuck...sorry. You're so tight. I don't want to hurt you." And he didn't want to come before he'd even got halfway inside her either.

Her legs slid up and around his waist, ankles locking at the small of his back, opening her up more fully to him. "It's been a while. Two years. Apparently I've been saving up for the good stuff."

He grinned and leaned down for a quick kiss. "You trying to get in my pants with all that flattery, Ms. Gambol?"

"I believe I'm already there, Sheriff Chase."

"Indeed you are." With one last grunt, he seated himself fully within her.

With slow intensity, he dragged nearly all the way out before sliding back into her. Before too long, she matched his movements with a roll of her hips, her body meeting his, swallowing him, pulling him back inside.

The thought that she was made for him, her body was a haven for his own, flashed through his mind. He cupped the back of her head in one palm, protecting her from the ground below.

He wished it was as easy to protect her from her ex, from the past that had her flinching in the presence of unknown men.

Cassie looked up into his face as her body met his in an easy rhythm. Their breath mingled, the scent of honeysuckle and star jasmine hung thick in the warm night air. The lap, lap, lap of the lake against the shore was like a metronome to their movements.

The way he sliced through her pussy as he thrust into her was so intense it rode up her spine. Her body just molded to his, made room for him like he was meant to be there.

His gaze tenderly roved over her features and there were moments when she felt like he saw straight to her soul.

"Are you with me, darlin'?" His voice was soft and he held his weight off her with his upper arms.

She nodded. "Yeah."

"You feel so good, Cassie. I want you to feel good too. Are you all right? Am I squishing you?"

Somehow, the tenderness, the concern in his voice just got to her. He wasn't coddling her, he *cared* about her. Part of her that she'd closed off because it had simply been crushed into nothing by Terry, sparked back to life. And when it did, she felt what she'd been missing for four years. Not the intensity of someone's attention that she'd mistaken for love and adoration from Terry in the early years. No, this was a man who truly wanted her to be okay. Thought about her feelings.

Tears blinded her as he changed his angle and his pelvic bone crushed into her mound and created friction over her clit. A deep moan broke from her lips.

"Baby? Those good tears or am I hurting you?"

She laughed through her tears and reached up to wipe them away with the back of her hand. "Good ones. Now shut up and fuck me."

Her thighs began to tremble as each press and grind of his body against her clit brought her closer to orgasm.

"Cassie, darlin', I'm really close. You with me?"

"I..." And it broke over her, shattering her into wordlessness, eyes blurring and back arching. She heard his muffled curse and felt his cock jerk and spasm deep within her as he came as well.

With a long, satisfied sigh, he rolled off her and to the side, quickly dealing with the condom and coming back to lie beside her. Panting, sweat cooling on their bodies, they both looked up into the night sky.

He reached out and linked fingers with her.

"Thank you."

He turned to his side and looked at her. "Darlin', the pleasure was all mine, I assure you. God, I can't believe I fucked you on the ground. You deserve a soft bed and candlelight. I just had this vision of you, bathed in moonlight, making love to you with the sweet smells of night against our skin. I hope you don't think I was disrespectful. I'm sorry."

"Shane, don't." Tears laced her voice. "I can't seem to stop crying. I hate that. You have nothing to be sorry for. It was beautiful. You were wonderful. Gentle and patient. I enjoyed myself, believe me. Twice."

He laughed. "I'm sorry about that. It should have been at least three times but I had to have you. I'm usually more finessed than that."

"Three times? Wow. Well, I'm quite pleased with two. Hell, I'm thrilled with one."

He looked at her, shocked. "Do you know how fucking beautiful you look when you come? Your neck arched, eyes desire-blind, mouth slightly open, your nipples hard and pretty—just thinking about it right now makes me hard. Any man should want to see that as much as possible. Your ex needs his ass kicked. But then I suppose if he'd taken care of you I wouldn't be here beside you now."

"They aren't very nice anymore. They used to be lovely. But time. Well you know."

He sat up on his elbow. "No. I don't have any idea what you're talking about."

Her hands moved to put her bra back in place but he stopped her, kissing each hand and putting them back at her sides.

"My breasts. They used to be higher. They're sort of saggy. I'm sure you're used to tight bodies and perky breasts. I've seen some of the women in town, the ones who give me the dirtiest looks, their bodies are nicer than mine."

Shane exhaled sharply. "Cassie, how old are you?"

"Thirty-three."

"And you think you have saggy breasts?"

She sat up and moved to fasten her bra and button up her camisole. "Yes. And my belly has this little pooch and my thighs are flabby."

"Cassie, I'm just telling you so as not to spook you, I'm picking you up now." And she found herself tossed over his shoulder as he walked her, bare assed, into his house.

"Hey! I don't have any panties on," she hissed.

"No one can see but me and I like your ass." He took her up the stairs and into his bedroom and set her down in front of mirrored sliding doors in his closet.

"Now, I want you to look at yourself." His hand smoothed over her hair. "Your hair is truly beautiful, thick, black, long, tousled from sex." A thumb traced her bottom lip. "Luscious. I want to nibble it every time I see you."

He moved behind her and unbuttoned her camisole and popped the catch on her bra in record time. He held her breasts in his hands. "Gorgeous." And let them go. "They do *not* sag. You have large breasts and they're not in a bra and you're not twenty-one, Cassie. But your breasts are fucking phenomenal." A finger traced the valley between them. "I'd very much like to put my cock here sometime in the future. I think about that. A lot."

She shivered.

His hand slid down her stomach. "This is not a pooch. It's your stomach. You are not flabby. You're beautiful. Your thighs are beautiful. Your calves are beautiful. Your pussy is pink and pretty and beautiful. Your eyes are beautiful."

He picked up her hand and kissed it. "Your hands are beautiful." And paused. "Did you break your fingers?" He held up his left hand and the index finger was slightly crooked. "I broke it when I was twenty-five."

In the year since the attack, she'd had time to heal. Time for physical therapy. But her middle and ring fingers still bore the scars of the break. Bore the odd bend of what she knew she was lucky to still have working fingers after he'd done so much damage.

"Yes."

His face hardened and he met her eyes in the mirror. "He did this to you." It wasn't a question.

Her eyes closed for a long moment and she nodded. Shane brought her hand to his lips and kissed the fingers. "Beautiful. Cassie, one of the things that surprises me the most about you is how you don't see your own beauty. You walk into The Pumphouse and men bump into things from staring at you. I believe book readership has skyrocketed in Petal since you started working at Paperbacks and More. You speak and I get hard. You breathe and I get hard. I get jealous. Even when I walked in and caught Sandra with my best friend, I wasn't jealous. I was just betrayed and hurt and then pissed off.

"And let me clarify the jealous thing because don't think I didn't see the fear flare in your eyes when I said it. Yes, it drives me a little crazy to see men watching you and practically drooling. But I'm not going to hurt you over it. I may want to whack 'em in the back of the head with my pool cue, but baby, I want to cherish you, not hurt you."

Gaze locked with his in the mirror she leaned back into his body. "If I try to talk about this right now, I'm going to cry. And I am sick of it. So, I'm not going to except to say thank you."

He bent and as she watched in the mirror, he took her neck between his teeth and she gasped. "You're so beautiful, I want you right now. Again. Show me, Cassie." One hand moved up to cup her breast and roll and tug a nipple between his fingers and the other slid down her belly to her pussy.

Automatically, she adjusted her legs, widening her stance and he put his thigh between them, enabling her to lean back against his chest. Unable not to watch, her eyes caught his fingers parting her and sliding through the still very wet folds of her sex.

She watched the pull, roll, tug of his fingers on her nipple and then two of his fingers disappear into her pussy and his thumb sliding from side to side over her clit.

Her eyelids slid halfway shut as the lethargy of desire stole over her. His eyes watched his hands on her in the mirror. Watched his fingers fuck into her and she didn't miss the widening of his grin when she rolled her hips to meet his hand.

But she was past embarrassment. She wanted to come. She'd turned off her expectations of climax during sex with anyone else and the need came back, sharp edged and starving after so many years denied.

"Give it to me, Cassie. I can feel your pussy beginning to flutter around my fingers. I know you want to come, I can see it in your eyes." His words were whispered into her ear and she shivered. "Let go."

Even as she was getting ready to tell him she couldn't possibly come again, she did. Not the explosion of pleasure she'd felt on the grass outside but a muscle-deep series of contractions. Wave after wave of pleasure rolled through her until she was nothing more than a boneless heap of satisfied woman laying against him.

"Oh, I wish I had a camera." He chuckled and she raised her hand in a half-hearted one fingered salute.

They cleaned up. He refused to let her reciprocate for the moment and ran outside to retrieve her panties, skirt and shoes which, to his disappointment, she put back on.

They stood side by side in his kitchen, made sandwiches and ate them. Later they brought root beer to his couch, snuggled and watched a movie. The normalcy of the moment fed her heart.

When the movie ended he stood up and stretched. "So, darlin', you staying over?"

"I have an appointment in Shackleton at ten. I should probably go home so I won't disturb you."

"What do you have to run all the way over there on a Saturday for?"

"My therapist is there." It wasn't as hard as she'd thought, saying it aloud.

He sat again and nodded. "Good. Is it helping?"

It felt slightly odd to talk to him about it but at the same time, good.

"I think so. Sometimes I have all this stuff in my head and I can't say it to anyone. But I can to her. She doesn't know me or my family, she doesn't judge me. It's very freeing."

"I imagine so. You can always talk to me you know. I'm not going to judge you."

"No, but you get mad about stuff. And sometimes, having to deal with other people's emotions over it is more than I want to. Sometimes I want it to be about me just saying it and being rid of it."

He bit his lip against what he wanted to say. He *did* get mad at some of the things she told him. When he'd seen the damage to her fingers and she'd revealed it was her ex's doing, a wave of rage so deep and dark swallowed him for a moment he was quite sure he could have killed the man over it.

Instead he nodded. "I understand. I'd still like you to stay over. We can get up early and I'll run you home. You can shower here with me." He waggled his eyebrows at her lasciviously, making her laugh.

"All of my stuff is at home. I'm very particular about my hair products. I know it's terribly shallow of me. And I don't have any night clothes."

"Sleep naked. Or, I can loan you a T-shirt if you like. I'm sorry if I'm pressuring you. I just want to wake up with you in my arms tomorrow. But I do understand if you'd like to go home."

She still had dreams, she had the scars. The weight of the hiding she'd have to do lay on her heavily. It warred with her yearning to be held in Shane's arms all night.

"I can't. I'm sorry. There's...it's..." She shrugged her shoulders, not able to find words, not knowing if she could trust him or herself to reveal more. "It isn't you. I know that sounds like a cliché. But I can't. Not yet. And I really do have to get up early tomorrow. Please don't be angry."

He pulled her against his body and kissed her temple. "Darlin', I am not angry. I won't say I understand because I don't know all of it and I couldn't possibly be in your place. But I do understand your wanting to go home and I'm not hurt or upset. I keep telling you we have time. And we do." He moved to look into her face. "We do don't we? I suppose I've just assumed that we're in a relationship but I haven't really asked you."

"I told you, I'm not a casual person. But I don't know what I have to give anyone just now. If you're asking if I'd like to continue seeing you and that I have no interest in anyone else, yes. What I have to offer above that right now? I don't know."

He stood and helped her up. "That's all I need for now. We can work through the rest as we go."

The drive back to her place was quiet but comfortable. His hand lay gently on her thigh as he drove. When they got to her place he walked her to the door.

"Good night, darlin'. Would you like to come to dinner at my parents' house on Sunday night? My momma's been bugging me to bring you. I won't lie to you, I think she's got a bigger crush on you than I do. There's a running competition to see who can talk about you more. She also tells me you've promised to come to dinner sometime soon. And I'd love for you to get to know them all better. Maggie will be there too."

She smiled. "I did promise her. It wasn't like I could do anything else. She's called me twice about it. And I do like her, even if she's the world's worst driver and a total menace behind the wheel."

"Yeah? And what about me?"

Coyly, she cocked her head. "You? Hmm. Well, it appears that your driving is decent. Safe enough. Clearly you didn't learn to drive from your mother."

He laughed, the sound echoing through the quiet of the post midnight evening. "My dad taught me. And you know that's not what I was asking."

"I know, I just wanted to tease you. I happen to like you too, Shane Chase. More than is probably wise."

"Good. Wisdom is overrated. Now, let me come in just to be sure everything is okay." Her back went rigid and he sucked in his breath, making an agitated sound. "Okay, so I didn't really phrase that like a request. And I know I'm pushy and I know you don't want to hear that I just want to protect you. I'm trying you know. Would it be all right with you if I came in just to check the place out?"

Her posture relaxed and she put a hand to his cheek. "Thank you for that. It means a lot to me. And I'd appreciate that."

He did a quick check of the apartment and all was well. After kissing her good night, he told her he'd pick her up on Sunday and waited on her doorstep until he heard her locking all her locks.

Whistling softly, he jogged down the steps and to his car, entirely sure he'd not been that happy in a very long time.

Chapter Nine

When they pulled up to the curb in front of the Chase's beautiful home, nervousness clawed Cassie's insides. Sure, she knew Polly casually and she saw Matt pretty much every day, but this was like a meet the parents date. What if they didn't like her for their son?

Shane grabbed her hand and brought it to his lips to kiss across her knuckles. "Darlin', don't be nervous. They already know you except for my daddy and he's going to love you. Trust me. Now come on." He jerked his head and she laughed.

He had to put his hands in his pockets to keep from going to open her door but the smile she gave him for letting her do it herself was worth it.

She took his arm though as they walked up to the porch and he wanted to shout to the whole neighborhood that Cassie Gambol was his. Long, curvy and absolutely astonishingly beautiful, he couldn't believe this woman beside him trusted him as much as she did.

Before he could reach out and turn the knob, the door opened and Marc stood there, grinning. "Hey there, Cassie. My, that blue does only good things for you." He leaned in quickly and kissed her, just a friendly greeting. But Shane felt her startle and stiffen. Putting an arm around her waist, he shot Marc a look and his brother stood back quickly.

Marc seemed to understand, winking at her but backing off to let them both in. She relaxed and he kicked himself for not talking to Marc about how to approach her. Matt, he knew, understood and Kyle didn't hug up on any women he wasn't related to after he'd gotten together with Maggie.

"I thought I heard someone arrive." Polly Chase came click-clacking into the hallway, wearing a big grin. "Hi there, honey. Welcome. Can I get you something to drink? Maggie and I were sneaking a beer in my sitting room. You want to come on in there after my Edward meets you? He's been dying to after hearing us all talk about you nonstop."

Shane tensed, not knowing how Cassie would react to his mother's stream of consciousness, mile a minute chatter but she smiled and let his mother enfold her into a hug.

"Mrs. Chase, this is just a beautiful home. I love the period pieces you have. Are they family antiques?"

Shane wanted to laugh out loud. Now Cassie was in for it. She'd hit on some of his mother's greatest loves. Antiques and the history of the house and the pieces in it.

"Polly. My mother-in-law is Mrs. Chase. I'll give you a tour. Let's go say hi to the boys in the family room. Dontcha know baseball is on and once the game starts you won't see any butts moving from seats until dinner." Polly took Cassie's hand and Maggie came out of the sitting room and after a quick hug for Shane, followed Polly and Cassie into the family room.

Shane watched his father's eyes widen when he saw Cassie. He'd told his father Cassie was beautiful but Shane saw his father really understand the full impact Cassie made. He waited for the voice.

"Well hello there. You must be Cassie." His father, ever the gentleman, took her hand, giving her a courtly kiss. Cassie blushed slightly. "I'm Edward Chase. It's very nice to meet you

139

and see you in one piece after my wife welcomed you to Petal in her own special way."

Cassie's delighted laugh sounded through the room and Shane wanted to laugh himself as he saw his father's eyes widen again and he snuck a quick peek at Shane.

"It's nice to meet you too, Mr. Chase. My neck has recovered from your wife's welcome and my car is good as new. I'm sure your insurance company is less thrilled than I am though."

"Edward, please, sugar. And my goodness, aren't you just a bundle of gorgeous? Shane told me you were beautiful but he was right that I had to see you, and hear you, to get the full impact."

"Okay, Daddy, enough. You trying to steal my girl?"

"Oh no, my boy! Your momma is more than enough for me."

Matt approached and paused a moment, making sure Cassie saw him before giving her a hug and kiss on the cheek. "Hi there, sweetie. You ready to run out the door yet?"

Cassie grinned. "Nah. I hear there'll be cobbler. I can't leave until after that."

Kyle laughed and stood up to squeeze Cassie's hand and reach around and smooch Maggie. It was an easy movement and Shane realized, not for the first time, just how good his brother was at making people feel safe.

Shane loved seeing Cassie so at ease and relaxed and hoped she'd come to be comfortable with his family enough to be like that all the time.

"Okay, we're off for the tour. You boys behave. Dinner in thirty." Polly took Cassie's hand and they left the room.

Shane grabbed a beer from the mini-fridge in the corner and sat on the couch, grinning at his father.

"Go ahead on and grin, boy. She's something else. Your momma sure does seem to like her and I don't believe I've ever seen you this way with a woman before. You watched her, made sure she was all right. I like seeing you that way."

"I'm sorry I spooked her, Shane. I didn't mean to." Marc might come off as cavalier in public but those who knew him, really knew him, understood he was a truly sensitive person.

Shane turned and patted Marc's arm. "It's okay. You didn't mean any harm. She'll get used to you in time. She's really easy around Matt since she sees him every day. Women don't seem to spook her at all."

"She's a totally different woman than the one who practically shoved me out the door when she first came to town. You're good for each other," Matt said.

CRSO

At dinner, Cassie marveled at how close they all were. Such an ease of communication and friendly banter. It was clear they all loved each other very much.

And they all went out of their way to make her feel included and welcome. She missed that kind of connection to family. Terry had interfered so much she'd backed away from her father until the very end and she'd had to sneak around to see Brian. Sitting there at the table, listening to the joking and the teasing, a pang of longing cut through her, and a tiny ember of hope flared too. She wasn't so far gone that this wasn't possible.

It was a scary thought but not as scary as it would have been even three weeks before. Suddenly she could see herself at this table with these people. See herself as part of their family. See herself with Shane.

The danger of hope was the very real chance of losing it. She wasn't sure she could afford it but her therapist seemed very happy and sure Cassie had the strength to succeed in a relationship with a man like Shane. She just had to find the strength to keep on believing in herself. To let go of the Carly she'd been and embrace Cassie and her future.

CRSO

"You ready to run for Florida yet?" Shane teased as he drove her home.

"I like your family, Shane. They're all very nice and worked to make me feel welcome."

"They like you too, darlin'. I'd ask you to dinner next Sunday but with the party on Monday, I think my momma will be cooking and getting ready. The woman loves to throw a party."

"But it's her birthday. Oh see, I'm putting her out. I'm going to call a caterer so she doesn't have to do all the work. I'd do it myself but I'm a terrible cook."

Shane laughed. "Cassie, my mother *loves* to plan parties. She does. She loves to cook and be with her family. She lives for this stuff. You'll see when Homecoming approaches. And I don't want you spending any money anyway. I know it must be tight with just being part-time at the book store. My dad wanted to talk to you about some work in his office but he didn't get the chance. You should call him about it."

"I don't need the job. I told Penny that. I really don't. I have some money set aside and with the jewelry beginning to take off, things are very comfortable."

142

"Comfortable? Come on, Cassie. I know you can't be making much more than your rent. Where is the money coming from for you to live?"

"I told you, I have some money set aside."

"From the divorce?"

Money was a sore subject. She'd fought over it with Terry many times as it was a chief way to control her movements. As a surgeon she'd made an excellent living but her checks were direct deposited and he kept a tight hold on their bank account.

"Shane, I told you all you need to know. I appreciate your concern but it's not necessary."

"You know, you have to give some too. It's not fair of you to expect me to do all the compromising."

"Do I ask you how you pay your bills, Shane? How is it a compromise on my part to tell you how much money is in my bank account and where it came from? I told you I had enough to pay my bills and be comfortable. I'm not sure how it's any business of yours where it comes from."

"I'm the sheriff; it's my business if it's from an illegal source."

He pulled in front of her building and stopped the truck.

"Are you accusing me of breaking the law? All because I won't let you snoop in my finances?"

He knew he was in trouble when he saw the set of her jaw and anger flashing in her eyes. Put the way she'd said it, he saw her point. Still, it frustrated him that she kept trying to keep him out. He was a cop. He couldn't turn it off even if he was dealing with his girlfriend. He knew that bookstore job couldn't pay very much and even if her jewelry business was doing really well, it couldn't be doing much more than paying her rent. He truly didn't think she was involved in something illegal but he hated not knowing and hated her not sharing with him even more.

"I'm sorry. Yes, I did insinuate that but I don't mean it. I'm just agitated that you keep hiding from me."

"I am not hiding from you. I've let you in further than anyone else other than my brother. That doesn't mean I'm going to let you snoop in my checkbook. I think I need to go in before we say something we regret." She grabbed the door handle.

"Are you always going to run away when things get difficult?"

She turned to him, shock on her face. "You don't know a fucking thing about it, Shane."

He knew he should shut up but damn it, his mouth wouldn't listen. "Then tell me! How can I know if you won't tell me?"

"You don't get every part of me! I am the only person entitled to all of me. If you need to know every bit of me and what I do, I can't offer it to you. I won't. I've been there and I will not go back."

"I'm sick of you comparing me to him, Cassie."

"Well, let me make it easy for you then. I won't compare you to anyone. Goodnight, Shane."

She got out of the car and began to walk to her apartment. He sat in his car and watched until she got inside and drove off.

Chapter Ten

For the next several days, he tried to tell himself he didn't need the aggravation of such a difficult woman in his life. He needed a woman who'd share with him without reservation.

He avoided the side of town the bookstore was on. Tried not to think about her. Matt was annoyed as hell at him. Gave him a lecture about how of course Cassie got her back up when she'd been controlled all those years and how Shane had a tendency to steamroll people to get what he wanted. Made the infuriating comment that Cassie was as stubborn as Shane was and that he'd met his match in her.

On Thursday he walked past the Honey Bear and saw the familiar fall of ebony hair and that long tall body. Cassie sat inside having lunch with Marc of all people. Shane stood at the door for a while, watching his little brother laugh and flirt and cajole Cassie. Just when he was ready to go in there and snatch his brother bald headed for moving in on his woman, Shane realized Marc was trying to get her to eat.

Marc looked up, face darkening when he saw Shane in the doorway, before moving his eyes back to Cassie. A sick feeling gathered in Shane's stomach and he went inside.

"Hi, mind if I join you?" He kept his voice light until he saw her face. Dark circles, impossible to cover completely with makeup, smudged the normally flawless skin below her eyes. Eyes that had lines of fatigue around them.

"I'm just leaving."

The caramel of her voice was flat.

"You haven't finished eating, sweetie. You promised me you'd finish half that sandwich. You wouldn't break a promise would you?" Marc cajoled her.

"I'll take it to go. I promise I'll eat it when I get home." She smiled at Marc.

"Cassie, please, can we talk?" Shane wanted to touch her, had burned to touch her since she'd walked away from him Sunday night but his pride had stopped him from calling her. Damn it.

"I think we've said all we needed to."

"I'm sorry. I've missed you. You look terrible. I'm sorry." He scrubbed hands over his face and took a deep breath. "Can I walk you to your car at least?"

"I'm going to go get this wrapped up for you, okay, Cassie?" Marc stood and grabbed her plate.

"Thank you, Marc." She turned back to Shane and met his eyes. Their connection sparked. "I didn't drive. I walked."

"Okay. Can I walk you home then?"

Marc brought her a bag and handed it to her, kissing her cheek. "You promised. Don't make me give you my pouty face. I'm told it's quite devastating."

Cassie laughed. "I promised. Thanks, Marc."

He shrugged and moved past his brother, shooting him a glare over her shoulder. "Of course, sweetie. That's what friends are for. Now I'll see you Monday. You promised that too."

"Okay, okay. I'll see you then."

She watched Marc go and then grabbed her handbag and the paper sack that held her leftovers.

Moving so she could see him coming, Shane reached out to touch her arm. He knew there was hope when her eyes closed a moment. "Darlin', I'm a pushy bastard. But damned if I don't just think you're the best thing that ever happened to me. I think we covered the arrogant ass part in an earlier conversation. I'd like to refer you back to that."

"You can walk me home," was all she said as she headed toward the door and out onto the sidewalk.

"Would you like me to drive you? It's awfully warm out here and you look tired."

"I can walk. It's five blocks. And I *am* tired."

"Okay. How about I carry your leftovers so you can hold my hand?"

Without saying anything she handed him the paper sack after a block and he took her hand in his. Relief rushed through him.

They didn't speak much on the walk but she invited him in.

"Only if you'll finish eating. I haven't eaten either. You have any food inside?"

She rolled her eyes and jerked her head, ordering him inside.

He'd been unsure what to expect. His own place was a pit, he'd been eating out a lot and sleeping on the couch but her apartment was clean enough.

"Sit down, I'll make you a sandwich." She looked him up and down. "Two. You want iced tea?"

He grinned and she made a soft sound, part annoyance, part affection. He watched her as she moved in the kitchen, making him sandwiches and putting her leftovers on a plate. Within moments she placed the plates on her small table and went back to grab the teas, sitting down with a sigh.

"You haven't called."

"Neither have you." It sounded petulant even to his own ears.

"No. Because I've told you I can't deal with feeling controlled. That may not have been your intention but I was up front with you from the start that I have hot button issues. What's your excuse?"

Damn she was direct. He swallowed hard. "I don't have one. Pride I guess. I'm a damned fool."

She looked him up and down and nodded shortly. "Yeah. But you're well meaning."

Unable to hold back a smile, he gave her one and took her hand. She let him. "Okay, the deal is, you and I have some major chemistry. But we're both stubborn. I think this will lead to fights."

"You're brilliant. You should have pursued rocket science."

He snorted but laughed anyway. "Sarcasm doesn't suit you. But I think if we know this and you absolutely know I'll not raise my hand to you ever, we can be mad, take a few steps back for a few hours and work it through. No more three days without speaking."

"Four days, asshole."

"You're a hard woman. Yes, four days. No more, okay? We'll work it through? Because you're worth it to me. I've missed you like crazy. Matt isn't speaking to me and I'm pretty sure after Marc tells my momma what you look like, I'm in big trouble from her too. My arms have been empty without you."

She softened. "You know I'm nearly helpless when you say that stuff. All right. I've missed you too."

"You look like hell."

"I haven't been sleeping well."

"I'm sorry."

"Stop saying that. We're done with that now. I'm sorry too. And I've just had some bad dreams. My therapist called in some pills to help me sleep better. I picked them up yesterday."

"And are they helping?"

"I haven't taken them. I..." She didn't want to be that far under in case Terry found her. If he broke in, she'd be helpless and he'd kill her. She'd dreamt of it over and over since Sunday night.

"You?"

"I just don't like narcotic sleep. It makes me feel out of control."

He nodded. "You working tomorrow?"

"Yes. Every Friday."

"I'm on shift until six tonight. I'll be back here with Chinese food and some clothes by seven. Don't worry, I'll sleep on the couch if you like. But you're going to sleep tonight and I'll be here to make sure you're safe. You'll take those pills and start feeling better because you're the guest of honor at a big party in just a few days."

She started to refuse but she wanted him here. He did make her feel safe. She didn't have the strength to refuse him. And she didn't want to.

"Okay. Thank you, Shane."

He came to kneel before her. "Cassie, I care very deeply about you. I'm sorry you've felt unsafe all this time while we've both been stupid. But you don't know how happy it makes me that you'll let me help, in even such a small way. Now eat."

CRSO

That night he'd slept beside her, her body in his arms, breath on the skin of his neck. They'd made love but she'd kept her shirt on and the lights off. He knew she had body image issues and he didn't push her but he wanted her to know how beautiful she was. He hoped she'd trust him enough to let him see all of her some day soon.

He'd gotten up and ready first. She was a bit groggy when her alarm had gone off but some coffee and toast helped her wake up. When he'd left for work she was already looking better for her full night's sleep.

Chapter Eleven

Labor Day morning dawned bright and warm. Cassie had deliberated on what to wear for the last several days until she finally decided on a pair of denim shorts and a deep red sleeveless shirt. The collar was enough to hide the edge of the scars and she was able to wear her hair in a high ponytail.

Shane had wanted her to sleep over at his house the evening before but then he'd gotten called out for work at nine-thirty and she'd just headed home, she wasn't comfortable enough in his house to be there alone just yet.

She'd headed to Penny's first thing but Shane was already there with his mother and brothers, setting everything up.

"I thought I'd be able to beat you here." Cassie smiled at Polly, her hands on her hips.

"Honey, you'd have to get up a lot earlier to beat me to it." Polly laughed and pulled her into a hug. "I'm glad to see you here. Come on out here and tell me what you think."

Penny's backyard had been transformed into the perfect place for a party. A canopy was set up near the big oak tree and several tables rested beneath it for shade. Several stations of tubs filled with ice and cans and bottles of soda dotted the area. Penny's dock had several floats and donuts for the kids to play on laying around.

"Wow. It looks great."

Shane saw her and dropped what he was doing to come and swoop her up into a hug. He dropped a kiss on her lips. "Morning, gorgeous. Sorry to have to duck out on you last night."

"Well, I suppose it's one of the hazards of being a cop's girlfriend. Is everything all right?"

He smiled at her and Polly laughed. "You just said you were my girlfriend."

"I am aren't I? I thought we'd discussed it."

"We did. I just like hearing it."

Cassie rolled her eyes.

"I like hearing it too. It's about damned time." Polly harrumphed and moved back out into the yard to order people around.

Before too long, people began to show up and two very large barbecues began to fill up with burgers and chicken.

Shane heaped food on Cassie's plate and got up to get her another glass of tea. He'd been very careful to make sure she stayed hydrated and ate well after she'd scared him several days before. At first she'd been testy when he insisted she take care of herself and eat better but to his relief, she finally let him take care of her. She did appear to be sleeping better though and the dark circles were gone.

"You're good together." Liv patted his arm after he'd gotten the glass of tea. "I wish...well, I'm glad for you and Cassie. She's a good person. And she clearly makes you happy. Love is a good thing, Shane."

He saw the sadness on her face and her eyes moved to Matt and then away. "I'm real sorry things didn't work out with Matt. I hope you find what I've got with Cassie. You deserve it."

Liv shrugged. "I wish it had worked too. But you can't make someone love you. They do or they don't. It was a nice time. He was lovely to me. He just didn't love me and after a while I couldn't deal with loving someone when they didn't love me back. Love changes you. Look at you. You were an asshole, Shane. God, you treated Maggie like shit. But you see now, you see in ways you couldn't then. That's good."

Brody called to her and she smiled and waved, moving to him after she'd said goodbye to Shane.

He stood there, thinking about the last thing Liv had said. That love changed how he saw things. Sure he'd been sorry he hurt Maggie because he liked her as a person. Liked her as a sister, even loved her as one. But loving Cassie had opened his eyes. He wasn't sure he liked what he saw of himself before. He'd closed himself off and it hadn't made him particularly nice to women. He hadn't been a cad, but he hadn't seen them in the way he should have.

He looked across the lawn at her as she laughed and talked with Penny, her back resting against the tree trunk. Damn she was beautiful. Yes, stunning on the outside, but her inner beauty shone like a beacon. He loved her. He didn't see her with love, he didn't love things about her, he loved her. Was *in* love with her.

"You love her, don't you?" Shane's father came to stand next to his son.

He looked at his father. "You're scary. I just realized it myself. I'm scared to death I'll fuck it up. I don't have the best track record with this stuff."

Edward chuckled. "That's love. Real love is scary. Because you know what you stand to lose. But she's damned strong, Shane. You need that. You didn't need some tough-as-nails woman to capture your heart. That's Marc. No, you needed a

153

woman who was as strong as you but who engaged your ability to empathize. To show you what it meant to truly rise above and live. She's a fighter, our Cassie. She's your equal and your other half because she gives you the ability to see beyond yourself.

"You're a good man, Shane. But you've been selfish with women after Sandra. It's been hard to watch you wall your emotions off the way you did. All we could do was hope like hell Cassie would come along and break your shell. And she did and you've broken hers too. Seeing you so gentle with her does my heart proud. I'm proud of *you*, son. You're a man now." Edward pressed a kiss to his son's cheek and squeezed his shoulder before Shane moved to walk down to his woman.

But before Shane got to her she was standing up and looking toward the water. She took off at a run and Matt ran the other way, toward the front of the house.

Shane yelled her name but she dove off the dock and he ran, balls out, to reach her. Dee was crying and, in what felt like slow motion, Cassie surfaced, holding eighteen-month-old Michael in her arms. He'd fallen from the dock into the water and at some point, he'd taken a knock to the head and a deep, ugly wound gashed into his forehead.

Matt shoved him out of the way and took Michael from Cassie. Breaking free of his trance, Shane reached out to help her scramble up onto the dock.

"Back up," she ordered and everyone did. Shane put his arm around Dee with Arthur on the other side of her.

Matt opened a medical bag and Shane watched in awe, as his Cassie melted away and a confident, in charge woman replaced her. Her face was set in concentration as she tipped Michael's neck up and leaned in.

"Matt, I'm going to need something for this head wound but let's get him breathing first."

Matt took orders smoothly as she began to give CPR to Michael, who'd turned blue.

Dee sobbed and he heard his father yell out that an ambulance was on the way.

Cassie broke her lips from Michael's and turned him onto his side and he coughed, water gushing from his mouth. She continued to give orders to Matt while she alternately spoke to Michael in a soothing voice to keep him calm.

Without taking her eyes from Michael, Cassie addressed Dee. "Dee, honey, can you hold it together? Just kneel down and touch his legs. He's scared. I'm going to get this gash on his head cleaned up and the bleeding stopped. He'll probably need a few stitches. Ask when you get to the hospital for a surgeon to do it. Preferably a plastic surgeon if one is available. That should help with the scar. He's going to be all right, Dee."

Dee took a deep breath and fell to her knees. She reached out to rub Michael's legs while talking to him, reassuring him. Cassie continued to work and Matt handed her everything she asked for. The siren sounded as the ambulance neared.

The paramedics ran over with a board and Cassie spoke to them clearly and quietly, explaining what had happened and what had been done. Dee moved to go with them in the ambulance, Arthur would follow in the car. Cassie followed until they got loaded in and drove away.

As she returned to the yard, Shane looked to her, amazement on his face. Matt wore an identical look.

She held up a hand. "I need a drink. The story is long and I can't tell it with everyone here."

Polly had already begun to shoo people out of the yard and Edward put a tumbler filled with an amber liquid into her hand. One handed, he pressed her into a chair in the shade.

When everyone but the Chases, Penny and Liv had gone, Cassie took a deep breath, and the smoky scent of good scotch filled her nose. Two swallows and it was gone. The heat spread through her, warring with the adrenaline crash.

"My name is not Cassie Gambol. It's Carly Sunderland. Or rather, it used to be Carly Sunderland, it's been changed legally. A long time ago in a galaxy far away, I was a successful vascular surgeon at a private hospital in Orange County. You all know the story of my ex-husband.

"I divorced him. He wasn't happy. He harassed me and my family. Showed up at my job until they had to bar him from the hospital and he lost his position and ability to practice there and his own practice group tossed him out. I kept quiet and was careful when I went home so he couldn't follow me. I thought I'd been successful. But I wasn't. Eight months later he found me. Broke into my condo while I was sleeping. I woke up with him on my chest and a hammer coming toward my face. I threw him off but I tripped leaving my bedroom and he landed on my back. He held me down while he used the hammer to shatter the bones in two of the fingers in my right hand. I tried to get free but he's a big man.

"Blood was everywhere, I was slipping in it as I tried to struggle. I'll never forget the smell. It wasn't like I'd never smelled blood before but it was different because I knew it was mine. I knew I was losing too much.

"He'd hit me so hard the handle of the hammer began to splinter, and it broke completely when he hit me on the back of the head with it. I worked to stay conscious as he began to stab me with the shattered handle. Repeatedly. In the back and neck. He left me for dead as I lay in a pool of my own blood. But I managed to reach my phone just as I passed out. Luckily 911 sends someone out when there's no response.

"I was in a coma for three weeks and then in the hospital for nearly another month. It's all more complicated than I want to dwell on but after that they found him and arrested him. Put him on trial.

"At first they thought he'd paralyzed me. The wounds really messed up some of my nerves in my right arm. But with physical therapy, and my good luck at having one of my colleagues work on me, they saved most of my movement and by the time the trial was midway through I could walk through the door on my own power.

"I testified. They convicted him. He was supposed to be remanded immediately, awaiting sentencing. But there was some sort of paperwork error and they let him go. By the time they realized their error he'd skipped town."

She held up her hand to silence Shane, as Edward handed her another drink. Penny pressed some crackers into her other hand, which she ate to stave off the nausea.

"He called and taunted me. Said he'd be back to finish the job. It wasn't like I could be a surgeon ever again. I don't have the fine motor skills in my hand to do it. I had a wonderful victim's advocate the court hooked me up with. She got me enrolled in a program to change my name and social security number. He'd tracked me to my new apartment with my social security information.

"My brother drove through Petal a few years ago on his way to Atlanta and he liked it here. I chose an apartment I saw online and Carly went away and Cassie moved to Petal."

"Jesus God." Maggie looked up at Cassie.

Cassie swallowed and turned to look at Shane, wincing as she saw him. "I'm sorry I lied. I'm a little messed up right now, but I'll go home and clear out of town as soon as I can. You must all hate me."

A deep, tortured sound came from Shane as he fell to his knees and pulled her into his arms. "How you survived that and had the courage to come here and start your life over I'll never know. Cassie, you're amazing and I love you so much it hurts."

Cassie blinked several times, trying to figure out if she'd heard him right. "What?"

Shane pulled back and kissed her and kissed her again for good measure. "I. Love. You. Cassie, you're so damned strong. I don't hate you. How could you think I'd hate you for not wanting to share that horrible fucking story?"

"I lied about my name."

"So what? Cassie Gambol is your legal name now isn't it? Honey, you must think I'm a grade-A prick if you think I'd be angry at you for having to give up everything to move here to protect yourself from a homicidal freak."

She put her face in her hands. "I don't know what I thought! You don't...you're all...shit. I don't know. I'm sorry."

He laughed. "You're sorry? Honey, let's get you to my house, okay? Get you tucked into bed for a rest. You just saved Michael's life and told us one hell of a story. That's got to take a lot out of a girl."

"I've got lake water all over me."

"Why don't I go to your place and get you some clothes? I'll bring them by Shane's." Penny squeezed Cassie's hand. "Honey, I knew you were good people the minute you walked into my shop and not a damned thing you've done has made me doubt that."

"I lied to you all!"

"Not about anything important. Your actions speak the truth, Cassie. You were in charge and strong out there on that dock today. Even though it exposed you, you did it. You saved

Michael's life without even a thought. You've been a good friend to us and you've, well, you've saved Shane too." Maggie fought tears.

Cassie couldn't deal much longer. She needed to be away from them all before she lost it. She also knew she couldn't be alone in her apartment. "My keys are in my purse. It's in the front closet."

Marc jogged inside and brought her purse back out and Penny took her keys and handed the purse to Shane, who took one look at Cassie and picked her up. "We're going to go to my house. I'll talk to you all later."

He started toward the car and Cassie laid her head on his chest and closed her eyes.

As the car pulled out of the driveway, everyone else stood on the front porch watching Shane take her to his house just three doors down.

"Holy hell." Matt leaned back against the front porch rail.

"I'm going to go to Cassie's and get her clothes." Penny moved to her car.

"I'll stay here until you get back." Polly sat in the porch swing and Edward joined her.

Penny waved and left.

"I can't even imagine. I knew it was bad. When she told us about the abuse I was horrified. I thought there was some big incident but she didn't say. I just had no idea it would be this." Maggie leaned back against Kyle.

Polly sighed. "I knew it would be a strong woman who'd finally captured Shane's heart. But she's braver than any woman I've ever met in my life. Imagine just up and leaving after suffering so much and starting over again halfway across the country."

Lauren Dane

"She won't be safe until this asshole is found." Kyle held his wife to him.

"Shane won't stop until he is." Matt spoke with absolute certainty.

૮ૠૹ

Shane took her up to his bathroom and turned on the water in his shower. "You can use a T-shirt for the time being. Let's get you cleaned up now." He tried to hold on to the tasks to get her comfortable. Anger and fear warred within him but he didn't want her to see either. He needed to be strong for her right then. Later on he'd go into his weight room and beat the hell out of the bag.

Woodenly, she let him help her out of her shoes and pull her shorts and panties down. As gently as he could, he freed her hair from the ponytail. Reaching down to pull her shirt off, he steeled himself. He knew seeing the scars would be shocking but he also knew he had to control his rage at Terry Sunderland to not make her feel bad. Her hands came down to stop him.

"Let me see you, Cassie. I think you're beautiful. You've told me the hard part. It doesn't matter to me. The scars don't make you less beautiful."

"You don't know. The scars..."

"Is that why you've left your shirt on when we make love?"

She nodded slowly. "That and well, my stomach and stuff."

"Cassie, please trust me. Your body is gorgeous. I don't care about the scars. They only make me think you're more beautiful."

More beautiful? Was he out of his mind? Angrily she pulled the shirt up and over her head and yanked her bra off. She

160

moved her hair away, giving him her back. "There! Still think I'm beautiful? Still think fourteen stab scars makes me *more beautiful?*"

She felt the press of his lips over each one of her scars until tears came from so deep she couldn't stand anymore. He was there though, taking her weight into his arms, pulling her into the shower with him.

She clung to him as he shampooed her hair and soaped her up the best he could with her arms wrapped around him.

"Come on, darlin'. Let's get you out of here and dried off." He helped her out of the shower and toweled her off after he'd wrapped up her hair.

Leading her into his bedroom he had her sit on his bed. "I'll be right back. I'm guessing Penny has been by and left your clothes downstairs."

And she had. Left a bag just inside his screen door without disturbing them further. There was a note that Cassie's keys were at Penny's house when she needed them.

He stood in his living room, a towel wrapped around his waist, thinking about her scars. Out of Cassie's presence he let the rage take him. The rage at seeing the pink skin of fourteen scars on her back and neck. Of knowing the man who'd done it to her was still out there, keeping her so afraid she didn't sleep at night. That the sick fuck had taken away her career and nearly killed her—all because she wanted a divorce. Took away her name and her home.

He needed to let it wash through him because the last thing Cassie needed was a pissed off man. He knew right then that he would track Terry Sunderland down and turn him over to the courts or kill him himself. Shane Chase was a man who lived by law and order, believed in the power of justice. But at the moment, he wanted to kill another man. Wanted it with a power he'd never felt before.

Forcibly unclenching his fists, he took several deep breaths and let it go. He picked up the bag to bring Cassie her clothes.

Cassie lay on his bed quietly, her hands folded over her abdomen. Totally naked. The shock of her beauty hit him in the gut like it always did but this time with greater force because she wasn't covering up. She was totally exposed to him emotionally as well as physically.

"Darlin'? I've got your clothes here."

"Do you want me to cover up? Do the scars creep you out?" She sat up, the wet strands of her hair moving over her shoulders and chest.

Putting the bag near the door he pulled off the towel and stood there, naked and hard. "Does it look like your scars creep me out, Cassie?"

She shook her head. "Shane?"

"Yes, darlin'?"

"Do you have condoms?"

"Yes."

"Will you come here and make love to me please?"

He froze a moment. "Are you sure, baby? I'd like nothing more to do that but I don't want you to do it if you don't feel up to it. It's been a trying day for you."

"It has." She nodded. "But I...I need to feel alive and you make me feel alive. When you're inside me, with your hands on me, I feel alive and vibrant."

He crawled across the bed to get to her. "You...Cassie, you make me feel so much. I love you. I've said it to another woman but I didn't even know what love was until I met you."

She moved to her knees and touched his chest and encircled his neck with her arms. "I love you too." Her voice was small but he heard it and his heart skipped a beat. "I love you but I'm scared."

"Let's work on that, okay? Because I'd give my life for you, to protect you. I love you and that means you're mine. And not in the way he meant it. You're not a *thing* to me. You're *everything* to me. I want you to be free from fear. Happy. You deserve that. Let's work to make sure I can help protect you."

She pushed him back on the bed and scrambled to straddle his body. "I love that you asked to protect me."

"I love this position." He grinned lasciviously. "And I'm trying. God knows I want to hide you and go to war for you, but I know that's not what you need so I'm trying to find a middle ground. Because I have to tell you, I want to find this bastard so you can live freely. I want you to be able to choose to be Carly or Cassie. As long as you're with me, I don't care what you call yourself."

Leaning down, she kissed his lips and then the cleft on his chin. Her hands skimmed over the hard, tight flesh of his shoulders and chest. Through the hair there and over the coppery nipples, his gasp of pleasure bringing her a smile.

"I like that you have hair on your chest. It makes you even more masculine. And my goodness are you masculine. It makes me all shivery."

His hands slid up her thighs and came to rest at her waist. "I'm glad. I like that I'm not the only one shivery all the time."

She brought her lips to the hollow of his throat and swirled her tongue there, tasting the salt of his skin. Over his collarbone and down, teeth grazing over each nipple. Scooting back, her ass rested on his thighs as her hands traveled over the flat muscle of his belly until she finally reached his cock.

"I like this too."

"I'm *really* glad. It likes you as well." His voice was strangled. "We can get to the making love stage soon, right? Because I really need to be inside you."

"In due time, Sheriff." With that, she bent down and took him into her mouth, bringing him off the bed with a hiss of pleasure.

She explored him slowly with her mouth, with lips and tongue. Around the head, tasting him, and then slowly taking him as far as she could before nearly pulling off him.

His hands gripped the sheets so tight she was surprised he didn't rip them. But his control, all for her, to make sure he didn't spook her, touched her. And she yearned for a time when he'd take her wild and hot, when she could be taken without fear. A time she felt would come someday.

Shane looked down his body at Cassie. Her dark hair, slowly drying, played peek-a-boo with her face so he got carnal glimpses of her sucking his cock. What he didn't see was just as hot as what he did see. One of her hands wrapped around the base of his cock and the other did something naughty and really good with his balls.

The hot, wet of her mouth surrounded him and he was awash in pleasure. He knew he had to stop her soon or he'd come and he'd already discovered just how much he liked being inside her when that happened.

"Baby? Cassie, honey? Stop now, I'm getting close."

She pulled off him with a slight pop and looked up. She looked so wicked and sexy at that moment his cock jumped in response. Her lips were wet and swollen, eyes half lidded, hair tousled.

"That's the point, Shane."

He laughed. "Ride me, Cassie. I'll come, but I want to be deep inside you when I do."

Pouting, she took the condom from him and rolled it on. He was fairly sure he'd never want to put his own condom on again, the way she did it, slow and precise, was damned sexy.

Crawling forward, she reached around her body to open herself and guide him to her gate. He took it all in as she slowly sank back onto his cock.

Hot. Fuck, she was hot and tight as her pussy took him in. Welcomed him. Each time she pulled her body up, he watched the flex of her thighs and her breasts swayed forward.

"You're amazing, Cassie. So pretty up there I don't have words. I could look at you for days."

A crooked smile slid over her mouth and she rolled her eyes. "I love that you're so full of shit."

"You know, you're snarky when you get warmed up."

"Ha! You should see me when I've known you a while."

And that little comeback settled around his heart. "Yeah." He smiled a moment, drawing a fingertip around her nipple, delighting in her pause and the way her lip caught between her teeth. "I can't wait."

She took a deep breath and added a swivel when she came back down on him. "That was very nice," he said, voice strained.

"I got the mad skills. I haven't used them in a few years, but I got 'em." She tapped her temple and he laughed.

It was important to her that he realize she was more than the sum of those years with Terry. There was a time when she'd loved sex and she was quickly back there. Something about the way he looked at her, touched her, made her whole, enabled her to think about a future.

"You got 'em all right." He continued to circle her nipple with one finger and drew another down her stomach, finding her clit. Gasping, she rolled her hips forward. At first it was a slow stroke, building the fire of her pleasure.

"Cassie, give it to me. Let me feel you come around my cock."

She shivered at his words and arched, putting her hands on his thighs.

"Oh that's a sight. I love the way that looks. Almost as good as how it feels."

His voice was strained as the new angle of entry dragged the head of his cock over her sweet spot. That, along with his finger slowly sliding back and forth over her clit, brought orgasm over her with a sharp shock.

Shane looked up at her, watched the arch of her beautiful body. As her pussy clutched and clasped around his cock, he pulled her down on him and came, her name a hoarse whisper on his lips.

Boneless, she fell to a sated heap on the bed. He murmured that he'd be right back, checked the house to be sure it was locked up and lay beside her, his arms around her body, until she was deeply asleep.

Tucking blankets around her body, he set the air conditioner to keep the room nice and cool and grabbed some shorts before heading downstairs.

In his weight room, he worked out for well over an hour, hitting the bag, imagining it was Cassie's ex. He pushed every last bit of his anger and grief for her through his fists until he was so exhausted he trembled.

He heard a tapping on the door and got rid of the gloves before going out to see who it was.

Matt stood there and held up a six pack and a bag of pretzels. Kyle held up a dish of chicken and Marc held a cobbler. Shane let them in and put his finger to his lips.

"Cassie is sleeping. Come on through."

They followed him into the television room and flopped down on the couch. No one said a word until beers were cracked open and the pretzels passed around and chicken tasted. Shane put the cobbler aside for Cassie.

"How is she?" Matt asked.

"She's exhausted but sleeping. I thought the nightmares were just about the abuse. Shit, he broke in while she was sleeping. It's a wonder she slept at all." Shane ran a hand through his hair.

"You'll find him, Shane. Tell us what we can do to help." Kyle sighed and sat back.

"I will. Now that I've got a name that's a start. I'll call the officer in charge of her case tomorrow and see what he'll tell me."

"How are *you*?" Marc asked. "I can't imagine it's easy for you to know the woman you love has gone through something so awful."

"I'm better now. I punched the bag for a while, did some judo. I'll get down to the range tomorrow and I want her to come too. She's a strong woman, I'm betting she'll feel even better with some basic proficiency with a weapon. She'll feel in charge and I'll be helping her. God knows how touchy she'd be if I just did it all for her."

"You really love her, don't you?" Kyle smiled. "I'm sorry she had to endure all of that. But she's a damned strong woman and she's good for you. Maggie wanted to come over but she's with Momma, holding her back."

Shane nodded, understanding. "Momma must be like a bumblebee in a jar right now."

The brothers laughed, thinking about their mother in protective mode but being unable to leave to come and comfort Cassie and her son.

"Thank you." Shane looked to each of his brothers, jerking his chin at the food on the table.

"You love her. She loves you. That makes her one of us now." Matt shrugged his shoulders matter-of-factly.

Chapter Twelve

The next week went by in a blur. Shane spent every moment he could with Cassie, getting to know her better, falling in love with her a bit more every day.

Holding a bag of sandwiches and cream sodas, he headed up the stairs to her apartment and froze as he saw her on the landing, hugging another man. She clung to him tightly, her face buried in his neck.

Shane saw red and then his heart broke into a million pieces. It was Sandra all over again. He'd fallen in love after so many years and it happened to him again. He wanted to fall to his knees and howl at the unfairness of losing a woman he'd thought cared about him as much as he did her.

"Fuck all if you didn't totally fool me with your act. I'm as damned as you're faithless apparently. If you're going to cheat on me, Cassie, you should do it out of the public eye."

Cassie froze and looked around the man. And when the man turned Shane saw three things. The look of horror and pain on Cassie's face; his brother Matt standing in the doorway of her apartment behind them and that the man looked a lot like Cassie. *Shit.*

He moved quickly toward her but she pulled back into the apartment and shoved the man inside who looked about ready to punch Shane. Of course, judging from the look on Matt's face, he'd have to stand in line.

"Cassie, I'm..."

"Let me guess, you're sorry? Shane Chase, this is my brother Brian. He's here to meet the man I fell in love with and to tell me that Terry has been sighted." She tried to slam the door but he put a hand out.

"Cassie, I'm sorry. I thought...when I saw you with another man...it just...I'm sorry. Please. Can't we talk about it?"

"No, I don't think we can." She put a hand on his chest, shoving him back and slammed the door in his face. He leaned his forehead against the frame and let out a ragged breath.

CRSO

"Oh honey, I don't know what to say." Matt sat down and watched Cassie as she fought back tears. He was so angry at Shane he held his hands together between his knees to keep from shaking. The man found this woman who loved him so much, who'd never do anything so bad, and he might have just thrown it all away.

"I appreciate you coming over, Matt but I think my sister needs to be alone right now." Brian stood and went to the door.

Matt looked back at Cassie. "He loves you, Cassie. He tries to pretend like what Sandra did didn't hurt him that bad, but it wrecked him. He couldn't trust anyone for years. I'm not saying he was right, but I want you to try and understand why he jumped to conclusions the way he did." He went to the door. "We'll see you tomorrow night at dinner then."

"Oh no you won't."

He sighed. "Cassie, don't. Please don't shut him out. You're good for him and he's good for you."

"I can see how good he is for her. Accusing her of being a whore on her doorstep, making her cry. Fabulous." Brian crossed his arms over his chest.

"It was wrong, I'm not saying it wasn't. But my brother loves her. He's a good man and he deserves a second chance. Everybody makes mistakes, Cassie."

"Yes, and they always tell you they're sorry after they hurt you. Until they do it again. There's always an excuse. I'm not her anymore. I won't go back to being her."

Matt realized the depth of Shane's mistake then but didn't say anything further about it. "I'm next door if you need me. No matter what is going on between you two, I'm your friend. Okay?" He moved to hug her and she let him.

"Thank you, Matt."

"Please don't judge my brother too harshly, Brian." Matt raised his hand in a wave and left, hearing the locks click into place behind him.

Shane sat on the bottom step.

"What the fuck is wrong with you, Shane?"

Shane shook his head, Matt saw tears shining in his eyes. "Oh shit. I hurt her so badly. It's just...when I saw her there it made me think of Sandra. I forgot who she was for a moment. I spoke before I thought and oh, her face." Shane rested his forehead on his knees and Matt knelt there, touching his brother's arm.

"I know why you overreacted, Shane. I understand."

"I may have lost her forever."

Matt took a deep breath. "I hope not. But. I'm sorry to say this, Shane but you attacked her and falsely accused her and your shit with Sandra pushed her buttons. Both of your emotional shit hit in the same place at the same time. She's really upset and her brother is pissed off."

"And the ex has been seen?"

"She didn't tell me much. She came home from work and saw me out front. Told me her brother was on the way and that she wanted us all to meet him and for him to meet us. Then she told me the brother had said the ex had been seen. She didn't know more than that and I came over to her place to watch over her."

"I need to go to her, work this out." Shane stood.

"Don't. Shane, not right now. Her brother is really angry and protective. She's a mess. Call her, leave a message. Go to her stall tomorrow. Let her know you're here but don't rush up on her. Give her some space. She's scared right now that you're like her ex. Hurt her and say you're sorry and hurt her again."

"Fuck. I'm an idiot."

Matt hugged his brother. "No you're not. You've been one in the past but you got scared tonight and reacted before thinking. You love her and you hurt her. But you're not her ex."

Looking back over his shoulder at her door, Shane let Matt drag him over to his apartment where he called and left her a message.

CR80

"Carly, what is going on, honey?" Brian sat next to her on the couch, brushing a hand over her hair. "I thought this guy was the one."

Cassie had successfully fought away her tears and now just felt numb. "I thought he was too, Brian."

"Who's Sandra?"

She told him the story of Shane's ex-fiancée who he'd found cheating with his best friend.

"So he saw you with me and he must have flashed back on that. He's already left you a phone message apologizing. He sounded sincere. What do you think?"

"I'm afraid, Brian. He's probably the most sincere person I've ever met. But I don't know if I can trust my own perceptions these days and I'm afraid if I take him back that it'll be like with Terry."

"I understand. Well, I don't, but I trust your feelings here. I don't know this guy well enough to say. Why don't you give it some time to see how he acts in the coming days? Because I'd hate to see you write him off if he's the one for you. But I'd hate to see you take him back and end up with another asshole."

She put her head on his shoulder and sighed. "Tell me about Terry."

Brian did. He told her about how her ex had been sighted in San Francisco three times before dropping out of sight again. All the more troubling was that one person claimed Terry tried to get her to use her state job access to search information about Cassie.

"We don't have any reason to think he knows you've changed your name or that you're here. But I think you should be aware at all times. I can't see that you should move away from Petal. You're building a life here and that's important."

Lying in bed that night, Cassie stared at the ceiling and felt the emptiness next to her in bed. She'd gotten used to Shane's body there at night. Reaching out and touching him. Knowing she was safe and loved. And that was gone and her heart felt empty. Everything felt empty as she tried to figure out what the hell to do.

Chapter Thirteen

Brian stayed in Petal over the next several days to visit and keep in contact with the investigators on Terry's trail. Still, Cassie tried to keep to a schedule.

Shane had come to her table at the Sunday market but she asked him to go. It hurt just seeing him.

He left messages on her voice mail every morning to tell her he loved her and every night to say goodnight. Her feelings were all over the map. She loved him. No doubt about that. Every time she saw him walk by the front of the book store, every time she heard his voice or found a note he left for her on her car, she missed him more than she had before.

Loving Shane and being with him had filled up her life. Not in an onerous way like being with Terry had been. Being with Shane hadn't weighed on her. It had been good, right. She felt like she'd belonged to something instead of to someone.

But it would hurt less to lose him now than to take him back and fall into the same traps she'd done before and lose herself in the process. She'd rather be alone than live in fear ever again.

CR80

Polly Chase parked her car on Main and got out for the short walk to Paperbacks and More. "Damn kids. I tell you, if you want something done..." she mumbled as she patted her hair into place and absentmindedly waved at someone who'd called out a hello.

She walked into the store and zeroed in on Cassie. Her heart ached for the girl her son loved so much. Men!

"Hello, Polly." Cassie smiled wanly.

Polly pulled Cassie into a hug and held her upper arms as she gave her a long up and down. "Honey, you look like hell. When you gonna forgive Shane so you can both get some sleep?"

"Polly, I appreciate you checking in on me, I really do. But this thing between your son and I is not only private but complicated."

"Oh that's a pretty way to tell an old woman to mind her business. I like you, honey." Polly chuckled as she sat in the chair behind the counter. "But I'm a nosy old woman, it's a perk of getting old. You can be annoying and people just call you *eccentric.*" Polly laughed at that. "Anyway, I know Shane messed up. I know what he did and how he reacted must have made you wonder if he'd be like your wretched sonabitch ex. But you and I both know after a day or two, that's not the case. My son is a good man and that bitch gave him, how do you kids say, *issues* or baggage. I'm not excusing his actions, you best believe I tore a strip off him a mile wide and his father has too. But no one is punishing him harder than he is himself."

Polly leaned in, peering intently at Cassie. "You've made mistakes before in your life. I know part of that is what makes you hesitate now. But also, can't you see your way to giving my boy another chance? Let's face it, you two are going to fight. A lot. There's enough chemistry between the two of you to make an old woman sweat."

Cassie blushed crimson and looked at the paperback in her hands to keep from looking at Polly.

"You two have chemistry and heat but you're both stubborn, headstrong people. Lord knows this won't be your last fight. But you can fight with your man and know it's going to be all right the next day. Edward is the kind of man that butter wouldn't melt. I like that. It suits me. But Shane isn't that man. He's got my disposition. We're a tad hot headed. We love fierce. Shane loves you and I know you love him."

Polly hopped down from the chair, grabbing the bag she'd put near the register stand. "Two things. This has a cherry and a peach cobbler. Eat them both, you look pale. The second thing is I already think of you as my daughter-in-law so I love you too. Please give Shane another chance, for both your sakes. Oh, okay a third thing. You call Matty or Marc or me and Edward if you feel spooked, all right? We worry."

With that she thrust the bag at Cassie, hugged her again and click-clacked out of the store.

From there she headed over to the police station.

"Shane Edward Chase! You hold up right there, boy." Polly thundered as she stormed down the hall toward where he stood with the county prosecutor.

"Mrs. Chase, ma'am." The prosecutor, a boy she babysat many a time, bowed and got the hell out of there.

"Coward," Shane muttered and then waved his mother into his office. "Have a seat, let me get some soda because I can see from the look of you this will be a long lecture."

With narrowed eyes, Polly sat as she glared at her eldest's impertinence. "You look here, boy, I brought you into this world, I will not hesitate to take your dumb ass right out of it."

Shane laughed as he handed her a soda. "Of course, Momma, I'm sorry. I imagine this is about Cassie and I know, it's my fault and I'm trying to get her to talk to me. I told you that yesterday and the day before and before that too."

"I just went to see her, girl looks like she hasn't slept in a week. She's on the fence about you. But she loves you. She must 'cause I didn't let her get a word in edgewise." Pleased with herself, Polly chuckled again. "I made a good case for you, I hope. You know you and her are gonna butt heads a lot, right? Makes it more interesting in the bedroom I imagine."

Shane winced and got a sour look. "I don't want to have that line of conversation with you, Momma."

Polly waved him away. "Pshaw. Boy, you'll have any line of conversation with me I tell you to. Your daddy and I have four children, you think we don't have some chemistry ourselves? Now listen here, you've got to let her know that you love her and won't hurt her, even though you'll be fighting with her regular-like. And don't deny it, you two are just that way. But Maggie and I made her some cobbler and you know how your sweetie loves cobbler. Sweeten her up a bit hopefully."

Standing she raised the soda. "Thank you, Shane. You've turned out to be quite a decent man. I'm pretty proud of myself for not tossing your butt in the lake all the times I wanted to when you were a kid."

Shane grinned and kissed her cheek. "You're the best, Momma."

"Yeah, yeah. Boy, you better work on this girl harder because if she's not at dinner on Sunday you're eating a tuna sandwich."

With a last wave, she headed out while he chuckled.

CR&O

Brian walked out of the apartment and saw Shane talking with his brother. Making his mind up, he stalked over to them.

Shane looked up and saw him approach and nodded. "I've wanted to talk to you for a few days now. Clear the air."

"I'm going to speak now. You have no idea what my sister told me every time I spoke to her. About how wonderful you were, how gentle and kind and loving you were. How you chased away her demons and made her feel not only protected but capable of protecting herself. She was so proud of you, proud of herself for finding a man who was worthy of her." Brian looked him up and down.

"And so I get this information about that fucking bastard surfacing, trying to find her and I think I can come here, meet you. Instead, I get to listen to her cry every night. You tell me, Shane Chase, why the hell you think you're worthy of my sister."

Shane took a deep breath. "You don't know me so I can see why you'd be suspicious. It must have been hard to watch your sister go through what she did. I love her. Cassie means everything to me. You don't know what it was like...what I was like before. She changed me." He shrugged.

"I fucked up. I'm sorry. I have this old stuff and seeing her brought it to the surface. I was wrong. I've told her that. I made a mistake. I want to make it up to her. I'm not that bastard. I'm nothing like him. You can be mad at the person you love and not try to kill them. I don't know how to communicate that to her. But I'm going to keep trying until she listens to me.

"And I want to protect her. Yeah, yeah, I know she doesn't want that. But I love her and I'll be damned if that freak gets another shot at her. I'm trying to respect her need to do things herself. I want her to learn to shoot a weapon and take self defense courses."

Brian looked at him funny and then chuckled. "I take it you haven't talked to her about this plan."

"Well, no. She just told me about the attack two weeks ago. I'd wanted to talk to her about going to the range and then we got into this fight. Why? Is she afraid of guns?"

"God help you, Shane." Brian shook his head and started to laugh. "She's not afraid of guns. After the attack, after she got out of the hospital she went to the range every day and learned how to shoot. At first with her left hand because the right arm was so damaged. She's a pretty damned good shot. She's got a license to carry, I took care of that. She's got a 9 mm. The self defense classes would be good. She didn't have enough mobility yet after the physical therapy to really get proficient but she started to take martial arts classes just before she decided to up and move here."

Shane smiled wryly. "Okay, so the fact is that I'm *not* worthy of your sister. I can't think of anyone who is. She's just that special. But I love her and I'll keep loving her. And she makes me a better person, but I'm not perfect and yeah, I have buttons but so does she. So if I'm willing to work around hers, she should be willing to work around mine. Not that I think I handled it well. I didn't. But damn it, I deserve a second chance."

Brian looked at him silently for long moments and nodded shortly. "Yeah, I think you probably do. I have it on good authority that she's having dinner with Maggie, Penny and Liv tonight at Dee's. She told me she'd be home by nine. I'll be out then if you think you might want to talk to her."

Without saying anything else, Brian turned and walked away but not before looking back over his shoulder and tossing back, "If you hurt my sister again, I'll make it my business, Shane."

Matt watched as the man drove away in his rental before turning to his brother. "I like him."

CR⬦SO

Cassie spent the evening with her friends, enjoying the time with Michael and the easy communication with people. She began to know them and they her. Mostly they didn't talk about Shane but in their own way, each of them encouraged her to at least talk things over with him.

And she began to think they were right. Oh who was she kidding? She'd wanted to talk to him for days but was afraid. Afraid that if she did she'd lose him. Indecision had frozen her.

She'd talk to him the next time he called, she resolved as she walked from her car toward her stairs. Stairs that Shane sat on, holding a bouquet of roses, a gold box of chocolates at his feet.

"Those will melt out here in this heat," she said, walking past him and up the steps to her door.

"I should probably get them inside then, huh?"

"The roses need water too or they'll wilt."

He stood but stayed down at the bottom of the stairs, looking up at her. "Can we talk?"

"The lives of roses are at stake." She unlocked her door and walked in, leaving it open.

When he got inside, she'd pulled out a vase and was filling it with water. He locked up behind himself and came into the kitchen, handing her the roses.

"So talk."

And he did. He sat at her kitchen table and laid it all on the line. "Do you remember our first real fight? We promised each other that we'd step back and then work it through. We said no more not talking for days. So I called you every day. Twice a day. I kept my end of the bargain.

"I was an asshole. Stupid. I got caught off guard and when I saw you there it wasn't you, it was her for just a brief second. But I didn't let it process, I just spoke out of pain and I hurt you and I'm so sorry. I didn't mean to hurt you and I did but I'd like the chance to make it up to you."

"I'm not her! I would never do that to you! How could you even think that of me? I love you. I trusted you with my heart and you hurt me."

"And I'm not him! Come on, Cassie, give me a break here. I said some not very nice stuff, yes. I take responsibility for it. It was wrong but I didn't hit you, I didn't blame it on you. I made a mistake, a stupid mistake. I love you, but we both know it won't be the last mistake I make. I'll make more because I'm a clumsy guy and I do clumsy guy stuff. I'm a tool. But I love you more than words can say. I want you to be with me forever. I'm serious about you, about this, us. I want us to move forward and build something. Please let's move past this. Please forgive me."

She exhaled and looked into his face. A face she loved. She didn't see arrogance there, not anger or calculation. His words seemed genuine. She wanted to believe him so badly.

"Okay. We both have our buttons and I realize what Sandra did to you changed you and made you gunshy. I'm sorry she hurt you so much and I wish you hadn't been so devastated. Honestly, the woman is out of her damn mind. So in the offing, after all is said and done, you have baggage and you unloaded it on me. Problem is, you heaped a lot of nasty on me. Even for just a moment. And that intersected with six years of my life that I don't care to repeat, even as a sick, vague memory caused by your behavior.

"You can be a tool and do stupid guy shit, that's normal. But derision like that is another story. I can't deal with it. I won't ever again. I won't." Reaching out she took his other hand in hers as well. "I know. I know what it feels like to have that shadow of who you used to be come up and surprise you."

He closed his eyes a moment and let out the tension that'd built up in his muscles. "I love you so much, Cassie."

She smiled. "Yeah, yeah. I love you too, Shane."

Standing up, he pulled her to him, hugging her tight. "We'll just work it through. You and me, we're it, right? I've missed you this week. My bed has been empty, my arms, my life. I was getting used to your presence in my life and then you were gone and I didn't know quite what to do. Don't tell anyone that last bit."

She laughed. "Yeah, wouldn't want to blow your cred as a hard ass or anything. I missed you too."

He moved slowly, bringing his lips to hers and kissed her. Relief, joy, reconnection, desire, love—all rushed through him at once at having her back. "Bedroom?" he asked, breathless as he broke the kiss.

"Can't. Brian is due home any minute."

"I'd say I'll be quick but that's not really a good thing in this situation. Can I stay over? And you and Brian can fill me in on everything about your ex too. I want to know not just as the sheriff but as the man who loves you. Share your life with me."

"You hate my bed. You think the mattress is too soft."

He grinned. "It'll absorb the sound of the make up sex."

"Uh." She blushed. "Well go on home and get some clothes and bring back some cobbler from The Sands, it's still open. And then I'll let you have the side closest to the door."

He brought his lips back to hers, brushing his mouth over hers softly and nipping her bottom lip between his teeth for a moment. "When you put it like that, how can I refuse? Peach or berry?"

"I had peach yesterday so berry."

"You ate an entire cobbler?"

"So sue me. Your mother and Maggie made me some but I get hungry when I don't get sex regularly. You were an ass. I needed the comfort."

"I'll help you burn the calories." He waggled his eyebrows.

"You saying I'm fat?"

"Oh, you're just torturing me for fun now, aren't you?"

She laughed and tip toed up to kiss his chin quickly. "Yeah. G'wan then. I'll see you back here in a bit."

CRSO

The minute Shane walked into The Sands and asked for a berry cobbler, Ronnie looked at him and smiled at him for the first time in a week and exclaimed how happy she was that he and Cassie were back together.

When Shane returned, Brian had gotten back and Cassie had a pot of decaf brewed to drink with the cobbler.

Shane relayed the story to Cassie and Brian. "The whole damned town took your side, I'll have you know. They didn't even know what the hell happened and still they took your side. My mother hasn't spoken three words to me other than how I had to fix it between us. My brothers wouldn't play pool with me. At dinner last Sunday you should have seen it. My brothers all got these big juicy steaks and I got this tiny piece of gristle."

Unsuccessfully stifling a laugh, Cassie put a plate with cobbler and ice cream in front of him and then filled his coffee cup. "Your mother came over on Tuesday. She called every day this week too. Came into the bookstore every day I worked as well. Brought me cobbler to sweeten me up on your behalf. She's Machiavellian, that woman."

Cassie got her brother and herself a cup of coffee and joined them at the table. "She likes Brian. Maggie even baked tartlets for us. Lemon because it's his favorite."

Brian started to laugh, pleased to see his sister so lighthearted and silly. His reservations about Shane had faded over the week as he watched the man continue to reassure Cassie that he loved her but also didn't crowd her. And his family was just what Cassie needed. Brian didn't like the heartache she'd endured but he did like the fact that the man owned up to it and made it better. It was more than Terry had ever done.

"Tell me about him. Give me the details." Shane continued to eat but his expression darkened and by the end of the story, his eyes were narrowed and his mouth set in a tight line.

"Here's what we're going to do...with your permission." He looked quickly at Cassie who'd tensed up and then relaxed. "I hear you're a crack shot, we'll keep you going to the range, we can both go together so neither of us gets rusty. I'd like to put in a full security system here. We talked about it a little bit a while ago. I've got a list of available options and one of our contractors can put it in as soon as you decide on which you want. I even spoke with Chuck and he said he'd pay for half of it and not raise the rent if you paid the other half. If it's more

Lauren Dane

than you can afford right now, we can work out a payment plan."

Brian looked at his sister from under his lashes. "Don't worry about the money. It's not a problem. Carly...Cassie, I'm with Shane on this. Please put in the system. I can't be here, you can't come back to California and live with me at my place, it's hard enough having you so far away. If you have this system, I'll feel so much better."

"Don't think I don't know you're both working me," Cassie said, eyes narrowed. "But I'd be stupid not to do it. Shane, if your friend can do it on a Tuesday, Thursday or Saturday, let's get him scheduled."

"If he can't, I can be here or Matt can or someone. I'd like to do it as soon as possible. If that's okay with you of course."

"Fine, fine. Thank you. And I'm not a crack shot. I just know my way around a gun. I've got a license for it."

They finished up the coffee and cobbler as it got late. Brian stood up and stretched. "I'm going to go to bed. I've got a plane to catch tomorrow afternoon."

They said their goodnights and Shane and Cassie went into her room and shut the door.

Cassie sure hoped Shane was right and the softness of her mattress drowned out the sounds of their reunion or they probably kept Matt and Brian up all night long.

Chapter Fourteen

Petal was filled with activity as Homecoming Week activities took over the town. Cassie loved the pretty banners that went up on Main Street with the school colors.

Nervously, Cassie tried to figure out what to wear to the picnic she'd been invited to attend with Shane and his family. Terry didn't have any family and she'd rarely attended events like the picnic when growing up. She'd been to the Governor's Ball a few times, swanky restaurants and parties but none of them had her as excited or nervous as the picnic did.

She wasn't expected to bring anything. There'd be food at the picnic. Shane told her they had big tables of barbecue and peach pie with home made ice cream—and she was sure he smirked slightly as he said it—and all sorts of other goodies. That was a relief as she was a terrible cook. Anything more complicated than salad, grilled cheese and soup and she was lost.

She had an appointment with her therapist in the early part of the day so she told Shane she'd meet the Chases at the park after she got back to town.

After running home, she changed out of her jeans and into Capri pants and a T-shirt. Early fall was still warm but she tossed a sweater into her bag as she left.

The park was already filled up with people when she arrived. Shane had told her the Chases always sat beneath a big oak tree on a rolling hill just as the park sprawled toward the lake shore. There'd be fireworks after dark and he'd promised the view there was the best around.

She should have known she'd be able to find their patch of ground by the sheer population of women gathered nearby and clustered around the blanket.

She knew she really didn't like the way one tall blonde was looking at Shane like he was a piece of pie with ice cream on it. What Cassie did like was the hostile look on Polly's face and the way Shane kept moving away from blondie.

"Hey, Cassie." Maggie waved and grinned as she approached them. "Come and sit, Shane's been saving you a place."

Cassie winked at Maggie.

Shane turned and when he saw her, the annoyed look on his face melted away. His features lightened and a smile tugged at the corners of the lips she loved to feel over every part of her body. He held his hand out to her and helped her sit down. Leaning in, he gave her a quick, but solid kiss. "Hi, darlin'. I've missed you today. You look beautiful."

Cassie rested against him for a moment and waved at the whole Chase family, sprawled out on the series of blankets there under the tree. "Hi, Shane. Hey everyone."

"I just brought back a whole bunch of food, Cassie. Eat up." Edward indicated the pile of food in the middle of the blankets.

"And here, honey, iced tea." Polly put a cup in Cassie's hand before shooting another dirty look at blondie.

"You want to tell me who your fan club president is?" Cassie murmured into Shane's ear.

He barked a startled laugh and kissed her again. "You taste good." He winked. "I thought you were the president of my fan club."

"Mmmm hmm. So?" But before he could answer, blondie moved in closer on his other side.

"Hello, I'm Kendra. And you are?"

"This is my girlfriend Cassie Gambol. Cassie, darlin', this is Kendra."

Cassie just tipped her chin and waited for blondie to move back.

"Your girlfriend?"

"Yes, that's what he said. I take it you're a friend of Shane's?"

"You could call it that." Blondie smirked.

"Oookay." Cassie raised a brow at Shane and he moved closer to her. "Kendra, you really don't need to be in our laps. We get it. Everyone within a mile gets it. You dated Shane before he met me. Oh, snap. Okay now, point is made."

Shane tried not to smile but the corner of his mouth trembled a bit. He turned to blondie and said quietly, "Kendra, I've asked you to move back. You're being disrespectful to Cassie and me and my family too. Come on now, don't embarrass yourself."

Maggie sighed and Cassie craned her neck to see her around blondie. "How are you today, Cassie? I really like your hair that way."

Out of the corner of her eye she saw Kendra get up and storm off. "I'm glad you tried not to embarrass her, Shane."

He looked surprised. "You keep doing things I don't expect. I like that. And I like that you've got a big heart, even for people who don't necessarily deserve it."

She shrugged. "She's got a thing for you. How can I not understand that? Plus, I've been told that I'll have to deal with stuff like that all the time. They should suck it up now while I still have patience."

Polly laughed in the background.

"You sure you want to keep her, Shane? Because I'd be glad to take this fine young thing off your hands for you." Marc waggled his brows at them both and the tension was broken.

"Punk. You'll see when it happens to you, Marc. And then we're all going to tease the hell out of you." Shane put his arm around Cassie and squeezed her against him.

CRSO

And that night was what solidified Cassie's entrance into the Chase family. Every Sunday she sat at their dining room table and shared dinner with them. Every Friday night she had beer and junk food with her friends while Shane played pool with his brothers. Toward the end of the night, she'd wander back and play a game or two with them.

The awful heat of summer cooled into the more moderate temperatures of autumn and Cassie realized that for the first time in nearly six years she was leading a normal life.

Penny hired her on to work full time at the bookstore, which came with healthcare benefits, which was very nice. She kept busy and worked hard and began to feel like Petal was really her home and not just a place to wait until Terry got caught.

"Go ahead on and lock up, Cassie. It's nearly closing and I know you'll want to go and get ready for the Grange." Penny smiled as she came out to the front of the store where Cassie was rearranging the front tables.

"Thank goodness for you, Penny. Every time I asked Shane about what to wear he'd do that guy thing and shrug. *Oh you know, it's just the Grange. Wear some skirt or something.*"

Penny burst out laughing. "You do a great Shane impression."

"Well, I do think it's nice to have the community doing something like this for the local charities. I used to be more involved in charity work but I haven't done much since...well anyway. I've spoken with Polly and she's put me in touch with the woman who does the holiday drive for the soup kitchen and food pantry so I'm excited about that. *And,* I can't wait to meet this mystery date of yours."

Penny blushed. "I told you, he's an old friend of my family's. He went to school with all of us here. No big deal, he's just visiting from Atlanta for the weekend and I bumped into him."

"Yeah, old family friends always make me blush like a schoolgirl. I'll see you tonight." Laughing, Cassie squeezed Penny's hand and headed out after locking up.

Cassie's nervousness had been making her slightly nauseated all day. This Grange thing was a big community event and the Chases would all be there in force and it was like some big step for Shane to have her there with him. She'd gotten used to the stares in town of the jealous women but from what she understood taking a date to this event was a big deal for a Chase. None of them did it until Kyle brought Maggie.

Things had gotten very serious between her and Shane. As she put on her makeup, she realized that. Realized that she either spent the night at his house or him at hers at least five nights a week. They went out every weekend and saw each other or spoke on the phone every day.

In truth, she'd never expected to find love after her divorce and the attack. She certainly didn't figure she'd end up with a man like Shane, strong and protective who also gave so much. He respected her space and continued to be nothing but gentle and kind toward her. They'd had some minor disagreements but she'd never felt threatened or worried about them. And he simply put up with her skittishness. How he did was beyond her. She knew she brought a lot of issues with her but he never made a big deal of it. He accepted and loved all of her, warts and all.

She also realized that the holiday season was upon them. Brian was coming back for Christmas but they'd been invited to celebrate with the Chases at their home. It warmed her heart to be included and thought of as one of them.

ℭℬℰ

Shane showed up right on time looking and smelling positively fabulous. She'd never seen him so dressed up.

"Wow. You sure clean up nice, Shane Chase."

He spun her in his arms and kissed her neck. "I have to keep up with you. It's hard when a man's woman is the most beautiful woman in town. You set a tough example. I love red on you, by the way. That dress is hot."

She laughed, pleased by this compliments. "I don't think I've been called hot since college."

"Ah, there's more where that came from. I'm a silver tongued devil."

Her eyes slid halfway closed at that. "Yes. Yes you are."

He stilled and then looked toward the front windows. Reaching back, he hit the lights, leaving them both in the dark.

"What are you up to?"

"Oh, well. Just proving you right. Do you have panties on under that dress?"

"What?" She laughed nervously. "Of course!"

He moved toward her and she stepped back until she bumped against the kitchen island. He dropped to his knees and a soft moan came from her lips.

"No matter, I'm good with my hands too." He slid his palms up her calves and stopped when he got to her thighs.

"Surprise."

"You're wearing stockings and garters."

"I know."

"We should be at the Grange in fifteen minutes."

"You'd better be quick then, huh?"

His chuckle brought the brush of his warm breath against her thighs as he pushed her dress up. "You'll be showing them to me later. In my bedroom with the lights on. I think you should leave the shoes on too."

Her hands dropped to his shoulders as her upper body leaned against the island behind her.

He pulled the panties out of the way and she widened her stance as his fingers slid through her pussy, hissing when he found her hot and wet.

Leaning in, his mouth found her ready for him, her clit already swollen and sensitive. Her taste seduced him. He loved the way she felt on his tongue, loved the scent of her body, of her skin and the honey that rained on his tongue. Loved the long, lean flanks of her legs.

Two of his fingers pressed up and inside her as he took quick, whisper-light licks over her clit. A gasp tore from her lips and her fingers dug into his shoulders.

This was an appetizer, something to whet his appetite for her and get him through the next hours. When he got her back to his place he planned to get a better look at those sexy stockings as her legs wrapped around him.

He recognized the change in her taste, the tremble in her thigh muscles and the quickening of her breathing and knew her orgasm was on the way. He loved to give her a hard, fast climax, leaving her for a few hours, knowing he'd be back for more later on. Knew she'd be wet for him for the rest of the night and it was only fair because he'd be hard for her all night long too.

With a soft intake of breath and a long moan, she came with his name on her lips. He loved hearing it that way. Often thought of how it sounded during his day.

After her pussy had stopped fluttering around his fingers he withdrew them slowly and rearranged her panties before standing and kissing her. Hard and possessive.

He was glad they'd reached the stage where he could be a bit more dominant with her and it didn't spook her. Just thinking about her made him want to grab her and head for the hills. She brought out something very primal in him and he liked it. No one else ever affected him on that level.

"You ready to go?"

Eyes opening slowly, she brought her fingertips to her lips. "I...uh yeah. What about you?"

He was glad she couldn't see how predatory his grin must have looked there in the dark, as he thought about once they were back at his place. "Believe me, darlin', I'll collect later on."

At the Grange, Cassie was sure everyone would know Shane went down on her with the drapes open in her kitchen in the dark. But if they did, none of them seemed too bothered by it.

That's when she noticed Penny walk in with a tall, handsome man about their age.

"Ryan Betts. How are you?" Shane stood up and clapped the man on his shoulder.

"I'm good. Just squiring Penny around for the evening. It's only taken fifteen years to get a third date with her. You look well, Shane." He turned his green eyes to Cassie. "You must be Cassie. Penny talks about you all the time. I'm Ryan, it's nice to meet you."

Cassie took his proffered hand and shook it before turning her eyes to a very pinkfaced Penny. "Nice to meet the mystery date. I've been bugging Penny for the last week but she kept telling me I'd meet you when I met you."

"And you did. It's a good thing you're such a good employee because you're a pest." Penny's laugh sounded different than Cassie had ever heard. It was nearly a giggle.

There were long minutes of back slapping and drink getting and a few toasts as Cassie watched them all. She hadn't felt like an outsider for a few months but realized that's what it looked like when you had lifelong friends.

She felt the edge of that divide rather sharply although she knew none of them intended it. Cassie didn't have friends she'd known all her life. People left a lot. Her mother died, she went to boarding school for several years until high school. She did stay in LA to go to college at UC Irvine and then medical school at UCLA. The only permanence had been Brian.

"Why the long face, gorgeous?" Matt sat down next to her and put a mug of steaming cider in front of her.

"Oh nothing. I was just thinking about how I didn't really have lifelong friends like all of you. I suppose I was just feeling a bit sorry for myself."

Matt took her hand and squeezed it. "You have us now. And once you're a Chase, you don't want for company. Of course, that also means we're always up in your business too."

"You making a play for my girl?" Shane turned and smiled.

"In a perfect world, Shane, your lovely woman would realize what a tool you are and run away with me. But alas, the world is a flawed place and for some crazy reason, she loves you." Matt put a hand over his heart dramatically.

"Come on, darlin'. Let's grab a dance or two before dinner gets started."

Cassie stood, taking Shane's hand and let him draw her onto the floor and against his body.

"You were meant to be here against me. You know?" he murmured into her ear.

"It feels that way, yeah."

"God it makes me happy when you accept all of this. This thing between us."

"It makes me happy too. I was just thinking tonight as I got ready about how lucky I am in you. You're so good to me."

Dinner was the usual Chase affair—organized chaos of arms and hands and talking in all directions. Cassie watched, amused as Penny and Ryan flirted and grew smitten with the other. She knew she'd be demanding the full story from her friend on Monday.

"You're staying over at my place tonight, right?" Shane leaned into her and kissed her temple.

"I have to get up and out early. I haven't done a damn bit of shopping for Thanksgiving yet. I'll invite Penny I think."

"Shopping for what?"

"Uh, food. I imagine you'll be at Chase central all day. You can come over afterwards."

"I can come to your apartment after I spend the day with my entire family eating turkey, ham and roast beef? Just stroll on in and say hey after I've done that?"

She drew back, looking at him. "What's with the attitude?"

"I've got an attitude? Cassie, did you really think you weren't invited to Thanksgiving at my parents' house? And if you weren't invited, did you really think I'd be with them and just come on over to your apartment after you ate by yourself? Is that how little you think of me and my family?"

"I didn't want to presume."

"Presume? And they say I'm the dumbass. My momma told me to invite you weeks ago but I assured her you knew you were invited. My manners are bad apparently. Well okay, that's not a surprise. Anyway, you're eating dinner with me at my parents' house on Thanksgiving. Afterwards, we play cards and then you all sit on the porch and talk about us while we play football. It's a tradition. You can't buck tradition, Cassie."

"Oh. All right then."

He looked at her askance and then chuckled. "I wish you'd agree to everything that easily."

"I do to all the important stuff."

The way he looked at her made her all tingly.

"So you're staying over then? Now that the Thanksgiving situation is all cleared up and all."

She leaned in and put her lips to his ear. "I've been waiting for a while for you to take me. I feel how much you control yourself to keep from scaring me. Show me, Shane. I want it all."

He sat very still, she wasn't even sure if he breathed for long moments. Slowly, he turned to look her in the eye. His pupils were so wide it was hard to see the color. He turned to his family.

"Folks, Cassie and I are going to cut out early. I have a headache. We'll see you Sunday for dinner."

He stood and helped her up, grabbing her wrap and putting an arm around her, steering her toward the door.

"Goodnight, everyone." She waved as they moved to leave. Everyone just looked at them, amused.

CRSO

Shane didn't say much as they drove to his house. Cassie watched the scenery pass through her window, smiling.

"What are you smiling about, darlin'?"

"I love the sound of your voice. It's deep and masculine and so sexy. Sometimes it's almost a growl. If you weren't mine I'd be working to grab you every day."

He pulled into his driveway and turned to her. "I...when you say stuff like that it does something to me. You held yourself away from me for so long and now to see you like this, saying I'm yours, it..." He took a deep breath as he shook his head, unable to find words.

"I'm sorry if I don't say it enough. I'm smiling because my life is normal. Because I trust you. I'm smiling because I know you're going to take me into that house and make love to me."

"You got that right." Leaning over, his upper body pressed her gently to the seat. Lips just above hers, his eyes stared deeply into hers. "I want you to tell me if I go too far or scare you. You have no idea how much I want to take you a dozen times a day against every conceivable surface just to know I'm the one making you feel the pleasure, just to hear the sound of you coming in my ears. But we need to go slow with this. I know that. All you need to do is tell me to stop or slow down, all right?"

Moving just a bit, her lips brushed up against his. "All right."

Quickly, they got out of the car and went into the house. "Bedroom."

Cassie looked back over her shoulder at him and then took the stairs with a sexy sway.

"You're playing with fire, darlin'."

"Mmm, good. You'll have to make me wet to put it out."

He chuckled and she found herself tossed on the bed, his body above hers on his hands and knees.

Lifting her hands to his chest, she worked the buttons on his shirt and exposed his chest. His heart beat reassuringly against her palm as she slid it over the hard muscle of his pectoral muscles.

Sitting back, he pulled his shirt off, tossing it to the side and moved to her again. This time he undid the tie at her hip and pulled the dress apart, exposing her body that way.

He sat there looking at her for a long time, quietly taking her in. A month ago she'd have felt embarrassed at his close perusal but he'd made her realize that he thought she was beautiful. Her scars did not matter to him. If her thighs were an issue, he hid it well and so she just let him look, loving that he wanted to.

Reaching out, he traced a fingertip along the scalloped lace of her bra, skimming just over her nipple.

"I like this. Red looks good on you with all items of clothing I see."

The catch on the front was a black rose and he popped it with one-handed ease. Her breasts spilled into his hands, his thumbs coming up to flick back and forth over her nipples. Each movement of his fingers against her sent an answering pulse to her clit.

Her fingers dug into the muscle of his upper back as he leaned in, the heat of his mouth closing over the pulse-point at the hollow just below her ear.

Moving her hands, she pushed him back and scrambled atop his prone body, wriggling out of her dress and bra.

"Now that's a reward for a long hard day. A beautiful woman sitting over my cock in nothing more than garters, stockings, a wisp of red lace pretending to be panties and some very sexy shoes."

"There's that silver tongue, I see." Her hands made quick work of his belt and the button and zipper of his trousers and she kissed down his neck, over his chest and belly. The way his hands felt on her, so large and warm, confident and gentle, always made her want to cry.

"Pants off!" She struggled to get his trousers off and he laughed, setting her aside and standing to do it himself.

"Well, lookit you." He moved toward the bed, his cock so hard it pressed against his stomach.

When he'd stopped, his cock was right at eye level. She looked up at him, up his body and saw the look on his face. He waited there, making sure her comment at the Grange wasn't just made in the heat of the moment.

"I do want you to take me, Shane."

One of his hands caressed her face, down her neck. He watched her face until he appeared to be sure.

"Well then, I think there's a little rain check to be collected and then I'm going to fuck you with those garters on."

She grabbed him and angled his cock to slowly take him into her mouth. Loving this, loving how much pleasure it gave him, she took it slow, doing all the things she'd learned he liked so much.

Her tongue swirled around the head, digging into that sweet spot just beneath the ridge of the crown. The salt of his skin, of his essence, sprang on her tongue, filled her with desire, made her feel like a goddess that he wanted her so much.

Shane looked down at her, watched his cock disappear between her lips and pull out again. He loved the way her eyelashes swept over her cheeks.

His fingertips traced over the raised marks of her scars on her back. He'd found it reassured her that he thought she was beautiful. As if anyone could look at her and think anything else. Her scars were as much a part of her as her eyes or those long-as-sin legs. So he loved them too, even as he wanted to take the man down who'd given them to her.

When she'd told him she wanted him to take her, he'd nearly come on the spot. He dreamed of being able to show her the depth of intensity of his desire for her but kept it in check to keep from scaring her. He wanted to take her hard and fast but he'd watch her, especially this first time, to be sure she was all right with everything.

"Cassie, stop. Lay back, leave your legs over the side of the bed."

She did as he told her to and he marveled at her, lying there on his bed. Her dark hair spread around her head like midnight. Her breasts, breasts she thought were sagging, were capped with puckered pink nipples, just begging for his mouth.

Her belly, with no pooch he ever could divine, led to the neatly trimmed patch of hair that shielded her pussy. Only right then the pretty red panties covered her.

"Next time, put the panties on after the stockings."

She laughed, a slow, sexy sound that never failed to make him crazy. Reaching down, she pulled at the sides of the panties and they untied. Lifting her ass, she pulled them off and threw them over his shoulder.

"Oh. Very nice. Very nice indeed. You know, I wanted to see these legs wrapped around me but I'm thinking we can save that for another time."

He pulled out a condom and sheathed himself quickly before flipping her over with relative ease. He did sense her stiffen and he drew a fingertip down her spine. "Shhhh. I want to take you from behind, Cassie. Feel you from this angle, be able to reach around and touch your body, have your clit right where I want it."

He paused, giving her time to stop if she was freaked but she relaxed. Pulling her body toward him, he brought her feet to the ground and bent her just so, moving to check her readiness.

When Shane touched her pussy and found her so wet she was slightly embarrassed by how much he turned her on, he made a low sound.

"Fuck. Cassie, how do you do this to me? Make me want you even more when I feel the evidence of how much you want me?" As he finished the last word, the blunt, fat head of his cock pressed against her, nudging his way into her gate.

She pushed back into him and they both grunted in satisfaction as he seated himself fully inside her.

Losing herself a bit as he began to thrust, her hands gripped his comforter, cool against her heated skin. He felt so good as he filled her up over and over. Her body molded itself to him, took him in and made itself his.

"I want to feel you come around me," he murmured, leaning down and kissing her shoulder. One of his hands found her clit, fingertips strumming through the wet flesh, bringing the skin of the hood to stroke against the clit. The friction was delicious, right on the edge of just enough but not quite there.

His lips pressed over each one of her scars as the fingers of his free hand stroked lightly over her arms and back and down over the curve of her ass and thighs.

"More."

In answer, he began to thrust into her hard and fast in deep digs. He gave up the slow tease of her clit and squeezed it gently between slick fingers over and over until she came, screaming into his mattress. All the while he continued to fuck her.

"Damn, you're so fucking sexy I don't know what to do. I just want to spread you on a cracker and eat you up. I want to kiss every inch of you. You walk past the front window of the bookstore as I drive past and my cock throbs. You've bewitched me, Cassie."

His voice was slightly breathless, staccato even, as he continued to move within her. She felt, for the first time, the full power of his thighs as his muscles flexed against the back of her thighs. Felt the strength in his arms as he held her, the uncoiled desire in his movements and heard it in his voice.

And there was no fear. This wasn't how Terry used her. He'd used this strength *against* her to hurt her. Shane used his strength for her, on her to bring her pleasure. Even with the strength he had, he did not abuse it, he kept it under control and she gave into her need to moan and cry out as he built the pleasure within her.

"Pleasepleaseplease," she whispered.

"Please what?" His voice wavered a bit, she knew he was close and she wanted him to come deep inside her. More than she'd ever wanted anything and she wasn't quite sure why. She just knew she wanted him to find pleasure inside her, to know her body gave him safe haven when he needed it. When he wanted it.

"Please come inside of me, Shane. I want that so much." Her words escaped her mouth in a quick flow before she could worry that he'd be disgusted by her brazenness.

"Hell..." His word was stuttered as he pressed once and then once again, deep into her, his fingers holding her hips tight as he pressed deep, his cock jerking within her as he came.

Long moments later, he kissed her neck and left the room. Returning in moments, he helped her into bed after he'd taken her shoes off and removed her garter belt and stockings.

"You'll wear those again, right?"

"I couldn't deny you the chance to see my legs wrapped around your waist with them on."

"I don't know what I did to deserve you. I haven't always been the nicest man to women, you know. But you're the best thing that's ever happened to me. I love you, Cassie." He kissed her deeply, pulling her against his body.

Chapter Fifteen

Cassie paused as she picked up the cashmere sweater from the table where it'd been stacked in a pile of folded luxury. The hair on the back of her neck stood on end and a chill settled at the base of her spine.

She turned and looked around the area but nothing seemed amiss.

"Cassie? Honey, are you all right?"

Shaking off the dread, Cassie turned and found herself looking into the face of Edward Chase.

"Edward, hello." She kissed his cheek and he gave her a hug.

"You looked upset just then. Is everything okay?" He looked around the area much as she had.

"It just felt like someone was watching me. Probably because I'm here buying Shane's Christmas present." She tried to believe the lighthearted laugh she gave but couldn't.

"Sugar, you should tell Shane. Do you think he's found you?"

"I don't have any reason to think that, Edward. My brother is keeping in regular contact with the investigators and they're all in contact with me and Shane. He hasn't surfaced since the summer. Maybe he's given up."

Edward looked at the charcoal colored sweater she held in her hands. "Shane will like that. Can I take you to lunch?"

Cassie really liked Edward Chase. She definitely enjoyed Polly but Edward was quiet and insightful and Cassie treasured their conversations on everything from post modernism to baseball.

"Sure, why don't I meet you at El Cid in fifteen minutes? I just need to pay for this."

He kissed her cheek and agreed, heading out while she went to the cashier to pay for the sweater and the shirt she'd found. With the assistance of a local artisan, she'd made Shane a bracelet of pounded copper and silver that she hoped he liked. The sweater and shirt were nice and all, but the bracelet had taken her a lot of time and effort. She'd never done anything like it before and wanted to create something that fit his personality perfectly. But now she had a new skill and had taken to working with silver to create earrings and necklaces that did very well.

Edward was waiting with fresh chips and salsa and waved as she caught sight of him.

After they'd ordered and the food arrived, Edward told her that he'd been looking into how she could go about practicing under her new name with her medical license.

"I don't want you to think I'm presumptuous but I'm asking around. The state board is going to want to have the ability for your patients to know who you are. This name change project has been around for several years but it's still hard to get professional licenses in the new name for many women."

"I appreciate that, Edward. I've been thinking on it long and hard. I miss medicine a lot. I know I'll have to go back to get more training but if I mean to make my life here, I'll need to figure out what I want to do. I like working at the bookstore and all, but it's not what I'll do forever."

"So you plan on making Petal your home then? Pardon my nosiness but my son loves you very much. The change in him is remarkable. I'd hate to see his heart broken."

Cassie reached across the table and squeezed his hand. "I never thought I'd want to be with anyone else again. I swore the last thing I needed was a big, domineering man and look who I went and fell for. I want to be where Shane is. He gets me. Like no one ever has. He understands me and makes room for my quirks and works around my crazy stuff. I adore him."

"Good. That's good to hear. I like you, Cassie, I like you being in my family an awful lot."

CR80

After lunch, Cassie went home and wrapped the presents and checked to be sure Brian's flight was on time. He was flying in for the weekend to celebrate Christmas with her and the Chases.

Shane managed to convince her that she and Brian should stay at his house because it was bigger and more comfortable for everyone. In truth she spent seventy percent of her time there anyway, and Brian knew they were a couple and was very happy about that fact.

Even though she had a key, she knocked on Shane's door and ignored his annoyed look when he saw she'd not used the key.

"Hi, baby, take these will you?" She thrust the packages at him and bent to pick up a bag of extra clothes she'd packed.

"Darlin', use your key. You're not a guest. And let me get that." He held the door and then went to put the packages under the tree they'd both picked out the weekend before.

"It feels weird just letting myself in."

He grabbed her and pulled her down onto the couch with him. "Move in here and it won't feel weird."

"What?"

"I'd ask you to marry me but I know that would be rushing you. But I want you here with me. I want to wake up with you every morning. I like that my bathroom has your stuff in it. I want to build a life together."

"I...I don't know if I'm ready for that."

His face lost a bit of its light and seeing that she'd caused him pain sliced through her. But she was afraid of making another Terry-sized mistake.

She put her hand to his face. "I love you, Shane. But it's only been five months since I met you."

"Almost six and I love you too. You're here or I'm at your place almost every night. What's the difference?"

"Shane I don't want to hurt you but I need the haven of my own place right now."

Kissing her he nodded. "Okay, fair enough. But you know how I hate it when you treat me like I'm him."

"This argument is really old, Shane. I don't want to have it again. I promise you that's not what I'm doing."

"Bull. If it hadn't been for him you'd move in here. How is that not making me pay for his behavior?"

"If it hadn't been for him I wouldn't be here so that's a moot point. Stop making this about you! I am not wanting to take this slow because I think you're Terry. I *know* you're not Terry. I'm taking this slow because the last man I lived with nearly

208

killed me after beating the hell out of my body and soul for years. The difference is pretty major, Shane."

"It feels the same to me."

She stepped back, out of his embrace. "I'm sorry. All I can do is feel what I feel and tell you the truth of it. I'm being honest and trying my damndest to explain the inexplicable to you. This is about me. If you choose to make it about you, I can't stop you."

"Why are you so difficult? Why don't you let me love you?"

"I do. I've given myself to you, heart and body. I'm not giving anyone my soul, Shane. I love you, more than anyone I've ever loved but that's not going to stop me from using my common sense. I'm sorry it offends you that I want to wait to move in together. I'm not doing it because I don't trust you or want to be with you. I'm asking you to respect my feelings and to give me time. But I can't make you what you aren't any more than I'll let you make me into what I'm not. So if you can't live with that, tell me now so I can walk away. I'm in deep enough with you and your family, if you're going to break it off, do it now."

Pacing, he shoved a hand through his hair. "I'm not going to break it off. I love you. Things would be so much easier if you just agreed with everything I said."

Cassie snorted a laugh and he moved to where she was standing to pull her close. "You're a very complicated, difficult woman."

"You're a very arrogant, difficult man."

"Perfect match." He grinned.

"So you say."

"I do. Wanna get lucky? I'll let you open a present early."

"Oh you think I'll fall for that one twice?"

Laughing, he took her down to the carpet.

CR80

"I can't believe you gave me rug burn on my ass," Cassie murmured in Shane's ear as they had Christmas Eve dinner around a table filled with only about four hundred of his family members.

He chuckled. "It was worth it."

"For you! I was on the bottom."

"Next time roll me over, darlin', I'm quite happy to have you on top."

She fought off laughter. "As if I'm not nervous enough meeting all these people, I have rug burn."

"And a bit of beard burn on your inner thighs too, I'd wager."

The charming devil had the audacity to leer at her and she burst out laughing. Luckily, everyone seemed to find their interaction wonderful and amusing and his grandparents only dropped marriage and great-grandchild hints about every twenty minutes.

"Did you tell Shane about how you felt like you were being watched at the department store earlier?" Edward's voice was casual but Cassie heard steel there and fought annoyance as her brother and Shane both rounded on her.

"I just felt weird, not necessarily watched. And no, I hadn't had the chance to tell either my brother or Shane about it. Thanks for that, though." She rolled her eyes at Edward and Polly sighed and smacked her husband on the arm.

"Cassie, you promised to tell me!" Shane glared at her.

"And me," Brian echoed.

"Look, as much as I'd *love* having this conversation here with the family of my boyfriend looking on, I'm not going to. I hadn't had the chance to tell either one of you. Brian, your plane was late and Shane, you waylaid me when I got to your house. I appreciate your concern but it was nothing. And that's all I'm going to say right now."

"Cassie..."

"Shane Edward Chase, let it go. Your daddy made a big enough mistake, don't compound it. She'll talk to you about it later." Polly narrowed her eyes at him and he backed off with an annoyed shrug.

Maggie changed the subject quickly to the trip she and Kyle were taking in the spring to Italy and Cassie sent her a grateful look. Penny was there with Ryan, he'd come to town once or twice since the Grange night and had spent quite a bit of time on the phone and email with her. Cassie approved, she'd never seen Penny so glowing before.

After dessert and a game of cards so cutthroat that Cassie just watched in awe, they made their way back to Shane's. They'd promised to be back at seven the next morning in exchange for not sleeping over. Cassie felt self-conscious enough, she really didn't want to sleep with Shane at his parents' house.

On the way out, Edward took her aside. "I do apologize, honey. I didn't mean to put you on the spot like that. I just spoke while thinking about it and then realized that you must have felt nervous with all those new people and all. I know it seemed nosy of me, but I care about you like one of my own. I was just concerned. I hope you're not mad at me."

She kissed his cheek. "Thank you for explaining. I feel a lot better now. I do appreciate you caring about me, honestly. I'm not angry. It takes a bit of getting used to, being part of your circle, I'm trying."

"You're not part of our circle, honey, you're part of our family. You're one of us. Even if it was only that Shane loved you we'd think of you that way. But we love you too. You're an eminently lovable woman. Now go on, Shane's going to want to hear all the details along with your brother. We'll see you first thing."

All she could do was nod. It was a simple thing, the acceptance and love from the Chases but it meant so much more than she could ever begin to put into words. Swallowing back her tears, she smiled and walked out, garnering hugs and kisses from a whole host of Chases before she reached Shane who waited for her on the porch.

CR§O

In the car she got belted in and held up a hand as they pulled away from the curb. "I will tell you everything. I was shopping and felt odd. Like a cold chill. I looked around but there wasn't a damned thing wrong. Your father bumped right into me, asked if I was all right. I assured him it was and we had lunch. That's it."

Shane sighed hard. "All right. But I want you to tell me this stuff right away. Call me from the restaurant."

"Me too! Damn it, Carly—Cassie, I can't be here, the only way I can keep from worrying to death over you is your assurance that you'll tell me what's going on."

"Brian, you were on a plane. And Shane, I wasn't going to call you from the restaurant over a funny feeling. I was with your father and you know why I was a bit busy later on. If it had been important I would have called you immediately. Now it's Christmas Eve, let's talk about something else, please."

Chapter Sixteen

The beginning of February had Penny and Cassie heading to Atlanta to pick up more supplies for Cassie's blooming jewelry business. With Valentine's Day approaching, Cassie found herself nearly out of the findings she needed for earrings and she wanted to pop in to a little bead shop she'd ordered from online.

Ryan joined them for lunch after they'd spent too much money on beads and clothes. The roads were a bit slick but not icy so they wanted to get back before it got too dark and cold.

Cassie had a sense of foreboding all day. She'd attributed it to the anniversary of her divorce from Terry and the news from a week before that Terry had been sighted in New York City and that it appeared his family had been helping him financially.

Shane had insisted on their driving his giant truck and in retrospect later on, it probably saved their lives. Halfway between Atlanta and Petal, Cassie noticed the lights of an SUV that had been with them for the last ten miles. It stayed right on her tailgate and felt aggressive. Not so unusual really, people drove like idiots all the time but she couldn't ignore her increasing nervousness. On top of that, Penny was in the car and Cassie didn't want to ignore something that could hurt her friend.

Swallowing back fear and nausea, Cassie reached out and touched Penny's arm. "Penny, I want you to get on that cell phone and call Shane. There's a car following us. A big SUV, Georgia plates. It's probably nothing but it makes me nervous. Crossed a few lanes to keep up with us several times." Putting her hands firmly on the wheel, she wrestled the demon of her terror and read the plate number to Penny, who calmly made the call.

Shane stayed on the line with her and patched a call into the state patrol to check the plates. He urged Penny to tell Cassie to stay watchful. They'd entered a more rural part of the drive back to Petal and there weren't many off ramps. So rural that even at most of the few offramps there weren't any services or places to go for help.

The SUV backed way off and Cassie breathed a sigh of relief and wanted to kick herself for her paranoia. She turned to tell Penny everything was all right when she caught the lights moving toward them from the next lane at a high rate of speed.

The truck skidded on the rainy road and flipped over twice into a ditch on the side of the road finally landing right side up.

Cassie returned to full awareness as the paramedics were cutting her free of the seatbelt and pulling her out of the car.

They spoke to her, asking if she was all right and what hurt where.

All she could think about was her friend. Sick dread coursed through her. "Penny! Is she all right?"

"Your friend? She's fine." One of the paramedics pointed over to the side. "She's there. Some cuts and bruises but she's conscious and alert. She said you might have some prior head wounds?"

Numb, Cassie recited her past history. They took her vitals and were discussing the need for hospitalization when she caught sight of the huge body of her man moving purposefully toward them. The lights of the ambulance and police cars glinted off the bracelet she'd made him for Christmas that, much to her relief, he seemed to love. Two state police officers stood in his way, speaking to him.

"That's my girlfriend and I'm going to her. Period."

The deep bass of his voice echoed up her spine and she felt safe then. So safe that the fear came over her in a wave so shocking she began to tremble violently.

"Ma'am?" The female paramedic touched Cassie's forehead. Cassie heard them speaking to her but the panic attack took over. Her teeth chattered and in moments Shane's voice vibrated off her skin as he reached her, kneeling at her side. Strong, gentle arms pulled her to him, encircling her with his body as he rocked her slowly back and forth. The prick of a needle and then the sting of medication hit her as she fell into the dark calm of unconsciousness.

CRSO

It wasn't until he'd brought Cassie back to his house afterwards that it all began to hit him. The terror of what could have happened felt clammy on his skin.

Running a hand through his hair and over his face, Shane hung up after speaking with Brian for nearly half an hour. Cassie's brother was understandably upset and feeling helpless. He was grabbing the next flight out to Atlanta and would be arriving the next afternoon.

He'd also spoken with the state police at the hospital while he waited for Cassie. The car that Cassie had given him the license plate for had been stolen. They'd done a fingerprinting check but the investigating officer felt that the prints they'd found were the owners' but would let them know once they heard back officially.

The hospital waiting room had filled up with Chases as they'd all waited to hear back. Kyle held on to Maggie tight—the scene was scarily reminiscent of the one several years before when Maggie had been kidnapped and assaulted by a stalker.

Polly click-clacked over and hugged her son tight around the waist, Edward held on to the other side. "She's going to be all right, Shane."

Shane had felt five years old again as he'd slumped into a chair and his mother stroked his hair away from his forehead and kissed his temple, speaking softly to him. His father's strong hand at his shoulder, Shane realized once again how important his family was to him and how much they meant to his life. They'd refused to leave his side at the hospital, knowing he needed the support.

Even at that moment Matt was downstairs, camped out on one sofa, Marc on the other. Both had refused to leave. Penny was recuperating in one of the Chase's guest rooms with Ryan in another. Family meant more than just being there when things were good.

After they'd examined Cassie at the hospital and watched her for a few hours, they'd sent her home in his care. There hadn't been any sign of a concussion but her therapist had come to the hospital and had advised them to sedate her. She'd also told Shane to expect some flashback behavior and perhaps some greater occurrence of panic attacks and jumpiness that Cassie had shown when she'd first come to Petal.

Standing in the doorway to his bedroom, he watched her, reassuring himself she was indeed all right. She lay in his bed sleeping soundly, a bruise marring the left side of her neck and face where the seatbelt had dug into her. He thanked her quick thinking and his insistence that she take his truck. The other car had struck just behind the passenger seat. The scene investigators told him the other car had to be going at least seventy miles an hour to cause that much damage and the roll over.

His fingers dug into the door jamb. It could have been a coincidence. Punk kids stole cars and caused accidents in them on joyrides every day. The car was stolen in an area of Atlanta that had suffered a rash of car thefts in the last week. Still, it was hard not to think Terry was behind this.

Truth was, Shane was pretty sure that it was his presence on the scene that lent credence to Cassie's story and not her history. The state police were looking into it more carefully than they would have if it had been a clear cut joyriding case. He didn't like it but the fact was, it was just all a coincidence and she hadn't received any threats and there wasn't a reason to believe that Terry had found her.

The way he'd felt when Penny had called hit him. He closed his eyes against the helplessness he'd felt, knowing Cassie was in danger and he was too far away to help. It had taken all of his strength to keep his voice level and talk Penny through as he'd called the state police on his other line. He'd wanted to hear Cassie's voice himself but he knew it was more important for her to keep focused on driving and being safe.

And then the screams and the dead air after the crunch. The phone line had remained open, the call never broke so he heard the shattering glass, the groan of metal, the screams and the sobs of pain. He'd stood up, yelling Cassie's name. The state dispatcher assured him the ambulance and response cars were on the way as he'd run to his city vehicle and headed toward the scene with the sirens on.

And when he'd arrived, seeing the glitter of broken glass on the pavement and the flashing red and blue against the bent metal, it was nothing compared to the feeling in his gut as he'd caught sight of her being treated on the gurney.

Single mindedly, he'd moved to her, the staties let him move past. He could see her trembling begin to start from all the way back where the staties had stopped him. He needed to get to her to help. Seeing her that way again, the panic attack sending her so deep into herself that she could barely register what people said to her, sent protective feelings warring with anger through him.

No, not anger. Anger was too mild a word. Murderous. Rage washed over him, made him see red until he clenched his fists imagining Terry Sunderland's neck there. It was war and there was not a fucking chance in hell Shane would walk away the loser. His woman's life was at stake for real and he would not stop until Terry Sunderland was in prison or dead.

He went to her quietly, brushing his lips across her temple, tucking the blanket around her. Her pulse was normal and her breathing was calm. Blinking back hot tears of impotent rage, he backed out of the room and headed downstairs.

Neither brother was sleeping and Kyle and Maggie had joined the group. Everyone looked up as he entered the living room.

"You all can go home, she's sleeping soundly. Her doctor said the sedatives would keep her sleeping deeply for several more hours. There's nothing anyone can do right now. I'm going to go to sleep in a bit too."

Maggie handed him a cup of hot tea and pushed him down onto the couch. "Nothing anyone can do but be there. Drink that. It's chamomile, it'll help you sleep. I imagine you're pretty wound up."

"Not every day your woman almost dies." Kyle watched Shane through knowing eyes. Leaning over, he poured a liberal helping of whiskey into the tea. "That'll help more than chamomile I expect."

Maggie sighed. "Why don't I go up and sit with her for a while? I've got a good book with me and you three can plot and not worry." She kissed his cheek. "I promised Mom I would. She wanted to be here so badly but Penny needed some TLC too. I'm her stand in."

Shane squeezed her hand. "Thank you so much, honey. I'll be up shortly, I promise. I'm just keyed up right now. I don't want to disturb her. But you must be tired..."

Maggie shook her head. "I slept already. I have tomorrow, or today I suppose, off. Kyle is going to make me brunch later on. Now go on, wind down and let me help. She's my friend, you know, I love her too."

Shane nodded. "Thank you. Really."

After she'd gone upstairs the brothers all looked at each other with perfect understanding. One of their own was threatened, no one hurt a Chase and got away with it. Cassie was Shane's therefore she was theirs too.

"Brian's plane comes in at two. He's driving straight here. I spoke with him a few minutes ago. Terry hasn't been sighted since last week in New York but his mother admitted to a friend that she'd seen him and given him a significant amount of money. More than enough to move around the country."

"How did he find her? She changed her social security number and name." Matt punched the arm of the couch.

"Money talks, Matt. You know that. If he knew where she was getting her domestic violence victim advocacy, he had a way of getting to people. I don't know anything for sure, but I do know that this is not a coincidence. He's found her."

"She can't stay here. We have to get her to another city and right away." Marc looked to his brothers.

Shane chuckled ruefully. "I wish she would go for that. But if you think Cassie would agree to it, you don't know her very well. She's not going to let him chase her away. And he'd just find her again anyway. No. We need to draw him in and take him down before he gets her."

"Her apartment isn't safe." Matt watched Shane through serious eyes.

"Nope. She's moving in here. I've asked her, hell I've *been* asking her for months now. I've got a great security system here. I'm going to do all I can to protect her and she's going to have to deal with that or I'll sic Momma on her."

"You aren't going to get married? Momma's gonna be hot." Kyle chuckled.

"What? *You* and Maggie lived together! And anyway, if I thought she'd say yes, I'd marry Cassie tomorrow. She's gunshy, you know that. We'll live together and then I'll ask her to marry me. I'm charming, she won't be able to resist me."

"You let us know what to do and we'll do it. Nothing is going to happen to her." Matt looked to his brothers who all nodded solemnly.

"We're taking Terry Sunderland down. It has to happen. Scum like him has to be taken out. What kind of man beats his woman? What kind of man hurts the person he should be cherishing? He had the best thing in the universe and he threw it away. He tried to kill my woman and I am not having it. It's her or him and I know how it's going to end."

CR80

Cassie awoke, sore and disoriented, mouth dry. Within moments, the night before came back to her in disturbing clarity. Terry found her and tried to kill her. *Again.*

The trembling started in her hands and she gripped the sheets to stop it. She was not going to fall apart.

"Darlin' I'm here."

A hand cupped her cheek and she turned to face those green eyes. She let herself fall into his warmth, allowing herself to feel safe with him, to relax. The shaking in her hands subsided a bit.

"Nothing is going to happen to you. I'm here and the alarm is on. You know where the handgun is on your side of the bed, right?"

Cassie opened her eyes and looked at him again. "You're very calm for a cop telling me where my handgun is."

"Cassie, if he breaks into this house you will shoot him before he can shoot you. Or beat you with something, he seems to like the up close and personal, fucking bastard. It is you or him now, I have no qualms about wanting it to be you and telling you so. Do *you* have qualms about that?"

"About what? How would you feel about me if I told you I wouldn't feel bad if I killed him? He's making it me or him." She sat up with a wince and he put pillows behind her. Carefully, he reached across her body to get her pills and a glass of water.

"I'd feel reassured that you're willing to protect yourself. Now, the doctor said you'd be sore. There's no major injury. You're bruised. Your therapist said you may have some panic attacks for a while and to take medication if you need it to sleep and keep calm."

She shook her head and pushed away the pills but drank the water. "No. I don't want that. I need to be clear headed now."

"There's no shame in it, Cassie."

"Don't you tell me what there's shame in, Shane Chase! I will not be sedated right now. My life is at stake. This man wants to kill me. He's tried and he almost succeeded. He's been controlling my life all these years. Making me afraid to even live. No more. Damn it! No more. I will not. If I need to sleep, I'll take the pills but I will go to work and live my life and I swear to you right now that if he tries to hurt me I will make sure he can never harm me, ever again. However I have to."

Shane nodded and put the pills back on the tray. "There you go. You don't forget that, either. Take that fury and hold it close, use it. It is you or him and damned if I want you to apologize for wanting it to be you. If you're in pain, take the damned pills. I have ibuprofen for that if you'd rather. If you get to a point where you can't function through the panic attacks, take the damned pills. But yes, defend yourself and your life. I will too. We can do it together but, Cassie, please, I'm begging you right now, please move in here."

"I will not be a burden or a charity case!"

"Oh shaddup. Seriously. I want to fuck you on demand. It's a lot easier if you're here. I wake up, roll over and bang, you're right there. Easy access. What more can a man want? Plus, honey, you are a shitty cook, I can keep you from wasting away after all that strenuous sex."

She rolled her eyes at him but at the same time, she realized she was an idiot to resist what she wanted anyway.

"I've been asking you for months now. It's not like this is a last minute pity request."

"Are you sure? Because I'm still going to be a pain in the ass you know. I won't be managed just because I live here."

"Darlin' perish the thought of you being managed in any way." He grinned and she swatted him playfully.

"I'd like that. Thank you."

He let out a long breath. "Whew. That's a relief. My brothers offered to help pack your stuff and get it over here. With your permission of course," he added with a sexy wink.

"Heaven save me. You're some smooth operator, Shane."

"Cassie, I was empty before you came along. You fill me up. I love you."

Tears stung Cassie's eyes. "Me too. When I saw you last night, I knew it was okay. I knew I was safe. Even there on the side of the road with broken glass in my hair I felt safe. Thank you."

"You wreck me, darlin'." Gently, he pulled her down to snuggle against his side.

Chapter Seventeen

Brian came and went back to Los Angeles after he helped with the move. He wanted to stay longer but he had to get back for a case and there wasn't much he could do anyway.

There'd been no conclusive evidence that the person in the SUV had been Terry. No witnesses to the accident or the theft to begin with and it remained quiet with no contact.

Spring came and heated up the landscape. Cassie realized she didn't miss much about LA except for the ocean and they could drive down to the Gulf for that if they wanted to.

Cassie's life became Cassie and Shane's life and it wasn't scary anymore. She loved him and loved waking up to his body next to hers each morning. Loved coming home to their big house every evening. They'd sit out on the back deck and look at the water or have friends and family over for barbecues.

As May approached, Cassie began to believe that the accident in February was just that, an accident. Nothing more than a stupid coincidence. Still, she set the house alarm every time she came and left, went shooting at the range twice a week with Shane and took judo classes with him. She was moving forward and arming herself for the eventuality where Terry did find her. It gave her a measure of control in some sense.

Walking into Penny's backyard on June first, Cassie halted at the unexpected sight of thirty people clapping and cheering. Brian stood next to Shane, and Penny beamed as she stood in Ryan's arms.

"Happy birthday, Cassie." Shane approached her and pulled her into his arms.

"Oh my goodness. A surprise party? Where did everyone park? I can't believe you did this and I didn't know it."

Brian pushed Shane out of the way and hugged his sister, kissing her cheek. "Shane's been planning this since the end of February. We all parked at the Chase's and came over in just a few cars that are tucked all around the neighborhood. Now come on in, there's cobbler and cake and food galore."

"And presents?"

Brian laughed. "Yes, doofus, lots of presents."

Shane watched, a wide smile on his face, as Cassie accepted hugs from everyone with ease. Gone was the woman who winced or trembled if someone she didn't know well hugged her. She still got spooked from time to time but she'd grown into an effusive person who loved to touch as much as be touched. It gladdened his heart to know he had a part in that.

Once seated at the head of a large table, she dug into the pile of presents. He'd noticed that she loved presents. Big or small, cheap or expensive, it didn't matter. It was the ripping of paper and ribbons, the surprise that she loved.

The day was a good one. The kind of day that memories were made of. Cassie wouldn't forget the smell of the cobbler and the sound of the salt and ice crunching in the old fashioned ice cream maker or the taste of fresh, home made vanilla ice cream. She wouldn't forget the way it felt when she'd seen all her friends and the people who'd become her family stood there, smiles on their faces as they shouted *Happy Birthday!*

The sun shone on the water, the day was warm and clear and absolutely perfect. Shane had given her something wonderful yet again, a memory to replace the bad ones.

They all cleaned up as the sun went down and Cassie looked up when Brian called out to her.

"What?"

"Your phone is ringing."

She trotted over to her bag and dug through it, wondering who the heck it could be since everyone she knew had been at the party.

"Hello?"

"Happy birthday, Carly."

Nausea bolted through her as she lost her legs, her knees hitting the ground as she heard Terry's voice.

Brian's eyes widened. "Cassie? What is it?"

"Are you having a good day? I hope so. This is the last birthday you'll ever see." With that same laugh he used as he'd berated her, the line went dead.

She looked up at her brother as he went to his knees. Dimly she heard someone call for Shane and then his feet pounding the earth as he came to where she was.

"Cassie? What is it?" He looked confused at Brian and then her.

"It was him." The phone dropped from her nerveless fingers.

"Him? Terry? Terry just called you? What did he say?" Brian demanded.

Shane grabbed up the phone and flipped it open. "Caller ID? There's a number here."

Cassie watched numbly as Shane went into cop mode and called the number on the phone and then hung up shortly. He then called into the state police and spoke to some people who told him within moments that the number was one from a disposable cell phone that could be purchased anywhere.

"Cassie, darlin', what did he say?" Matt helped Brian get her into a chair and Shane knelt before her, touching her face.

She told them.

"How did he get the number? It's..."

"What?" Shane looked up sharply at Brian.

"It's in my name. I didn't want to chance putting it in hers when I bought it for her last year. I'm an idiot. I've put her in danger."

Shane squeezed his shoulder as Cassie shook her head vehemently. "Brian, you didn't. Don't you see? He doesn't have to know her new name if you had this phone in yours. All he had to do was find out your phone information. He doesn't necessarily know she's here. You kept her safe by doing that."

"He called me Carly."

Shane looked back to her. "Okay, that's a good sign. He probably doesn't know your new name."

"He would have used it if he did, just to fuck with me. He doesn't know my new name and I'm betting he doesn't know I'm here. Don't you see, that means it probably wasn't him on the road in February."

"Oh honey, one step at a time. Could you tell where he was? Think carefully, any details at all could be important."

She shook her head. "No. It was loud here, people talking and laughing. All I heard on his end was his voice and that laugh."

"Okay, sweetie, let's get you home, all right? I bet you'd like a stiff drink and a shower." Penny put her arm around Cassie's shoulders and looked worriedly at Shane.

Once home Cassie stood on the top step and looked down at Shane and Brian and Shane's brothers. "Do not talk about me when I'm gone. We'll plan together. I won't let this happen *to* me. I will have a hand in this or I'll go crazy. Please."

"Of course we're going to talk about you when you're in the shower. But I promise to have you in on the plans when you come back down here," Shane negotiated back.

She exhaled and narrowed her eyes at him. "I will not be handled, Sheriff."

He rolled his eyes. "Go and shower, woman. I need to talk about you while you're gone."

"Honestly!" Throwing up her hands she walked toward their bedroom, mumbling.

"She's going to be okay if she can still get pissy about being managed," Shane murmured to Brian who chuckled.

"You two know each other pretty well. Now, what the hell are we going to do to protect her?"

"We don't know that he knows where she is. She seems to think he doesn't and she knows him better than I do. Only that he's tracked down this number." Shane held up the phone. "I need to call the California authorities to get a warrant so we can set up a trace on this phone. That'll be complicated, we'll have to get a warrant for her own company and then one for whatever company that handles the phone he calls from next. That means it may be a matter of days or even weeks once we find out who he's used on his next call and he'll have time to jump to a new location. But it's something. I also want to get someone to keep a watch on the house here."

"I'll hire someone to bodyguard her."

"Don't you think you should ask her?" Maggie walked in with Liv and Penny, and an agitated looking Cassie brought up the rear.

"Yeah, I hear she gets really pissed off when people try to manage her life the minute she steps out of the damned room." Cassie put her hands on her hips and glared at the men in her life.

"Of course I was going to ask you. It doesn't have to be invasive, I know you'd hate that. But I can hire someone to drive by the house here a few times a night. Nothing major." Brian's tone was calm but firm.

"And you know as well as I do that a trace on the phone is a good idea." Shane's jaw was set in a hard line.

"Look, I'm not arguing. But I am not a piece of furniture either. You can't just make plans about my life and my safety without including me."

"You're not arguing?" Brian looked surprised and Cassie sat on the couch beside him.

"I'm not an idiot, Brian. I just don't want other people making my decisions and choices."

And so they planned. Shane worked with the California authorities to get a warrant in place for a tap on her cell phone and they'd be ready to move on a warrant for the records from that company when and if Terry called again. That done, Brian arranged with Shane to have a local security company drive by the house every hour each evening after Cassie got home from work.

It wasn't fool proof, there was a lot left up to chance and it made Shane uncomfortable but it was all he could do short of keeping her with him every moment of the day and neither one of them would survive that.

CR∞

Later that night in bed after everyone had left or gone to sleep, Shane turned to Cassie. "Are you all right?"

"At first I lost it. I couldn't deal with hearing him, with him being a reality in my life again. But I have a plan to focus on and I feel better. I feel safe with the precautions you and Brian have set up."

"I'm not going to let anything happen to you, Cassie. I love you."

"I know. But you should show me. You know, just in case I forgot."

"Are you sure? I'm...well, I'm not sure I can be gentle right now. I'm so damned angry and worried for you. I hate seeing him do this to you. I hate not being able to stop it."

"I don't need you to be gentle right now. I need you to make me feel alive, Shane. And you *can* do something for me, you can touch me."

With a deep groan, Shane moved his lips to hers, crushing them in a kiss filled with desperate need to make everything all right.

Feverishly, his hands roamed her body and pushed her tank top up and out of the way, work-roughened palms finding her nipples hard and begging for his touch. His mouth swallowed her gasp as he pinched the nipples between thumb and forefinger.

Her fingers sifted through his hair, holding him to her, drinking in his kisses, the passionate need in him. She was his refuge more than he could ever tell her. She often said he gave her so much but in truth, she gave him more. Gave of herself and made him whole.

He would *not* lose her. Would not lose this battle with her psycho ex.

She writhed restlessly beneath him as he rolled onto her body after getting rid of her panties one handed. Her thighs slid up his rib cage, keeping his torso nestled there against her. His hands moved to bracket her body as he rolled his cock, the heat of her pussy nearly scalding him even through his boxers. Her hands were cool as she reached around their legs and bodies to pull his cock out and stroke him.

He loved the way her thumb slid through the slick of pre-come on the head. She knew him, knew how to touch him in small ways that totally devastated him.

With a gasp of his own, he broke the kiss and looked into her eyes. "I love you, Cassie. So much."

She nodded. "I love you too."

"Are you wet for me?"

He noted the catch in her breath, loved it. Loved it even more when she nodded, wordless.

Putting his weight on one elbow, he reached down and slid his fingers through her pussy, finding her ready. Superheated, slick and desire swollen. For him. He pressed two up into her and she moaned, her fingers tightening slightly around his cock.

"Let's get this party started, shall we?" he murmured. "First the appetizers and then the main course."

Latching on to a nipple with his mouth, he slowly thrust his cock into her fist while he moved his thumb up and over her clit in time with his fingers sliding in and out of her body. Her clit bloomed beneath the pad of his thumb and he knew it wouldn't be long before she came. And oh how he loved to make her come! It was like her body was tuned to his own, her responsiveness made him crazy with need.

Her back arched, pressing her nipple deeper into his mouth as she gasped. The muscles inside her clenched around his fingers and he felt her climax.

Without pause, he extracted himself from her grip and pressed deep into her pussy in one thrust. Back straight, he looked down at her, spread out below him, her hair a spill of midnight around her head, gaze locked with his. "So beautiful. You're so amazingly beautiful."

A smile curved the corner of her lips as her palms slid up his abdomen and the wall of his chest.

"You're one to talk. Look at you, all big and bad and masculine. So damned tall and broad-chested. I've never seen a more handsome man. That first night when I looked up from the steering wheel and deflated airbag and I saw you walking up my heart stopped for a moment. Part of me was screaming, *cop!* But the rest of me was like, *hello there!*"

His chuckle vibrated through them both. "Okay, the talking portion of the show that doesn't include, *oh fuck me harder* is now over." With that, he dragged out and pressed back into her, delighting in the flutter of those inner muscles around his cock.

"Oh fuck me harder!"

Laughing together, he set a rhythm as he thrust into her body, her hips rolling to meet him, take him back inside her as deeply as possible. The smooth skin on the inside of her thighs stroked against the hard muscle of his hips as she wrapped her legs around his waist, locking her feet at the small of his back. Each time he was inside her like this, the hot flesh of her pussy pulling at him as if she couldn't bear to let him go, her body

Lauren Dane

there laid out before him as she gave of herself, he knew he was home.

Cassie still had trouble believing this man was hers but he proved it to her every day. She hadn't exaggerated, he was the most handsome man she'd ever clapped eyes on. His size had been daunting at first, Terry was very tall as well. The similarities were scary in the beginning until she realized Shane would never use his size against her, not physically and not mentally to threaten her. They'd been in some heated arguments and he'd never made a move that scared her even when he was clearly losing his temper.

But this? His size dominating her as he sliced into her body with his cock? It was delicious and touched parts of her she was sure were long dead. She loved it when he took her hard and all she could do was hold on. Loved it that he desired her so much his eyes glazed over and his muscles bunched as he wrestled for control. It made her feel beautiful and special.

She'd never loved sex so much in her life. Simply put, she could not get enough of Shane. Except for those rare times when one didn't feel well, they made love at least once a day in some way. All he had to do was look at her and her body responded.

He'd chased away the demons and helped her slay them. Yes, the threat was still there but her response was different. When she'd first heard Terry's voice she'd lost it but by just a few minutes later she'd recovered and had a plan. The old Cassie, no Carly, would have hidden and fallen apart because she didn't know what else to do or experience, Terry had taken all emotion and response from her but fear. But Shane had pushed that away and helped her remember love and hope and courage and she'd be damned if Carly would come back now.

"You're thinking. Is that good or bad?"

His voice was low, nearly a growl and it caressed her skin. "Good. But it wasn't a fuck me harder thought so I'll save it for later." She grinned.

He rolled his eyes and lifted her ass, changing his angle and she gasped as the wide head of his cock stroked over her sweet spot. "Ah, I found it."

"Yes, ohgodyes you did. More. More, please."

"My hands are full of your luscious ass, darlin'. I think I need you to make yourself come."

Months ago it would have embarrassed her but now he'd freed her, made her feel so sexy that it didn't bother her. She did it not only because it felt wonderful but because she knew he loved to see it.

Eyes locked with his, her hand slid down her stomach to her clit. Still sensitive from the climax he'd given her just minutes before, she kept an easy touch while watching his face. His gaze broke from hers and moved to watch her hand on herself.

"I've never seen anything sexier than you making yourself come. The way you feel around me, when you start to get close, it's heaven. So hot and wet, your sweet pussy hugs me. Even right now I can feel it coming. I love that."

Her teeth caught her lip at the carnality of his words even has her body began to move toward orgasm. Each thrust brought a stroke over her sweet spot, lit up the nerve endings as he filled her and withdrew.

A low moan broke from her lips as a rolling, deep orgasm spread through her. Her head moved back and her eyes closed as she heard his muttered curse, felt his rhythm speed and deepen. As her body calmed from climax she opened her eyes to find him watching her with such an intensity that she wanted to sob with it. That look said so much, how much he loved and desired her, what she meant to him. It was utterly unguarded and a gift like none she'd ever received before.

Unable to find words she put her fingers over his lips and smiled, tears in her eyes.

"I almost hate to come, you feel so good. I want to feel this forever, right here on the edge..." he murmured against her fingers as he pressed deep one last time and came.

After a shower, they snuggled back in bed as they waited for sleep to come. "You want to tell me what the non *oh fuck me harder* thought was?" He nuzzled her neck.

"I was just thinking about how much I love and trust you. How you've helped me be a person I was pretty sure would never exist again."

She felt his smile against her skin. "That's a good one. You know, you've done that for me as well. For the last years I haven't trusted anyone, least of all myself. I kept my heart walled off and only allowed myself to love my family. I had this missing piece of myself, turns out that piece was you."

"You know I saw her. Sandra."

He stiffened and moved so he could look into her face. "When?"

"Last week. Penny and I were in Riverton, shoe shopping, and she walked past. Penny pointed her out."

"She's nothing to me. You know that right?"

Cassie laughed. "Shane, you were going to marry her at one point in time. You two lived together. She hurt and betrayed you with your best friend. Of course she's something to you. But I'm not threatened by that. I know it's in your past but I don't expect that not to have made a dent in your heart. It's okay to have feelings about her."

"I used to hate her. I don't even have that anymore. I just feel bad. We weren't right for each other, I should have seen it sooner. Hell, I miss Ron, my old best friend, more than I do her. Anyway, I hope it didn't upset you and I don't know why you didn't tell me."

"It upset me because she hurt you."

"She's married now, to Ron. It's all in the past." Shane shrugged. "If it had worked out with her and me, there'd be no you and I. So I can't be sad about it. Everything happens for a reason."

"She's sorry you know."

He raised a brow. "And you know that how?"

"She told me."

He sat up and pushed a hand through his hair in that way he did when he was agitated. It made her smile.

"You talked to her?"

"Of course I did." She snorted. "She fucked you over. I walked right out of that shoe store, Penny ran behind me trying to stop me. I called out Sandra's name and she turned and when she saw Penny she paled but waited. That took guts. Anyway, I told her who I was and she looked me up and down and nodded her head. Congratulated me, told me what a bitch she'd been and how sorry she was for breaking up two best friends and for hurting you so much. She's happy now with your old friend but he misses you too, talks about you all the time according to Sandra. He apparently stood in the back at the last two swearing in ceremonies when you were re-elected. By the way, even with saggy boobs and stab scars, I am way hotter."

He burst into laughter and pulled her against him, kissing the top of her head. "You are indeed way hotter, darlin'. I can't believe you confronted my ex on the street." He snorted. "Thanks for defending my honor."

"I was ready to smack the spit out of that woman but I have to say, after talking to her, I believe that she is sorry and while she hurt you and that can't be taken back, she did me a favor. But I'll tell you if I ever see Maggie's mother or sister on the street? Oh it's going down!"

"Look at you, like a gorgeous badger. If I weren't a man, I'd have smacked the crap out of Maggie's mother and sister too. Two more callous women I've yet to meet. But you'd have to stand in line behind my momma."

"Oh I know. I talked to her about the Sandra thing. She was hopping mad at me for a bit. It's okay now, she still hates Sandra and I can't blame her but she knows why I did it and I hope you do too. I want you to have closure on this. I want you to let it go because she's not worth it."

"A smart badger too." He kissed her upturned lips. "I have to admit that it does feel good to know she's sorry and also that Ron came to my swearing in. I can't say that I'd ever share a beer with him again but it hurts a little bit less now. No more going all Terminator on my ex-girlfriends though."

"Worried about your fan club president? Man does she hate me."

"Kendra? She does? Honestly, Cassie, I dated her a few times. I haven't in several years now."

"Shane, if I were threatened by every woman in this town with a torch burning for you, I'd be miserable. I trust you. That's all I can do." She shrugged.

"Well, if I get face to face with your ex things won't be so nice."

"Good."

CRIO

Summer broke with ridiculous fury. Cassie was pretty sure that she'd never been so damned hot in her life. It was only late June and she felt like melting candle wax every time she walked out onto the street.

But things were going well otherwise. No more contact from Terry, her job at the bookstore made her happy and she'd expanded her jewelry business to include several local stores as well as her booming market stall.

Shane's house was hers now. She no longer felt like a guest but comfortable enough to change around furniture and hang pictures on the walls.

"I'm out of here, Penny." Cassie called back to her friend as she got ready to leave for the day.

"Okay, see you later tonight at The Pumphouse." Penny was seeing Ryan every weekend now and he'd looked at houses in a town that was halfway between Atlanta and Petal so he could see her more often. He drove out every Friday night after work or she would stay with him while Cassie handled the store.

Just as she rounded the corner to the courthouse where Shane's office was, her phone rang. Moving fast now, she saw that the number wasn't one she recognized.

Picking up, she waved to Shane and pointed to her phone when he saw her. He ran to her as she said, "Hello?"

"And how are you, Carly?"

She took a deep breath and Shane moved the phone so he could hear as well. "I was fine until you called, Terry. Don't you have somewhere to hide?"

"Oh ho! I see my little mouse has found her roar. Talking tough when you think I don't know where you are, aren't you? I can find you. I did before, remember that night?"

Shane's arm tightened around her and she focused on the people milling around and tried to keep from losing it. She would not let him win.

"Which night, Terry? The one where you were convicted of attempted murder but then you scurried off like a coward? That night?"

"You fucking bitch! I told you you were mine, don't you forget it. I made you, you whore! I'll tell you when you can walk away, I'm not ready yet. When I kill you at last I'll be ready."

The line went dead and Cassie let Shane take her phone and lead her into the alcove outside his office. His secretary took one look and helped her sit down, pressing a glass of water into her hand. Shane grabbed the phone and went to work.

An hour later, the office had filled with Chases and Penny as well. Polly held one of Cassie's hands and Edward was on the phone with Brian. Shane came back and shook his head when she looked up.

"Disposable again. Your cell phone company told us who his cell phone company was. I've forwarded the info to your California guy and he's working on the warrant now. Because we don't know how long these companies keep records on what cell towers were accessed when a call is made, I'm hoping the warrant will go through quickly. I hate this waiting, Damn it!" He pounded the wall with his fist and Cassie jumped.

Seeing it he closed his eyes. "I'm sorry, darlin'. I didn't mean to scare you."

"You didn't scare me. It startled me. I'm not worried you'd do that to me. But here's the deal, we know we're not going to find him with the phone tracing thing. So even if you get a warrant tonight and they get it to the cell phone company and they give the records quickly and trace it to Topanga Canyon or Boston or wherever, he'll be gone. He's been on the run for over a year, he's not a stupid man. So why not get rid of the damned phone? I don't want to take calls from him again and if he can't find me and can't call me, I don't have to hear it."

"She's right, son. Why put her through it?" Edward shrugged.

"You need a phone. It's a basic safety issue."

"Fine, but Cassie can get a phone. I don't need this one in Brian's name." Cassie's voice was tired but steady.

They agreed that she'd get a new cell phone but also keep the other phone. Shane felt it was a way to keep track of Terry and in the end, Cassie agreed.

The warrant took a day and a half to go through and they locked the call location to Daytona Beach, Florida. He wasn't in Petal and that was at least one happy thing.

They sent out police to the area but found nothing. Terry was on the run again.

CRSO

In July, another call came as they celebrated at the Chase's house. Celebrated the one year anniversary of her arrival in Petal and at the same time, the one year anniversary of her crush on Shane Chase which was now a full out jones.

She danced with him under the stars in the backyard, surrounded by the people who'd become fixtures in her life. Happiness soared through her until she heard the ring of the phone, the old one.

"That's him."

Shane stood next to her as she flipped it open and answered it. "Hello, Terry. Don't you have anything better to do than ruin my Saturday evening?"

"You think you're so clever, don't you? I hear music in the background. You're whoring it up with some man? You're mine, Carly. I made you! Don't ever forget that. You'd be nothing without me."

"I was nothing with you, Terry. Move on. You have your freedom, why don't you get the hell out of my life and make your own better?"

"You and I have unfinished business, Carly."

The talking and laughing in the background began to die down bit by bit as people began to realize what was going on.

"We have nothing, Terry. You're nothing to me but a horrible period in my life. You tried to kill me and you sucked in bed so you had to rape me. Fuck off." She clicked the phone shut and Shane looked at her, surprise on his face.

"Bet that felt good."

She appreciated his simple response. "Yeah."

He pulled her into his arms.

This time the warrant came more quickly because he bought the disposable cell phone from the same company. He was in St. Louis. Again police went out to the general location, the area around Washington University. They found nothing.

Chapter Eighteen

The anniversary of Cassie and Shane's first date came and went without any further calls from Terry. Homecoming arrived and Cassie cheered on Petal at the game like she was a lifelong fan.

She'd looked into medical school again, she'd found out she had to go back and get more training to change specialties and there was still worry about her hand. And she would have to deal with her name change no matter what. Laws that allowed patients to know who their doctors were and to be able to file complaints were important, she realized that, but they also held her back. But she'd been discussing some possible avenues with her therapist and was really excited about one of them in particular.

In the mean time, Penny came to her with an offer.

Waltzing into the shop on a Monday morning, she put a cup of coffee in front of Cassie and said without preamble, "Ryan's asked me to marry him and I've accepted."

Cassie looked up from the inventory screen and laughed. "Oh my lands. What wonderful news. I'm so happy for you!" Moving around the desk she hugged Penny tight. "Congratulations. When's the date?"

"He'd like to do it as soon as possible. I'd be fine with living together but his family wouldn't be pleased and he loves me and wants to start a family soon. We're thinking November fifteenth."

"Wow, honey, that's a month away. Okay, it's doable. Let's get to work. What can I do? Obviously I can be here at the shop for you so you can take more time off. But I can help with other things, call around, make reservations, that kind of thing."

"You're such a good friend to me. You know, I always thought the idea of an adult woman having a best friend was sort of silly, the thing you only saw in books. But you're that to me. And I want you to be my maid of honor, or matron or whatever the hell, your marriage to Terry does not count." Tears ran down Penny's face as she laughed. "I never thought I'd feel this way after Ben. He was the great love of my life. This second chance is so special."

"It is, Penny. Ryan's loves you so much. I'm so happy for you and of course I'll be your maid doodad."

"Doodad sounds just fine and I promise I won't make you wear anything with tulle or a bow on the ass. It'll be simple, we want it that way."

"Fine, sweetie. It's your day. Where are you going to have it?"

"We just bought a house yesterday. It's an hour and a half from here. It has this grand stairway that leads into a formal living room with floor to ceiling windows. I want it there."

"Well, you're full of good news aren't you?"

"It's a wonderful house. As much as I love my house here, it'll always hold my life with Ben. I have to let go of that now. Take the memories with me as I build my new life. Which leads to my next thing. You interested in a bookstore?"

"What? You're selling this place?"

"Not all of it unless I have to. But I can't be here every day like I am now. I'll live far enough away that more than two days a week would be a pain to drive. I was thinking of breaking it down fairly, like seventy five percent yours, twenty five percent mine? We can talk to Edward about it and have him draw up the sales agreement. That is if you're interested.

"I know you want to practice medicine again but I also know it'll be a while before you can if you can at all. I'd like this place to belong to someone who loves it as much as I do."

"I'll need to talk to Shane and my brother but I can tell you I'm very interested. Truly, I don't think I can go back into medicine the way I was before. I was thinking about going into victim's advocacy. My therapist and I were talking about the difficulties in going back into medicine with my hand being so messed up and the name issue and what I want to do is help people heal. I can do that in other ways. She works with a doctor in Shackleton and has suggested that I speak with Doctor Wallace here in town to see what he'd think about me working with him on a volunteer basis. I'd need training obviously. But it solves some problems for me and gives me a way to help people."

"Oh my, Cassie, that's a wonderful idea. You'd be so good at it."

"Thanks. Okay, let me talk to Shane tonight and see what he thinks. I don't need his permission or anything but I want to run it by him. Brian is the person who deals with my trust and he'll need to handle payment. I suppose we'll have to get the store appraised too."

"I'll get on that today and talk to Edward as well."

Cassie left the shop with a bounce in her step, things were going well. The more she thought about victim's advocacy and counseling, the more she liked the idea. She could use the bad stuff she'd survived to help other people. And she loved the bookstore, it would be hers, something to hold her to town in another way.

At home, Shane was delighted with all her good news. They cooked dinner, Polly was giving her cooking lessons and she'd achieved at least a basic level of competency.

Of course, as it happened from time to time, Shane got a call after nine and had to run out. With a sigh, she accepted his kiss and went into her workroom to finish up some jewelry. As the holidays fast approached, she wanted to build up her inventory.

She'd lost track of time when she heard Shane come in. "I'm in the back here, honey. I'll be out in a sec."

Putting away her equipment, she turned to leave the room and saw not Shane standing in the doorway, but Terry.

Sick dread hit her, replaced by fear and then by fury. "What the hell are you doing here?" Backing up a bit, she reached behind her and hit the 911 button on the phone.

"Oh Carly, or should I say Cassie, why ask questions you know the answer to?"

"How did you find me?"

He laughed and it crawled over her skin like an insect. "The second time I called I heard someone say Chase. And the last time I heard someone yell out Polly and then Shane. What do you know? When I did a search for Polly Chase I saw a newspaper clipping and a picture of an event in small town Petal, Georgia. A drive for the local food bank and what did I see in the background but my faithless wife. Only her name was not Carly Sunderland anymore, it was Cassie Gambol. So unimaginative." He waved around. "I take it this is where you and Shane live? Nice. Not as nice as our house in the hills but for a small town backwater like this one, I expected shacks and hound dogs on the porch."

"Go away, Terry. I don't want you anymore!" In her pocket, she realized she'd dropped a pair of needle nosed pliers she used to tie off findings on a necklace she'd been working on. She slipped her hand inside and held on.

"It's not what you want, bitch! You fucked my life up. I gave you everything and you threw it back at me. You took my reputation and dragged it through the mud. I can't practice medicine anymore and it's all your fault." He came toward her and she stabbed at him with the pliers, felt them dig into the flesh just below his shoulder.

He bellowed in pain and rage and she ran past him, hoping the call had gone through, hoping the security guard would drive past and see something amiss, hoping Shane would come home. For that moment though, she was on her own and she needed to get to the table next to the couch to get her gun.

A hand, slick with blood but with a sure grip, closed around her upper arm and the weight of him rode her body to the ground. She tasted blood as her lip split open when he punched her in the face.

"You bitch! You won't make it this time. I'll make sure you're not breathing when I walk away." His fingers moved her to her throat and began to squeeze.

The world began to narrow as she lost oxygen. Desperately, she reached with both hands, trying to find something, anything to hit him with. Shane's coffee mug! Grabbing it with the tip of her fingers she put all her remaining strength into it and hit Terry up side the head as hard as she could.

Air rushed into her lungs as she coughed when he fell to the side, losing his grip on her.

She began to scream over and over as she scrambled around the coffee table and got to the drawer where her gun was. Fumbling, she heard him right behind her as her fingers touched the cool metal and pulled it toward her.

Her head yanked back as she continued to scream. She couldn't get to the safety to turn it off! Pain seared her as he bent one arm back so hard she felt the shoulder dislocate which probably numbed her enough not to feel the full impact when he broke her wrist. All she could think was thank goodness she knew enough to learn to shoot with her left hand. He hadn't seen the gun she'd been holding in it just yet.

"You can't have my life you bastard. You got enough from me!" she screamed.

"I'm going to fuck you one last time, you whore, and then I'm going to kill you. Leave you for your loverboy to find." His voice was in her ear, right behind her and she pulled her head forward and threw it back as hard as she could, hearing the crunch of his nose.

His pain-filled scream gurgled as she realized she'd broken his nose. Time slowed as she rolled, flicking off the safety and pointing the gun, steadying herself as best she could one handed.

She came to peace with the fact that she was ready to take his life, breathing out as her finger squeezed. Just before her arm took the brunt of the shot, a red bloom covered his chest.

Confused, she watched as he hit the floor, her ears ringing as the shot deafened her. Blinking back the sweat, she saw Shane running toward her and one of his officers going to Terry's slumped over body, checking for a pulse.

"Honey? Oh God, are you all right?" Cassie watched his lips more than heard him ask. Her hearing was still gone as Shane gently took the gun from her hand, wincing as he saw her other arm hanging at an odd angle.

"He's dead?"

"He can't hurt you ever again, Cassie. He's dead," the other officer told her as he stood up.

"Good. God damn it, good. My arm hurts now, Shane, I need to go to the hospital."

Cassie related it in a matter-of-fact voice right before she passed out in his arms.

CREO

Hours later, at the hospital, he paced back and forth through the waiting room. Another officer came in and took over the investigation. Obviously Shane did not have the ability to judge the situation without bias. Looking at her history and Terry's past and that they'd come in as he was attacking Cassie, Shane was sure his shooting would be justified. Still, he was placed on administrative leave while the shooting was investigated and that was all right with him.

Cassie's weapon was discharged but had missed. They found the bullet in the wall behind where Terry had been standing. She would have hit him in the chest if he hadn't begun to fall after Shane shot him. There wasn't any reason to do anything but see her as a victim in the situation. Another officer was questioning her as they patched up her arm. Shane wanted to be there but as he was the person who shot the suspect he couldn't. So one of his father's law partners was in with her and her therapist was on the way.

Chapter Nineteen

The months passed. Shane was cleared and came back to work right before Penny and Ryan's wedding. Cassie bought a three quarters share in Paperbacks and More and began to take classes to pursue becoming a victim's advocate.

Penny announced a week before Christmas that she was pregnant.

"Wow, you said you wanted to start on a family right away, you weren't kidding." Cassie laughed as she hugged her friend.

"We started a while before the wedding, don't tell his mother. Anyway, it's still new so don't tell anyone just yet, okay? I had to tell someone and I couldn't tell you over the phone."

"I can't wait to shop for baby clothes with you. Ryan must be over the moon."

"He is. He's already looking for a crib and I swear has a college fund started. I'm so happy, Cassie."

"Oh, honey, you deserve it. I'm happy for you too."

They agreed that Penny would tell everyone in Petal after New Years when the first trimester had safely passed. It was a delicious little gift for Cassie though, knowing that life continued even in the shadow of such ugliness.

Her cast came off three days before Christmas. "Thank goodness. I can only deal with so much. It's stressful enough spending the night at the Chases. I don't want to think about doing it with a cast on too."

Shane chuckled. "Honey, my mother loves you. My father loves you and my single brothers would steal you in a minute if I didn't keep an eye on them every second. It's no big deal. We live together, they know we sleep in the same bed."

"I'm only agreeing to this because of presents you know."

"I do know, you're very easy. I like that in a girl."

Cassie rolled her eyes.

ॐ

Even being used to the Chases for a year and a half did not prepare her for the insanity of Christmas morning in their household. Last year they'd driven over in the morning but waking up there was a whole different story. While they'd had a bedroom to themselves along with Maggie and Kyle, relatives slept everywhere. The pleasing picture of people young and old in pajamas around the eight foot high Christmas tree did her heart good. This was family. This was wonderful and normal and special all at once.

Brian smiled at her as she came and sat on the floor, resting her arms on Shane's thighs.

Shane's paternal grandfather handed out presents and the process took several hours as everyone ooohed and aaahed over each present from mundane to fabulous. The diamond bracelet Kyle gave Maggie was positively gorgeous and Cassie was proud that her jewelry was thoroughly loved by all recipients.

Still, she had to admit that her favorite moment was when Edward unwrapped the first edition Black's Law dictionary she'd found in an old bookstore in downtown Los Angeles when she'd visited Brian the month before.

"Holy cow! Girl, you're too good to be true. Shane, boy, you'd better keep this one around." Edward stroked the leather spine and beamed.

"She grabbed it before I could, Edward. Even with a broken arm and a bum shoulder she beat me to it." Brian laughed.

"That's my girl." Edward winked.

"Oops, I didn't see this last one. It's for you, Cassie." Pop handed the long, flat box to Cassie.

"From Shane, oooh!" Cassie set to unwrapping it. It was a card with a key attached. *Use me.* was written on it. She pulled the key off. The key to Shane's truck.

Everyone followed her out to the driveway, standing back as she opened the truck. "You giving me this monster, Shane?"

"My truck?" he sounded horrified. "No! Follow the clues, darlin'."

She saw a bow on the glove box and another note stuck there. *I need a key.*

Sliding the key into the lock she opened it and saw the light blue box. "Oh lordy! A blue box." Delighted, she pulled it out and opened it up. It wasn't until she saw the black velvet box inside the blue box that she realized what it was.

With trembling hands she cracked it open and a pear shaped sapphire sat nestled in the velvet, diamonds on either side of the deep blue stone. She turned to face Shane but he was on one knee. Tears began to run down her face.

"Cassie, will you marry me?"

"Holy cripes! Hell yes, I'll marry you." She jumped into his arms and they toppled onto the cold, wet grass, laughing.

Reaching around her, he grabbed the box and slid the ring on her finger. "Perfect. I knew you'd look better in something other than a diamond. I saw it and had to get it for you."

"You rock."

He laughed again. "Thanks, darlin', you do too. How about a Valentine's Day wedding? In that little chapel just outside town? You seem to really like it."

"Oh the one with the pretty stained glass? Do you think it would be available on such short notice?"

"Probably not but I booked it last year this time."

She stopped. "You did? Oh my. Awfully sure of yourself."

"We all know I'm an arrogant man, we established that early on. I wanted to ask you to marry me last Christmas but I knew you wouldn't be ready. But I wanted that little chapel for you when you were ready. Just in case."

"You're a giant marshmallow, you know that?"

"Don't tell anyone."

About the Author

To learn more about Lauren Dane, please visit www.laurendane.com. Send an email to Lauren at laurendane@laurendane.com or join her messageboard to join in the fun with other readers as well. http://www.laurendane.com/messageboard

Fly Away

Discover the Talons Series

5 STEAMY NEW PARANORMAL ROMANCES
TO HOOK YOU IN

Kiss Me Deadly, by Shannon Stacey
King of Prey, by Mandy M. Roth
Firebird, by Jaycee Clark
Caged Desire, by Sydney Somers
Seize the Hunter, by Michelle M. Pillow

AVAILABLE IN EBOOK—COMING SOON IN PRINT!

WWW.SAMHAINPUBLISHING.COM

GET IT NOW

LaVergne, TN USA
17 February 2011
216971LV00003B/14/A